The U.S. has **with**drawn from Iraq, now seething with resentment and **ci**vil unrest.

Saudi Arabia **has** fallen to the Islamists. Iran has nukes.

And everywhere, the scent of oil has begun to attract the **scor**pions...

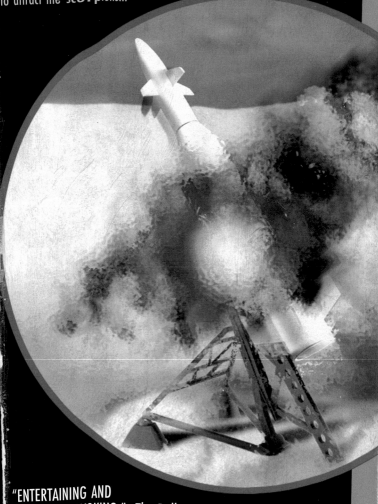

TITLES BY RICHARD A. CLARKE

THE
SCORPION'S
GATE

RICHARD A. CLARKE

BERKLEY BOOKS, NEW YORK

THE BERKLEY PUBLISHING GROUP
Published by the Penguin Group
Penguin Group (USA) Inc.
375 Hudson Street, New York, New York 10014, USA
Penguin Group (Canada), 90 Eglinton Avenue East, Suite 700, Toronto, Ontario M4P 2Y3, Canada
(a division of Pearson Penguin Canada Inc.)
Penguin Books Ltd., 80 Strand, London WC2R 0RL, England
Penguin Group Ireland, 25 St. Stephen's Green, Dublin 2, Ireland (a division of Penguin Books Ltd.)
Penguin Group (Australia), 250 Camberwell Road, Camberwell, Victoria 3124, Australia
(a division of Pearson Australia Group Pty. Ltd.)
Penguin Books India Pvt. Ltd., 11 Community Centre, Panchsheel Park, New Delhi—110 017, India
Penguin Group (NZ), Cnr. Airborne and Rosedale Roads, Albany, Auckland 1310, New Zealand
(a division of Pearson New Zealand Ltd.)
Penguin Books (South Africa) (Pty.) Ltd., 24 Sturdee Avenue, Rosebank, Johannesburg 2196,
South Africa

Penguin Books Ltd., Registered Offices: 80 Strand, London WC2R 0RL, England

This is a work of fiction. Names, characters, places, and incidents either are the product of the author's imagination or are used fictitiously, and any resemblance to actual persons, living or dead, business establishments, events, or locales is entirely coincidental.

THE SCORPION'S GATE

A Berkley Book / published by arrangement with RAC Enterprises, Inc.

PRINTING HISTORY
G. P. Putnam's Sons hardcover edition / October 2005
Berkley premium edition / December 2006

Copyright © 2005 by RAC Enterprises, Inc.
Cover illustration by Gallucci Imaging Inc.
Cover design by Richard Hasselberger.

ISBN: 0-425-21298-X

BERKLEY®
Berkley Books are published by The Berkley Publishing Group,
a division of Penguin Group (USA) Inc.,
375 Hudson Street, New York, New York 10014.
BERKLEY is a registered trademark of Penguin Group (USA) Inc.
The "B" design is a trademark belonging to Penguin Group (USA) Inc.

PRINTED IN THE UNITED STATES OF AMERICA

10 9 8 7 6 5 4 3 2 1

Dedicated to

the victims of terrorism,
to all who have fought against it,
and to their loved ones

ACKNOWLEDGMENTS

This book would not have been possible without the efforts of three close associates and friends: Neil Nyren, editor par excellence; Len Sherman, agent extraordinaire; and Beverly Roundtree-Jones, most loyal executive assistant. To them, my great thanks.

Some may think, as they read this volume, that they see themselves or others portrayed. They do not. This is a work of fiction, in which all the characters are fictional. The work is not meant to be predictive. We can and should hope for a better future. The issues the characters face, however, we will all face in the years ahead: the oil needs of competing powers, the requirements for accurate intelligence, the threat of weapons of mass destruction, the challenge of terrorist groups, the possibility of governments' being dishonest with their people, the responsibility and loyalty of those in government.

My hope is that this book will cause readers to think about those issues and will give them an insight into the real world in which such issues are addressed by real people, for we need a national and international dialogue—an informed dialogue—about exactly these matters.

R.A.C.

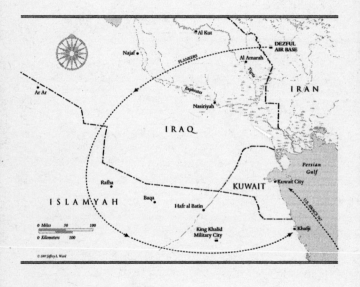

1

JANUARY 28

The Diplomat Hotel
Manama, Bahrain

The waiter flew through the lobby café.

Behind him came a blizzard of glass shards, embedding ragged-edge daggers of shattered windows in arms, eyeballs, legs, brains. The concussion wave bounced off the marble walls with a mule-kick punch he felt in his stomach. Then there was the deafening sound of the explosion, so loud it surrounded him with a physical force, shaking every bone and organ in his body.

Brian Douglas dove for the floor, behind a tipped table. His response was automatic, as if muscle memory had told him what to do, innate reflexes from those terrible years in Baghdad when this had happened so many times. As he flattened his body on the plush carpet, he felt the floor of the Diplomat Hotel shake. He feared the fourteen-story building would collapse on top of him. He thought of New York.

Now there were long seconds of silence before the

screams began, cries to Allah and God's other names, in Arabic and English. Once again there were the shrieking voices of women, painfully high-pitched and piercingly loud. Once again there were men moaning in pain and crying out as glass continued to shatter onto the floor around them. An alarm rang needlessly above it all. Just a few feet away from Brian, an old man wailed as the blood streamed down from his forehead and spilled across the front of his white robes, "Help, please! Help me, please! Oh God, please, over here, help . . ."

Although Brian had been through bombings, it chilled his bones, knotted his stomach, made his head throb, blurred his vision, and caused him to choke, gasping for air. His eardrums were ringing and he had a sense that he was somehow disconnected from the reality around him. As he tried to focus, he sensed something was moving inches to the left of his head. With a chill shudder, he realized it was the twitching fingers of a hand severed from a body. Rivulets of blood ran down the up-ended tabletop to his right, as though someone had thrown a bottle of red wine against it.

Sofas, chairs, carpets, the palm plants in giant ceramic pots were burning in the rubble of what had been elegant, the soaring lobby of a five-star hotel. Then Brian focused on the overpowering scent, a smell that made him gag again as he struggled to roll over. He coughed and spit as he inhaled the vile, heavy stench of ammonia, nitrate, and blood. It was a retching smell he hated but knew all too well. It was the stench of senseless death that brought back painful days of friends lost in Iraq.

Through the shattered glass that opened onto the driveway in front of the hotel came another sound he recognized as automatic gunfire. *"Brrrrt, brrrrt . . ."* Seconds later a cacophony of sirens blared, the European-made ones going up and down in singsong, the American-made sirens wailing their imitation of space aliens landing.

Suddenly, Alec, one of Brian Douglas's bodyguards, was over him. He wondered how long he had been down. Had he been out? "Does it hurt anywhere, sir?" Alec asked.

Brian now noticed that blood was dripping down from his scalp, matting his sandy hair. "No, Alec, somehow my luck has held once again," he said, getting up on one knee, grabbing the overturned table for support. Brian's head spun like a carnival ride. He tried to wipe away some of the blood and dust and rubble from his face. "Where's Ian?" For the three years that Brian Douglas had been Bahrain station chief of SIS, British intelligence, the staff at the station had insisted that he take two bodyguards with him wherever he went, driving to and from his house on Manama's northern beach, going on trips elsewhere in the little country, or visiting the subordinate posts in the other Gulf states. For the last year it had almost always been Alec and Ian, two former Scots Guards sergeants. They had watched over him with a mix of professional polish and personal attention, as if he were a favorite nephew.

"Ian was standing watch by the door, sir," the big man replied, helping Brian as he managed finally to stand up. "Ian is no longer with us." Alec said it with a slow sadness, in his soft Aberdeen lilt, accepting what he could not change, that their friend had been murdered.

"There'll be time for that later, sir, but right now we have to get you the hell out of here."

"But there are people here who need help," Brian stammered as Alec grabbed him firmly by the arm and moved him expertly through the mounds of wreckage and out the door to the pool deck.

"Aye, and there are experts coming to help them, sir, and besides, you're in no shape to be helpin' anyone." Alec had found the service stairwell next to the pool and was steering Brian toward it. "Hear all of that shootin' out front? This is not yet over."

The two men moved through the smoldering debris, trying not to step into the pools of blood or onto the pieces of pink and white and gray that had so recently been living flesh and bone and brain. Glass crunched under their weight as they moved to the stair and down to the exit door. An emergency lighting box provided a pale beam as the men headed down the darkened stairs. At the bottom, Alec tried the door.

"She would be locked tight, of course," said Alec as he motioned Brian to stand back. Pulling his Browning Hi-Power .40-caliber gun out of the holster beneath his left arm, Alec blasted three shots at the doorknob and lock. The roar of the shooting in the concrete stairwell brought the throbbing in Brian's head to a peak of pain. Kicking the door open, Alec smiled as he turned back to Brian. "Don't worry," he said as he reholstered the pistol, "there are nine more in that clip."

Brian followed Alec through a long service tunnel. At its end, he saw two other station men, standing by a door to the alley behind the hotel. "The station has had this route on the list for four years, since that foreign ministers' conference here," he heard Alec say through the ringing. The two big men by the door, folding Belgian machine guns slung under their windbreakers, rushed Brian to an unmarked white Bedford van blocking the alley. In seconds, the van was moving quickly down the streets of Manama, away from the burning tower of devastation that had been the Diplomat Hotel, from the fires, from the dead, and from those who wished through their pain that they were dead.

The van barreled past the Hilton and Sheraton hotels, where police officers and security guards scurried about the entrances erecting barricades in case they were the next to be hit. The van sped past Number 21 Government Avenue, site of the Kutty, the British diplomatic compound in Bahrain since 1902.

Alec and Brian nodded with appreciation as they saw the Gurkha guards, with their foot-long kukri knives and the Belgian folding automatic weapons, ready for action, lining the street in front of the embassy. They were members of the 2nd Battalion of the Royal Gurkha Rifles, headquartered in Brunei. These short soldiers were some of the few Nepalese left who still served as part of the British army, a tradition that dated back almost two centuries. Alec had helped train the 2nd Battalion when Whitehall had decided the Gurkhas would protect British embassies in the Gulf. "Silent, ruthless, dangerous little men," said Alec as the van continued down Government Avenue past the embassy. "They'd give their lives if they had to, to protect the Kutty."

As soon as they heard the bomb blast, the Station

began implementing the response plan for a terrorist action, bypassing the British Embassy, a possible target for a follow-on attack, and moving senior station staff to a clandestine facility off-site.

The Bedford slowed as it turned left onto Isa al Kabeer Avenue, just past the embassy, and headed to a compound two blocks down on the right. As it made the turn, Brian looked out the slit in the back-door window and saw three Bahraini army Warrior armored vehicles lumbering, black smoke snorting up from their exhaust pipes. The Warriors moved to the front of the Foreign Ministry building across Government Avenue. At the precise second that the Bedford reached the gray metal gate of the Al Mudynah Machine Works compound, the covert home of the backup station, a 15-foot-high gate moved aside. The van dashed forward into the courtyard and then braked hard. Armed men rushed around the vehicle. Seconds behind them, a British army medic in civilian clothes slid open the side door of the van and scrambled inside. He tended to Brian Douglas's head wound before the station chief got out.

Brian's number two, Nancy Weldon-Jones, was standing next to the van as he emerged. She flinched as she saw the bandage on his head. "No need to worry, Nance. I'm going to live." He paused and looked at the asphalt. "Unfortunately, Ian isn't." Then he looked up again. "Now, then, what's the report?"

"I got on to Admiral Adams over at the Navy base," Nancy said. "There's dead Brits and Americans, maybe a dozen each. Three times that many in local staff and guest workers. We think it was a truck bomb, probably an

RDX mix over ammonium perchlorate." She offered her arm to Douglas, but he shook his head and stepped forward. She continued her report: "A drive-by shooting followed, just as the rescue workers showed up. Word is that the drive-by shooter was in a Red Crescent wagon. An American Under Secretary for something-or-other was on an upper floor. Of course, the lucky bastard was unharmed. He wasn't in the lobby café because he had them open up the al Fanar Club on the roof for a private little breakfast with somebody."

With Alec urging them forward, gun in hand, the station chief and his deputy crossed the yard and went inside the white concrete-block building. "Okay, Nance, but we know first reports are usually wrong. Any claims of responsibility?"

"Not yet. No need, really. There's no question it's Bahraini Hezbollah, otherwise known as your friendly Iranian Rev Guards and their lovely Qods Force boys." Qods Force, or Jerusalem Force, was the covert action arm of the Iranian Revolutionary Guards Corps. "Is London up on secure vid yet?" Douglas asked as he forced himself slowly up the stairs to the station's backup communications center.

"Up and waiting. You should have the Big Four: the director, her deputy, chief of staff, and . . ." She smiled. "The ME division chief."

"Ah, good, what could we do without the ME division chief?" Douglas asked sarcastically. Roddy Touraine, nominally his immediate supervisor, seemed to delight in making Brian's professional life miserable.

Brian and Nancy made their way through two vault

doors to a room within a room, its walls, floor, and ceiling made of heavy see-through plastic. Exhaust fans buzzed loudly in the walls. The "boy in a bubble" room was just large enough for the plastic conference table that filled it. Attached to the far wall was a 42-inch flat screen showing the crisp image of a far more elegant conference room, complete with wood paneling and a china tea service. Just sitting down in her pale blue chair at the head of that table in Vauxhall Cross was Barbara Currier, director of the British Secret Intelligence Service.

As soon as she sat down, the director began the meeting. "Douglas, you look an awful mess. My deepest sympathies about Ian Martin. I will ring up his wife as soon as we are done here. We will, of course, take care of her." Currier took a cup of tea being offered to her by ME Division Chief Touraine. "Do we understand, Brian, that this is the beginning of an overt destabilization effort directed against Bahrain by the new rulers in Riyadh?"

"I agree it's unlikely a one-off, Director," the station chief said as he looked into the camera above the monitor, "unless they had it out for someone specific, perhaps that visiting American dig. No, I would advise Whitehall that this is the start of something, but not in our view inspired by Riyadh. More likely Iranian-inspired and intended to get the little king here to kick out the Americans from their Navy base."

"Will King Hamad fall for that, Brian?" asked Currier's chief of staff, Pamela Braithwaite, who had been chief of staff for three directors of SIS.

"Not bloody likely, Pam. They're a savvy group here. They may be close to the Americans, but they can and do think for themselves." Douglas leaned back, running his fingers through his unkempt hair and adjusting the bandage. "I think what we have here is the opening of a new terror wave in Bahrain, controlled by Tehran. And remember," Douglas continued as he glanced at some papers that his deputy slid in front of him, "the Shi'a are in the majority here, even though the king's government is largely Sunni. Iran has seen that as a potential weakness here for years. Failed every time they tried to exploit it, but haven't given up."

Douglas saw his nemesis, SIS Middle East Division Chief Roddy Touraine, lean into the camera's frame of view. "With all deference to our heroic and, I see, bloodied station chief, I think in the thick of it, as it were, Director, that he overlooks the obvious. This is not an Iranian attack. It comes across the causeway from Saudi. The Riyadh crowd wants to make sure King Hamad doesn't let the Yanks use this little island as a base for operations against their fledgling little caliphate."

"Whoever it is, Director," Douglas responded, his face reddening, "we will give all assistance to the king here, but we shall not be alone in that. The Americans won't abandon this place. The little Gulf states are all that they have left after the fall of the House of Saud and the creation of Islamyah, coming right after their pullout from Iraq. The Yanks are like sandwich meat spread thin onto the Gulfies between two very big hunks of hostile bread, Iran and Islamyah."

In London, Barbara Currier shook her head in sadness. "Kicked out of Iran in '79, politely pushed out of Saudi in '03, invited to leave Iraq by their Frankenstein in

'06. Then the fall of the al Sauds last year. Now they are just hanging on in the region, with only the little guys to help them: Kuwait, Bahrain, Qatar, the Emirates, Oman. And how long can they hang on there? *Sic transit gloria imperi.* Just ask us." She paused at a noise coming from the Bahrain end of the conference call. "What was that?"

A long, low rumble shook the bubble room in Bahrain. The exhaust fans seemed to cough. From London, Currier could see on her flat screen that someone who had just entered the room in Bahrain was bending over Brian Douglas, whispering something. Douglas had his hand over the microphone. He spoke briefly to those around him, and then he looked back up at the camera.

"The attack on the Diplomat was not a one-off, Director. The noise that you just heard was the sound of the Crowne Plaza, down the street from the Diplomat, pancaking."

Near the As Sulayyil Oasis
South of Riyadh
Islamyah (formerly Saudi Arabia)

"That white smudge on the black of the night is the backbone of our galaxy," Abdullah said softly. The two men lay back on the pile of pillows and pondered the infinite sky. The galaxy was bright above the desert, far from the lights of the city and the flares of the refineries. Abdullah sat up on the carpet and smoked the apple-flavored tobacco of the hubbly-bubbly. Except for the gentle gurgling of the water pipe, no sounds broke the stillness that covered the rolling sand.

Ahmed rose and walked toward the embers of their fire. "You are such a poet, brother, but you try to change the subject." He stirred the charred wood. "The Chinese are no different from the Americans when their troops were here," he said as he spat into the dying fire. "They too are infidels."

"Yes, they are infidels, Ahmed, but without the Chinese weapons, we will lie naked before our enemies. Many of our American weapons do not work anymore, without the American contractors and spare parts. My brothers in the Shura aren't always right, but they may be right about this. We may need those weapons, and the Chinese must be here to make them work until we can."

Ahmed shook his head in disagreement, prompting his brother to continue. "We must have weapons to deter our enemies. The al Sauds have bought important Americans to help get themselves back on the throne. The Persians stir up trouble among our Shi'a and those in Bahrain. And the Persians now have nuclear weapons on their new mobile missiles." Abdullah stood up and walked slowly toward his younger brother. "We will keep these few Chinese inside the walls, deep in the desert." He stared down at the remaining hot coals. "They will not stain our new society. The Chinese need the oil; they will stay in line. Besides, it is done. The missiles are here now."

The two men walked away from the fire pit, with its semicircle of carpets and pillows, heading up to the crest of the dune. Below them the desert was bathed in the dim blue light of the stars and the half-moon. "You know, Ahmed, the Prophet Muhammad, blessings and peace be upon him, camped very near here, just at that oasis. And our grandfather used to come here as well. Both of them loved the beauty of this place."

He grabbed his brother's arm, turning him to look into his eyes. "I did not come all this way just to be bound in chains again. While you were in Canada learning to cure people, Ahmed, I was learning to kill them. I personally slew al Sauds last year, and before that, in Iraq, I attacked their American masters. I am not going to hand our nation back to those swine, or anyone else. Allah, the merciful and compassionate, has given us the mission to create Islamyah from the fetid carcass that was Saudi Arabia.

"Those so-called Saud princes sit in their unclean mansions in California, drinking and dancing as they count the money they have stolen from our people. They buy whores in the American Congress to deny us the parts to make our American weapons work. They bribe the Jewish reporters to whip up support for invading us. They connive with the greedy British diplomats to spy on our embassies and steal our papers.

"They will stop at nothing until they have regained control of this land. Even now, the al Sauds, and those criminals in Houston who help them, are hiring assassins to kill all of us on the Shura. The Persians, too, infiltrate agents into Dhahran and the rest of the Eastern Province, pretending to champion the Shi'a."

Abdullah released his grip on Ahmed. He loved Ahmed, younger, taller, with the deep brown eyes of their late father. He wanted to persuade him. "But what we have done now may not be enough. What do both the Americans and the Persians have that lets them think they can intimidate our infant nation? You know the answer. It is the bomb of Hiroshima—the killer that turns the sand into glass and poisons the land for generations. If we resist, they will char our cities and incinerate our people, so they can again steal the oil beneath our sands. That is why, Ahmed, my so-called friends on the Shura Council think we need our own bomb."

Ahmed did not back down. "What about the Pakistanis? The al Sauds gave them the money for a bomb. You found the records yourself. The Pakistanis will defend us."

Abdullah turned and began walking slowly back down the hill to the camp. "Yes, perhaps, Ahmed, but the only thing that concerns the Pakistanis is India. They say the right things about Islam, but they will keep their few weapons to scare the Hindus. The Pakistanis cannot be relied on. Besides, their missiles are primitive. We need more than a few little Pakistani arrows."

A low cough and then a high-pitched whine stirred beyond the next dune. A wisp of sand flew above it into the desert night. The helicopters were starting. It was time to return to the city.

"So why did we come here tonight, Abdullah? I doubt that it was just to stare at the heavens and reminisce about Grandfather." Ahmed was seven years younger and four inches taller than his brother. He had marked his twenty-ninth birthday only two weeks ago, when he had returned home after eight years in Canada, ending his residency early, because Abdullah had become a member of the new ruling Shura Council. And Ahmed wanted to be part of his big brother's team now, just as he had wanted to play football with Abdullah and his friends twenty years ago. Since his return, Ahmed had pressed his brother on how he could help him with the new government of their country. But each time the answers were vague.

"No, not just to remember Grandfather." Abdullah looked down at the sand and placed both hands inside his robe. "It has been very hard for me to gain agreement from the Shura for you to work in my ministry. Many members distrust you because of your years away."

"But there are no decent medical schools here," Ahmed shot back.

"Not yet. Someday we will again lead. And you must stay in medicine, Ahmed," he said, looking back up the dune.

"But Abdullah, I want to work with you. I want to help our country, help bring back the pride of our people!"

Abdullah smiled. Ahmed sounded just like a little boy again. "And you will. You will start at a hospital next week." Seeing the disappointment on Ahmed's face, he ended the teasing game. "But you will actually be working for me, directly. The hospital job will be only a blanket thrown over your real work. You will be my eyes and ears in the nest of vipers across the causeway." Abdullah smiled broadly, as if he had just handed an expensive present to his brother.

"Bahrain?" Ahmed asked in confusion.

"Yes. It may be only sixteen miles away on the causeway, but that place is home to thousands of infidel sailors and their boats. The Persians are there, too, smiling and pretending to be merchant traders as they go back and forth in their dhows, but actually plotting against our new nation.

"You will go there, publicly estranged from me and supposedly upset with our new government. You will do your work at the Medical Center in Manama, but what you will also do is collect special information, just for me. You are going back into the belly of the enemy again, little brother." As he said that, Abdullah playfully punched hard against Ahmed's soft abdomen. Ahmed did not flinch.

A white Land Rover appeared from over the far dune, to drive them to the improvised heliport on the sand. As they came upon the Black Hawks, Ahmed turned and poked back at his brother, punching him in the arm. "Abdullah, you're really sure these American helicopters are still safe without the spare parts?"

"For that the Pakistanis are useful. They can find parts for us, at least for now." With that, Abdullah bin Rashid, Vice Chairman of the Shura Council of the Islamic Republic of Islamyah and Minister of Security, jumped into his personal Black Hawk. Beneath the tan-colored coating of the helicopter, the outline of the green seal of the Saudi Arabian air force could still be seen through the new paint.

As the Black Hawk rose, kicking up a dust storm, Ahmed placed the helmet on his head. He did not plug in the long cord that connected to the intercom system. He wanted to think, not to listen again to the incomprehensible babble of the crew. They flew low over the dunes, the Black Hawk's rotors beating through the thin air, speeding toward a light that spread across the horizon.

The aircraft's side door was open and Ahmed could see camels below, standing like statues, unfrightened by the aircraft's noisy appearance. Off beyond the camels, Ahmed saw the towers of the refinery, shooting giant orange flares that danced in the night sky.

They are the problem, he thought, the towers and the corrupting blackness that oozes from below our sands. It gives prosperity for our people, he thought, but it is also like the blood of a wounded camel on the sand. It draws deadly scorpions. And, Ahmed thought, Islamyah is now like a wounded camel. The Americans, the Iranians, the Chinese smell the blood of this land, oozing out from below its sandy skin.

As the Black Hawk rose to match its flight with the contour of the giant dune below, Ahmed thought, these nations are like the scorpions. And the scorpions are coming again.

Intelligence Analysis Center
Foggy Bottom
Washington, D.C.

"It's sixty-eight degrees on January 28th and the White House still claims that global warming isn't a problem? The Artic ice cap is melting, the polar bears are dying, the Eskimos are drowning, the trees and flowers are blooming three months ahead of schedule, and they still say that there isn't enough evidence?"

Russell MacIntyre flicked his wrist to see his watch. It was a cheap digital model that displayed the time in military style. It read 19:28, almost 7:30 P.M. He was going to be late meeting his wife at the Silversteins' in McLean, again. "Anything left, Deb?" he said, looking over at his attractive assistant, asking her a question that was actually intended to evoke an answer, unlike so many that he posed about politics and weather.

"Ms. Connor is still waiting down there," she answered, in a voice that suggested that the waiting young staffer had been sitting in the reception room for a long time.

"Shit," he replied and instantly regretted it. Connor was one of the best of the crop of newly minted analysts that he had recruited from the nation's top graduate schools. He had promised them an exciting job. He had promised them that they could make a difference. He had promised them access. MacIntyre sighed. "Okay, Debbie, please go get her and send her in."

Russell MacIntyre was, at thirty-eight, the Deputy Director of the new Intelligence Analysis Center, or IAC. Although it was sixteen years since he'd been on the Brown swim team, he still tried to work out in the pool at the Watergate twice a week. There were only slight flecks of gray in his auburn hair, but his wife Sarah wanted to "touch them up."

The IAC, where MacIntyre was the number two, had been created as the final piece of the intelligence reorganization started by the report of the 9/11 Commission and the fiasco over weapons of mass destruction in Iraq.

The combined failure of both the CIA and the new Director of National Intelligence to foresee the coup, or "revolution," in Saudi Arabia had finally convinced Congress to do something about analytical capability. The IAC was that something. It was empowered to see everything gathered by all the branches of the U.S. government and to order those agencies to try to get whatever information IAC wanted.

At the insistence of Senate Intelligence Chairman Paul Robinson, the analytical function was separated from the intelligence collectors, so the analysts would be unbiased, uncommitted to their agency's sources. Robinson also dictated that the new IAC have the resources to utilize open sources—press, blogs, academic papers, television from around the world. "I am determined that I will never again have to chair one of those 'oh my God' hearings after something critical happens that we should have seen coming, but didn't," Robinson had fumed on the Senate floor.

With an elite staff of two hundred handpicked specialists, the new IAC was bureaucratically independent from the intelligence collectors in the other so-called three-letter agencies: CIA, NSA, NGA, FBI, and NRO. The analysts were a mixture of old and young, top career specialists taken from longtime niches and new whiz kids who had just parachuted into their first government job. When Robinson and a group of key Senators and Representatives from both parties had essentially forced the President to name Ambassador Sol Rubenstein to head the new agency, the sixty-eight-year-old government veteran had almost turned them down. It was only after he'd gotten every possible operational and budget issue resolved in his favor that he'd turned to the issue of the location for his new agency.

When he had cocktails on the roof of what was then the new Kennedy Center for the Performing Arts, over thirty years ago, Rubenstein had been fascinated by the complex of old buildings he had seen nearby on the hill above the Potomac. They sat across the street from the State Department in the Foggy Bottom section of the city. Called Navy Hill, it had been the first home of the Naval Observatory. After the Observatory had moved in the nineteenth century, the Navy's Bureau of Medical Affairs had taken the Hill. In theory, they were still there, but at the outset of World War II some of the Navy buildings had been emptied out so that America's first real intelligence agency, the Office of Special Services, the OSS, could move in.

Ambassador Rubenstein had insisted on the ten-acre site for his new agency. He took as his own office the suite on the ground floor that had been home in 1942 to Wild Bill Donovan, the first OSS director. Rusty MacIntyre, the first Deputy of the Intelligence Analysis Center, had the office next to his new boss. Both men loved their river views, but the two spent as much time as they could wandering through the three buildings they called "our little campus."

MacIntyre had been Rubenstein's first hire for the new agency. The silver-haired retired ambassador picked him out of the executive suite of a defense contractor because, as Rubenstein had said, "You have a reputation for getting shit done and not worrying about who you run over while you do it." MacIntyre worked hard to live up to that reputation. Rubenstein had also been very clearly told by Senator Robinson that MacIntyre would be a good pick.

"I'm sorry that I pushed Debbie so hard to see you tonight, Mr. MacIntyre. I know you are busy with the Bahrain bombings, but you said that whenever we really needed . . ." Susan Connor was clearly nervous as she walked into the big room and sat on the edge of the couch, sweat showing on her high forehead.

"It's Rusty. Mr. MacIntyre was my late father," the Deputy Director reassured the attractive twenty-three-year-old African American. He then fell into his beaten-up leather chair by the window. "I said that whenever you really needed to see me, anytime, day or night, you could see me. So what's up?"

"Well, sir, you told us at the off-site that intelligence analysis was 'literally looking for needles in haystacks. The trick is looking in the right haystack, the one where they don't expect you to look.' Right?" Connor seemed to be reciting the lines from memory.

"That does sound like something I might have said." MacIntyre smiled, amused to hear his own words bounced back at him and pleased at the impact they had clearly made on at least one listener. "So, have you found an interesting haystack, Susan?" What the hell was Connor's assignment anyway, Saudi—he corrected himself—Islamyah military?

"Maybe, sir. Maybe an interesting needle." Connor began to relax, warming to the story she was about to tell. "I found this 505 report this morning." A 505 report was a type of dissemination from the National Security Agency, the electronic listening headquarters at Fort Meade, Maryland. It was a routine, low-priority report without special restrictions on its distribution. The NSA issued thousands of these reports every day, jamming the e-mail in-boxes of intelligence analysts connected to the highly secure interdepartmental Intelwire network.

"Okay. Well . . . ?" MacIntyre wanted to cut to the chase. He stared out at the river, which was now being pelted by a January rain. He pushed the intercom button for his assistant. "Deb, call my wife on her cell and tell her I can't make dinner with the Silversteins. Tell her I'll call her in a bit, but they shouldn't wait dinner on me." MacIntyre's friends were well used to his frequent no-shows, and had long ago learned not to ask why. He motioned for his eager staffer to continue.

"Well, sir, it was a frequency not used by the Saudi military, but it was coming from the middle of the Empty Quarter, the open Saudi desert. Burst transmissions, heavily encrypted, narrow beam straight up to the *Thuraya*." The *Thuraya* was a commercial satellite over the Indian Ocean. Connor was now unfolding a map of Saudi Arabia on top of the coffee table.

"Yeah, so . . ." Oh shit, he thought, this kid is talking about some standard 505 report, just the usual low-level crap . . . Maybe I should have gone to the Silverstein dinner . . . Sarah will be pissed at me again.

"So I called NSA, like you said we should when we needed more information than they gave us in the reports. I got the runaround almost the whole day, but finally, just after five o'clock, the assistant chief of D-3 called me back." The young analyst started taking coffee mugs from MacIntyre's collection of agency cups on the nearby stand, placing them on the corners of the map to keep it from coiling back up. Connor carefully secured the northwest corner with an NSC mug, the southwest with a NORAD cup, the northeast corner with one from CinCPAC, and the southeast one with a chipped blue cup with a gold SIS on it.

"D-3?" The Deputy Director sat up in his leather chair, which had been with him since his first job on Capitol Hill. "That's NSA's branch for Chinese military, not the office that handles Saudi."

"I know, sir." Susan smiled for the first time since she had entered the room. "The freq in the report is used only by Chinese Strategic Rocket Forces. It's their nuclear command link."

"Huh? What did the guy from D-3 say, what's his explanation?" MacIntyre was looking at the map. The red X that Connor had marked on it was certainly in the middle of nowhere. "That site makes no sense. Chinese? It's right in the heart of the damned Rub al-Khali. Why the hell would that transmission be coming from the center of the Empty Quarter? There's nothing there but a quarter million square miles of sand dunes."

Susan rearranged the mugs. "He said that it was unexplained, but he didn't seem too worked up about it. Sounded like he wanted to go home. He said that his car pool was waiting and . . ."

MacIntyre popped out of the chair and moved quickly toward his desk.

Connor began to mumble, "Maybe I shouldn't have bothered you, sir, since NSA didn't . . ."

The Deputy Director grabbed a gray phone. "This is MacIntyre at IAC. Let me speak to the SOO." There was only one place in the government where there really was "a boy named Sue"—namely, NSA's Senior Operations Officer, who ran the spy agency's command center. "Hi. I need a confirmation on the freq reported in your serial 505-37129-09. We were told that it was PRC strategic c-cubed."

Connor listened nervously, envisioning her career ending before it had even begun, especially if the answer was that it was really nothing more than Panamanian shipping comms. "Okay, and the lat-long places it where?" Another pause seemed to take forever. MacIntyre had turned his back to Connor and was fumbling through a directory. "Okay. Little odd, no? Okay, thanks."

The Deputy Director switched from a gray to a red phone. He looked again at his watch and then punched a speed dial. "I have a priority-two late insertion for the Placeset bird; my code is IAC-zero-two-zulu-papa-romeo-niner."

Connor was trying to remember what Placeset was: maybe the high-resolution electro-optical satellite.

"Coordinates, lat five zero degrees, three zero minutes east; long two three degrees, two seven minutes north," MacIntyre said as he stretched the phone cord while reading the location off the map on the coffee table. "I want a ten-mile radius at Focal Level 7. What time will you have it?"

The Focal Level System was like a lens opening, or stop, on a camera, only the camera was 200 miles up in space. Connor remembered that seven was a real close-up, the kind that almost let you read the words on street signs. She realized that MacIntyre had taken her seriously enough to play a special chit, an after-hours personal request to divert a satellite from the targets that had been agreed upon just that morning by an interdepartmental committee from CIA, DOD, NSA, and the IAC.

MacIntyre put the red phone back in the cradle with his right hand and simultaneously picked up the intercom handset with his left. "Deb, order us the usual pizza, then go home, thanks." The Deputy Director plunked down heavily in the chair again and smiled at his young analyst. "Now we wait. I hope you like anchovies."

At moments like this, Rusty MacIntyre felt like a one-armed paperhanger. He and Rubenstein had tried and succeeded in keeping the IAC small; that way they avoided the bloat that had made the CIA so ineffective. But small also meant that Rusty usually ended up doing everything from editing reports to arguing with OMB and the Congress for more money, to hanging out and eating pizza late at night with young analysts.

It also meant he hardly ever got to see his wife. After ten years they still hadn't gotten around to having a kid and now—with Sarah at thirty-eight—it was almost too late for them to start a family. She never complained about it. "Not to decide is to decide," Sarah would say to him, "and I'm fine with that." Maybe she actually was fine being childless, since she enjoyed her work at Refugees International so much, but Rusty wasn't fine with it.

"Oh, I forgot: here's your change from the pizza," Susan said, placing four quarters on the small tabletop.

Rusty MacIntyre smiled at his young analyst. Then he took his empty glass and placed it under the table. Susan gave him a double take but said nothing. Silently, MacIntyre palmed the quarters, placed one in the middle of the table, and pressed his thumb on it. *Clink.* The coin had disappeared. And then another. *Clink.* Susan Connor looked under the table, where two quarters sat in the glass. Then MacIntyre did it two more times, apparently pushing the coins through the table.

Susan Connor ran her hand across the tabletop. "How did you . . . ?" she asked, picking up the glass.

"Amateur magic, a hobby of mine. But it's also a lesson. Not everything is as it appears," Rusty said, sitting back in his chair. "Here's how . . ."

"Blttt . . . Blttt . . ." It was the secure phone. It was almost eleven o'clock and the satellite's ground site manager was calling. The image MacIntyre had requested could now be called up on the Intelwire. As Deputy Director of IAC, Rusty had few perks, but one he did have was a 72-inch flat screen connected to Intelwire. On it popped an amazingly high-resolution image of the Arabian Desert, in the middle of which a red crosshair cursor was blinking.

Using a handheld control, MacIntyre zoomed in and out and moved the cursor, quickly scanning the circle he had asked for, with its 10-mile radius. Connor could not keep up with her boss's search and was getting vertigo from the image on the screen as it zoomed and swerved in front of her. It was as though she were looking down on the Arabian Desert from a blimp just yards above the sands. Suddenly MacIntyre stopped and sat back down behind his desk.

"Helluva haystack, Susan," the Deputy Director said, shaking his head at the perplexed analyst. "Helluva needle."

"I'm not sure I understand, sir. What was that on the image?" Connor was perched again on the edge of the couch, a plate on her lap filled with pizza crust ends and tomato-stained anchovies.

"That, Ms. Connor, was twelve underground missile silos and a central support base for mobile missiles. Judging from the one missile that was on a truck at the base, I would say it is the Chinese CSS-27, Beijing's latest medium-range ballistic missile. Except they're not in China, they're in Saudi Arabia—ah, Islamyah."

Susan Connor stood up, whistled, and then, slowly, said, "Ho-lee shit." The anchovies were now on the carpet.

Aboard the USS Ronald Reagan
in the Persian Gulf, also known
as the Arabian Gulf

Although the carrier was moving at 25 knots, prepar ing to recover a squadron of F-35 Enforcers, there was only the slightest sense of motion in the admiral's suite, buried just under the flight deck of the 77,000-ton floating air base.

"Would you like a cigar, Admiral? It's a Cohiba," the new flag ensign offered. The three-star vice admiral, Bradley Otis Adams, grinned as he reached into the open mahogany cigar box. "First of all, Ensign, smoking a cigar in here is prohibited. Second, a Cuban Cohiba is contraband. And third, your predecessor briefed you very well."

Leaning forward from his seat at the end of the table in the admiral's dining room, one-star rear admiral Frank Haggerty took the beat-up Zippo lighter his boss offered. It was engraved with the words "HVT Bar, Baghdad." Haggerty smiled, remembering Adams had a role in going after the high-value targets, the leaders of Saddam's Iraq. Frank Haggerty lit up his Cohiba. "Ruck, you get these in Jebel Ali?"

Andrew Rucker was captain of the USS *Ronald Reagan,* a 1,040-foot behemoth with two nuclear reactors and a crew of 5,900. He looked across the table at his boss. "You can buy anything in Dubai," he answered as he, like Adams and Haggerty, lit a cigar.

Smoking indoors on a U.S. Navy ship had been banned for years, but no one was going to tell that to the commander, Fifth Fleet, or his subordinate, the admiral in command of the *Reagan* battle group. So for the captain in charge of the *Reagan,* there was one slight benefit to having the brass dine in. "I think, sirs, that once Castro finally goes we are going to switch from being enemies of Cuba to its greatest friends. Real fast."

Admiral Adams drew a long puff from his cigar and savored the aroma as it filled the room. The roly-poly fifty-year-old flag officer was young to be a three-star.

Although his blond hair was thinning, he looked even younger than his age. He had been young to be in every position he had ever been assigned to for over twenty-five years. He joked that salt water ran in his veins, since two Otises and three Adamses had been U.S. Navy admirals over the past two hundred years. He had been in the Bahrain job for one month, acting as both commander of U.S. Naval Forces (Central Command) and commander, Fifth Fleet. Already he was getting cabin fever in the little island nation of Bahrain. He had choppered out from Bahrain to join his friends Haggerty and Rucker for dinner under way aboard the carrier. He also just wanted to be on a moving ship again, not tied to a shore desk.

Tonight he also needed to deliver a message, one that was for their ears only. He made a slight gesture toward the two aides standing nearby, and Rucker instantly caught his meaning. "Lopez, Anderson. That will be all, thank you." The ensign and the seaman left the dining room and quietly closed the door behind them.

Adams stood up and took another long drag on his cigar. "Although he was a little shaken up by the lobby of his hotel turning into a charnel house, Mr. Kashigian did eventually emerge and come by the base for his briefing. Only, turns out he was actually here to brief me." Adams handed Haggerty a sheet of paper, with the engraved seal of the Secretary of Defense on the top and the looping signature of Under Secretary Ronald Kashigian at the bottom. "Take a look."

As the two read the documents, Brad Adams walked over to the wall and looked at the aerial view of the Gulf and the countries surrounding it. From space it seems as if nothing had changed at all, he thought, but now the al Sauds are gone and Iran had nukes, and we are in the middle of it all with not much more leverage than this fleet gives us.

"Does SECDEF really expect us to carry out all this while revealing nothing to anyone?" asked Haggerty. "I'm not sure that we can get the force prepped to do everything that he wants that fast without someone getting wise."

Rucker shook his head as he looked at the document in front of him. "Admiral, I don't mean to be out of place, but isn't it SOP for orders like this to be transmitted over ARNET, not delivered by hand?"

Adams turned back to the two men. Rucker, now forty-two, had been a little iconoclastic since his Annapolis days. He thought independently, didn't just accept the company line. It was amazing he had made captain. "They're worried about leaks. Of course, they're always worried about leaks. But this time they seem to be almost paranoid about it. It's almost as if they are certain that if CIA or NSA or IAC gets word of what we are up to, then somehow it is going to get out." Adams sat back down at the table as Rucker placed the orders on the table.

"Well, given the size of what they are planning, how do they expect it not to leak?" asked Haggerty. "They must realize that someone is quickly going to see not only what we are doing here, but all the movement in CONUS and the Med, too. You can't move this many men and ships and position that many people for action without someone getting wind of it."

"You're right, Frank, and I tried to explain that to Kashigian," Adams replied. "But SECDEF is locked into this thing with a religious fervor that makes the Shura look like a Unitarian Sunday-school class. I don't understand it exactly, but they are moving ahead with this at a pace like I've never seen before. The only thing I can figure is that they've gotten some bit of intel that they haven't shared with us or anyone else, or else—"

"Or else what, Admiral? This just doesn't make sense. The Iranians are a threat to blow up the whole damn region, Iraq is still a mess, sending terrorists after us wherever we turn. Why the hell would we pick right now to stage a major amphibious exercise with Egypt in the Red Sea and pull most of the Fifth Fleet out of the Gulf for ten days?" Haggerty got up from the table and walked over to the aerial photo of the Gulf that Adams had been studying. "I really am not sure that I can do everything that they want in that time frame, Admiral," Haggerty said as he looked at the picture. "There is a lot going on here, and we should not be denuding the Gulf of American forces for some silly exercise. What do you want us to do?"

"I expect you to follow orders, Frank. Remember, civilian control of the military? Even if sometimes the civilians don't make sense. You and Ruck do what you have to so that you can get us ready to do these missions while keeping them quiet. The largest amphibious exercise in memory, two carrier battle groups, most of our assets from the Gulf, all for a landing on the Red Sea coast of Egypt? It might be meant as a message to Islamyah. When does that say the date is of the amphibious landing?"

Captain Rucker looked down again at the Planning Order. "Marines will assault Green Beach on 15 March."

"The Ides of March. Guess somebody has a sense of humor, or history. That gives us some time to get ready . . . and to find out what's really going on. Not much time, but some," Adams said, smiling at Admiral Haggerty and Captain Rucker.

Vice Admiral Brad Adams drew a last puff. As he snubbed out his cigar in the big brass ashtray, an F-35 Enforcer executed a perfect nightime carrier landing. It hit the flight deck immediately above the Admiral's Suite with a noise that the inexperienced would have thought was a crash. All three men's eyes went to the video monitor hanging from the ceiling, to make sure that the jolt they had just felt was only an F-35 landing.

2

JANUARY 30

The White House, West Wing
Washington, D.C.

The lead and chase Chevy Suburbans pulled to the curb after being waved through the first checkpoint near the Ellipse. The black Chrysler 300M they had protected moved swiftly to the second guardhouse. The uniformed Secret Service officer dropped the metal V barrier designed to stop an eighteen-wheel tractor-trailer.

MacIntyre watched his young analyst's eyes grow big as they approached the fence line and the large gates that opened onto West Executive Avenue. "Ever been to the White House before, Susan?" he asked.

"Just on the tourist line in high school. Red Room, Blue Room, Green Room, but we never saw anything over here." Susan Connor fumbled for her badge as MacIntyre showed his to the Secret Service officer through the car window.

"Well, the thing to remember is it's just a government building filled with civil servants—and, of course, the guy who lives above the shop." The car stopped outside an awning-covered set of double doors that led to the basement, or ground level, of the West Wing. "You'll be amazed at how small everything in the West Wing is. It's a one-hundred-year-old building that hasn't been enlarged in half a century.

"This street, West Executive Avenue? It's the most sought-after parking lot in town. Tourists and local residents used to walk down it whenever they wanted to. Now it's behind three layers of security. Most of the White House staff is actually in this big building behind us," he said, pointing at the Eisenhower Executive Office Building, the EOB. "At one time, the entire Departments of War, Navy, and State fit into the EOB. That was when an Army general named Dwight Eisenhower would go get a voucher to pay for the trolley ride to Capitol Hill when he had to brief the Senate Armed Services Committee."

As MacIntyre spoke of the military leadership of seventy-five years before, the motorcade of the current civilian leader of the Pentagon screeched to a halt in front of the West Wing awning. Surrounded by civilian and military aides with briefcases and binders, Secretary of Defense Henry Conrad alighted from his armored Lincoln Navigator and strode through the open doors with barely a glance at MacIntyre and Connor, all the while jabbing his finger at another man.

"Well, hello to you, too," Susan snorted. "Who was the horse's ass on the receiving end?"

"That was the go-to guy, by far the most important of the many faceless princelings who do the bidding of the great one," MacIntyre said. "Sorry. I mean, that was Under Secretary of Defense Ronald Kashigian, getting reamed out for something by his highness, the National Command Authority."

Connor shot her boss a glance. "I thought the President was the National Command Authority."

"Half right. The President and the Secretary of Defense are both the NCA. Either can give orders for the use of force, including nuclear force." Seeing Susan screw up her face in doubt, Rusty explained, "It's meant to make a decapitation attack difficult, and also to prevent a slow response as someone tracks down the President while he's getting his picture taken with the Red Sox again. Let's go in."

Once inside the ground level of the West Wing, Susan was surprised that the hallways were dark, with low ceilings. A Secret Service guard in a blue blazer asked to see their badges and checked their names on a computer as young White House staffers breezed by with food trays. MacIntyre continued his tour-guide role. "The White House Mess is down the hall. It's a Navy-run restaurant that also does take-out for busy staffers who prove their importance by eating at their desks. Navy does the Mess, Air Force flies *Air Force One*, the Marines fly the chopper, and the Army runs the comms."

"You worked here once, didn't you?" Susan asked her boss.

"Clinton National Security Council Staff for three years," Rusty whispered.

"I won't tell a soul," Susan whispered back.

They walked down a few steps and turned to face a

wooden door, a television camera, and a telephone. On the door was a large colored plaster-of-paris Seal of the President of the United States and a brass plaque reading, "Situation Room, Restricted Access." Rusty picked up the phone and looked into the camera. "MacIntyre plus one." The door buzzed and they walked into a cramped anteroom.

Off the anteroom was a small, wood-paneled conference room. Ten large leather seats were forced in tightly around the solid, one-piece wooden table. A brass sign holder sat in front of every seat with a name of a principal, or member of the Cabinet-level National Security Council's Principals Committee. A dozen smaller seats lined the walls. On the wall above the chair at the head of the table there was another presidential seal. In one corner Susan noticed a closed-circuit camera behind a darkened glass globe. A door with a peephole was in another corner. A large white phone console sat on a sideboard near the head of the table. The far wall had three digital clocks: "Baghdad," "Zulu," and "POTUS." Zulu, Susan knew, was military speak for Greenwich Mean Time, or London. Doing the math quickly, she realized that today POTUS was Los Angeles time, the President of the United States was on a West Coast swing. POTUS time was whatever time zone the commander in chief occupied.

"I never saw the final talking points for your boss's meeting with the Chinese Premier," Defense Secretary Conrad was complaining as he leaned over the table across from Deputy Secretary of State Rose Cohen. "You guys have to be tough with those bastards. They are after the same oil we are." Cohen was sitting in for the Secretary of State, who was in Asia. Before she could even start to respond, Dr. William Caulder, the National Security Advisor, moved quickly into the room and sat at the head of the table, under the President's seal.

"Let's begin. This is mainly about China, but we will do some current odds and ends as well." He opened a loose-leaf binder to the agenda. Reading aloud, he ticked off the business at hand. "China: strategic assessment and then Chinese missiles in Islamyah, MacIntyre, IAC; bombings in Bahrain, Peters, National Counterterrorism Center; Bright Star Exercise, General Burns, and then you wanted to raise a restricted item, Henry?" The National Security Advisor looked above his half-glasses at the Secretary of Defense, who nodded back.

Like Deputy Secretary of State Rose Cohen, MacIntyre was also standing in for his bosses, Sol Rubenstein at the IAC and Anthony Giambi, the Director of National Intelligence, both of whom had begun skipping more and more of the contentious sessions. Rusty had, therefore, briefed the Principals Committee many times before. The PC, as it was known, was all the National Security Council members except for the President and Vice President. If the national security departments and agencies made up one big conglomerate, then the PC was their board of directors.

"Okay, first, the summary of the latest intelligence estimate on China, a briefing from the Intelligence Analysis Center, Mr. MacIntyre," the National Security Advisor intoned, sounding as though he were chairing someone's Ph.D. oral exam.

As MacIntyre opened his briefing book, a wooden panel receded into the wall, revealing a large plasma screen. On it flashed the first slide of his briefing, "China Emboldened by Economic Power." He began, "The stunning economic growth that China experienced over the last decade has enabled it to modernize its cities, create a domestic automobile industry that is now successfully exporting here, develop its own impressive technological research capability, and deploy a potent, although smaller, military." Pictures of the Beijing Olympics venues, the Gwangju skyline, and a research park appeared on the screen, followed by charts showing China's dramatic economic growth.

"With this progress has come the usual downsides of modernization, including social disruption, particularly in rural areas and in the old industrial cities, industrial and vehicular air pollution, and, most important, a growth in their oil and gas requirements. As you can see from this chart, China is now a close second to the United States in oil and gas imports. It may surpass us in the next two years. They are still well below us in electricity generated per capita, so we can expect the import curve to continue up as they will need more gas to generate higher amounts of electricity.

"This makes China dependent, again, on Russia and the former Soviet states in central Asia, from which they get the bulk of their oil and gas imports. Intelligence sources report that the Chinese leadership does not like that dependence and is seeking to diversify its sources. That may be why we see their new presence in Islamyah, which I will get to in a minute." MacIntyre realized he had their rapt attention.

As Rusty was about to launch into the military brief, Treasury Secretary Fulton Winters seemed to awaken and broke the trance Rusty had induced on the Principals. Winters usually stopped rolling his tie up and down long enough to deliver one delphic pronouncement per meeting.

"Usually people talk about the Chinese military threat to America," Winters began. "There really isn't one. The Chinese economy is tied completely to ours. We are their market. Now, it's true that they hold most of our government debt through purchases of T-notes and, theoretically, they could sell them or stop buying them. That would spike inflation here and probably burst the real estate bubble. But they won't"—Winters smiled—"because an economic divorce would hurt them much more than it would us."

No one commented. Winters returned to rolling his tie.

Rusty continued, "Well, actually, one of the more surprising strategic developments has been the growth of the Chinese navy. For decades, they had utilized Soviet castoffs and small, low-technology coastal ships such as frigates and destroyers. Then they bought some modern cruisers and primitive aircraft carriers from Ukraine and Russia. Now, within the last five years, they have put into service three modern, indigenously designed aircraft carriers with strike and fighter aircraft, the *Zheng He*, the *Hung Bao*, and the *Zhou Man*. They also built a port at Gwadar in Pakistan, at the mouth of the Persian Gulf.

"They have also launched their own air defense cruisers and nuclear-powered submarines. The visit of their *Zhou Man* carrier battle group to Sydney last year gave us a good chance to take a close-up look in many ways, and these are impressive ships," MacIntyre said, showing photographs of the Chinese ships at port in Australia.

"*Zhou Man* sounds like something my fourteen-year-old son would say," General Burns joked.

"Actually, General, Zhou Man was a Chinese admiral whose fleet explored Australia and much more around 1420," MacIntyre replied. "The other carriers are also named for admirals from the 1400s whose fleets explored the Pacific and Indian oceans. The message in the names is that the Chinese navy once ruled the world's seas supreme and may again. But enough about the Chinese navy: to more immediate matters . . ." MacIntyre said, hitting the clicker that brought up a new image on the flat screen.

It was a stunningly vivid picture of the missile base in Islamyah. Rusty began his presentation. "IAC analysts discovered this new Chinese-made missile complex in Islamyah two days ago. It appears ready to go operational. In 1987 the Saudis secretly acquired Chinese medium-range missiles. Confronted by the Reagan administration, they pledged that the missiles would not be nuclear-armed. The CEP of those missiles was such that they could have done little damage to anyone, except perhaps their own launch crews who handled the liquid fuel in the aboveground launch facilities."

The National Security Advisor, who was reading his briefing book, looked up above his glasses. "CEP?"

"Circular error probability, Billy. It's their accuracy," the Secretary of Defense chided. "Go on, go on," he said, flicking his wrist at MacIntyre.

"Now, two decades later, replacement missiles show up. Some mobile missiles on trucks and some silo-based, solid-fuel, highly accurate. In the Chinese strategic forces, they carry nuclear weapons, three per missile. Intelligence indicates that there are twenty-three hundred Chinese personnel at the main base, in the middle of the Empty Quarter. We estimate twenty-four missiles on launchers, probably some reloads.

"Beyond their military value, this secret deployment indicates that the Chinese have a much closer relationship with the revolutionary regime in Riyadh than we had earlier estimated. Although the missiles were originally ordered by the al Sauds, the delivery and deployment went ahead in secret after the revolution. We believe that the cash-strapped Islamyah government, suffering from our sanctions, is paying in oil.

"There is no indication yet from a variety of special intelligence programs and sources, nothing that indicates the presence of any nuclear weapons. We estimate that China would be reluctant to provide such warheads in violation of the Nuclear Proliferation Treaty and that the accuracy of these weapons is such that . . ."

"Bullshit, MacIntyre!" Secretary of Defense Conrad interrupted, leaning forward once again, his scowling face and dark eyes focused like a laser on Rusty. "What the fuck do you think they bought these things for, Chinese fireworks for Ramadan?" The Situation Room was suddenly still; all eyes were on the SECDEF, who continued his tirade.

"I'm telling you that these al Qaeda murderers in Riyadh are out to get nuclear capability. Maybe Beijing won't give them the bomb, maybe. But they can get it from the nuts in North Korea or their al Qaeda East buddies in Pakistan. You mean to tell me those guys in Islamabad won't sell their ideological brethren a few of their bombs? Hell, A. Q. Khan was doing it a decade ago out of the Pakistani larder." No one spoke as Conrad shook his head and pursed his lips. "IAC just doesn't understand the threat these regimes pose."

Finally, MacIntyre raised his hand with two fingers up and spoke slowly but forcefully. "I disagree, for two reasons. First, these weapons were clearly ordered by our friends the al Sauds while they were in power. The lead time is such that they could not have been both ordered and delivered in the year since the Sauds were thrown out. Second, only a Chinese-made warhead could be mated to these missiles. You can't just take a big Pakistani aerial bomb and fit it on a CSS-27. These things are precision weapons. I think for now what we have is a very accurate, high-explosive delivery system, a blockbuster in the original sense of the term, a weapon that has been brought in to deter Iran by bringing downtown Tehran under range of conventionally armed missiles."

The Secretary of Defense emitted a sound, "Pfffft," as he flipped through his briefing book.

"Well then, thank you, Russell. Now the bombings in Bahrain. NCTC?"

National Counterterrorism Center Director Sean Peters described the techniques used in the attack on the hotels in Bahrain, the effects, and a possible culprit. "Most likely Iran's Qods Force, or Jerusalem Force, a combination covert-operations and special-forces group that has been active in bombings in Bahrain and elsewhere in the Gulf for years," Peters concluded.

"Nonsense! Dr. Caulder, I despair of these supposed intelligence briefings. It wasn't the Iranians." This time the SECDEF actually pounded the table. "Ron, tell 'em. After all, they were trying to kill you."

From the back bench behind Secretary Conrad, Under Secretary Ronald Kashigian cleared his throat and stood. The thick glasses and buzz-cut hair made Kashigian look like a college basketball coach. "Well, I was in the hotel as it was attacked. And our intelligence people assume I was the target." Red was rising into his ears. "They, the experts in the region, say this was definitely the Islamygians . . . Riyadh." Kashigian sat back down.

"We are convinced, Billy," the Secretary of Defense said, stabbing his finger in the air at the National Security Advisor, "that this al Qaeda regime in Riyadh is sending a message to King Hamad in Bahrain to kick the Americans out, or else they will destabilize the place with bombings like these. These people are not satisfied with just their fanatical caliphate in Saudi Arabia; they want to export their revolution throughout the Gulf!"

Dr. Caulder, a former University of Chicago professor who had stepped in as National Security Advisor six months ago after his predecessor had suddenly died of a stroke, asked meekly, "Who do the Bahrainis think did it?"

The NCTC Director stood at his seat along the wall, said, "They don't know, Dr. Caulder," and sat down.

"Well then, moving on, maybe we can agree on, what is it, Exercise Bright Star? General Burnside."

"Burns, sir." The handsome and relaxed Air Force

four-star had spent a career flying and was now the second most senior military officer in the United States, the Vice Chairman of the Joint Chiefs of Staff. "Bright Star is a CENTCOM exercise series with the Gypoes, ah, the Egyptians, going back over twenty-five years.

"It lapsed for a while and in recent years has only been carried out on a small scale, but now with the revolution in Saudi, Cairo is interested in a show of force in the Red Sea, to demonstrate to Riyadh that Egypt has the full military support of the United States, just in case the Islamyah government is thinking about exporting their revolution to Egypt.

"We plan the largest amphibious operation in recent history, the largest airborne drop, and one of the largest bombing exercises we have ever had. Three MAUs, Marine Amphibious Units, will go ashore at three points along the Egyptian Red Sea coast, about fifteen thousand men." He used a laser pointer to put a red dot on the flat screen. "Two brigades of the 82nd Airborne will drop in behind the beachhead, about nine thousand personnel. The target areas will be softened up by Air Force B-1s and B-2s from CONUS and by Navair from the *Bush* and the *Reagan* battle groups in the Red Sea.

"The Marines and Airborne will link up with the Egyptian First and Second Armored Divisions and then move up the Nile Valley in a combined operation to demonstrate interoperability. All of this will be done in a way that allows the folks in Riyadh to see on TV and through their sources what the awesome firepower of the United States of America can do." General Burns turned off his laser.

"Any questions of General Burns? No? Then thank

you all. If I could ask everybody to leave except the principal or acting principal from each agency," Dr. Caulder said.

"I'll meet you in the car, Susan." MacIntyre turned from the table and whispered to his analyst, who had been back-benching behind him.

After the shuffling had settled down, National Security Advisor Caulder turned to the Secretary of Defense. "What was it, Henry, that you wanted to talk about in a smaller group?"

Tall and broad-shouldered, Conrad, dressed in what appeared to be an expensive double-breasted suit, radiated overflowing energy, fidgeting in his seat. "Well, it's just very sensitive, you know, Billy," Conrad said in a softer tone than he had used to the full house. "The reason I was so adamant, MacIntyre, I'm sorry, is that we have sources, really good sources, inside the PLA, the Chinese People's Liberation Army.

"These sources tell us that there was an order given to the PLA and its navy to prepare to send, secretly, a division of infantry to Saudi using roll-on/roll-off cargo ships and, get this, Air China 777s. The movement is to be protected by a Chinese navy expeditionary force, including two of the new aircraft carriers, accompanied by their cruisers with their new antiship missile, and their subs.

"The naval movement will be couched as a show-the-flag thing, with port calls in Perth, Pakistan, and then in the Saudis' ports.

"'Course it will scare the shit out of the Gulfies, I mean the smaller Gulf states, and Iran and drive the Indians bonkers, which is good for us, but all in all this is a bad deal. Red Chinese infantry in Saudi. Their fleet in the Indian Ocean for the first time.

"See, this is why I don't think it's impossible that they will deliver the nuclear warheads to accompany MacIntyre's missiles. When there are lots of Chinese troops in country, they can deliver the nuclear warheads for the missiles because they think we won't bomb a bunch of Chinese troops.

"They are bucking up this I-Salamie regime when it is new and weak, just to get long-term access to all the oil they got there.

"Here we are depleting the strategic oil reserve, freezing from Michigan to Maine, because we sanctioned Saudi oil. Paying top dollar in the spot market, where we are probably buying the Saudi oil anyway but getting it from middlemen. We're pumping Alaska dry, dealing with the very people who told us to get out of Iraq, and the Chinkos are going to lock up Saudi oil in long-term deals protected by their goddamn army!"

Once again, the Secretary had silenced the Situation Room.

"When is this supposed to happen?" Deputy Secretary Cohen asked meekly.

"Sometime in March," the SECDEF answered without any hesitation. "We may have to confront them, block them from getting their troop ships into the Gulf."

Deputy Secretary Cohen had had enough and slapped her hand on the conference table. "There is absolutely no legal authority for you to do that, Henry. It would be an act of war to embargo military shipments, like the Cuban

Missile Crisis, which almost ended in a nuclear war. What the hell are you after, a war with China, a nuclear war?" she asked.

"There is a draft finding, which I wrote," Conrad responded. "It's now on the President's desk. It will order us to overthrow those murdering, fanatic pretenders in Riyadh. We could add the naval embargo to that decision package. We need to act before the Chinese take over. The Chinese will back down in the face of firm U.S. action. They know we could sink their entire fleet in an hour. And the Indians would help us, too." Secretary Conrad slammed closed his briefing book.

"Dr. Caulder, I know of no such finding," said Cohen, almost quivering with anger as she turned with indignation to the National Security Advisor.

"That's because you're not cleared for it, dear," Conrad sneered as he got up from the table and pushed his way out of the Situation Room.

The National Security Advisor turned to Rose Cohen and said, "It's not under active consideration, Rose. That's why he's so mad." Dr. Caulder then quickly followed Secretary Conrad out of the Situation Room, leaving his briefing book on the table and calling, "Henry, wait up."

"Well, I guess that means this meeting is over," Rusty said to no one in particular. Kashigian, who had stayed when the other back-benchers left, brushed by MacIntyre, bumping his shoulder. "Don't get in the way of this, MacIntyre. Otherwise you and your boss Rubenstein will be on the wrong end of history, if you know what I mean."

"I have no idea what any of what you just said means,

but it sounded like you threatened me," MacIntyre said in a loud voice so that others could hear.

"Just swim in your own lane, okay?" Kashigian said, and he spun about as he left the Sit Room, moving quickly to catch up with the SECDEF and the motorcade waiting outside.

The Situation Room conference room was suddenly empty. MacIntyre headed over to the Mess, where he stood at the take-out window and ordered two frozen yogurts. Balancing the two cups on a tray and his briefing book under his arm, he walked outside past the Secret Service guards, and headed over to Susan Connor, who was standing next to the black Chrysler on West Exec.

"Rusty, it's February. Who the hell eats ice cream in February?" Susan blurted out.

"Glad to see you got over the Mr. MacIntyre thing. They're yogurts, not ice cream, and after that meeting I wanted to cool down," MacIntyre said, handing her a cup.

"They're nuts, boss," Susan said, taking the cup of frozen yogurt. "The whole damn Pentagon is nuts!"

The two got into the warm, waiting car. "The Pentagon is a building with about thirty thousand people. The Defense Department is about three million. Not all of them are nuts." Rusty spooned the yogurt as the Chrysler and its two escort vehicles pulled out through the Eisenhower Building's courtyard and crossed through a second courtyard to exit onto 17th Street. A Secret Service agent threw the traffic lights to red for the outside street traffic to stop as the lead Suburban pulled out of the gate.

"Well, their Secretary certainly is certifiable," Susan chortled. "I've never seen anything like that."

"Welcome to the big leagues." MacIntyre smiled. "You missed the best part. Secretary Conrad is so gung-ho to get the Sauds back on the throne that he is willing to risk a shooting war with China. In the next few weeks."

"Where does he get off acting like God made him Viceroy of Earth?" Susan lisped, her tongue now frozen from the yogurt. "Where'd we get him anyway? Does he have pictures of the President and a goat or something?"

"He was a takeover expert on Wall Street. Buy an ailing company on the cheap, fix it, then sell it for a multiple of six or seven what he paid for it." MacIntyre looked out of the car at the few tourists on the sidewalk, all trying to see what big shot was in the car leaving the White House. "Then he ran for Governor of Pennsylvania, where he's from. Some Main Line blueblood, out to 'help the people help themselves.' Or so his campaign claimed. Supposedly turned Pennsylvania around, too. And he delivered the state to the President, along with three hundred million in Wall Street cash. The President thinks Conrad is brilliant."

"What magic are you going to do?" she asked, again serious.

"As Otter told the boys of Delta Tau Chi, it's time for a road trip." MacIntyre took a big bite of the frozen yogurt as their car sped past the Corcoran Gallery and headed toward Foggy Bottom.

Susan Connor frowned. "Was that some kind of seventies reference?"

Returning to the Intelligence Analysis Center, MacIntyre went straight for his boss's office to debrief him on the meeting. Sol Rubenstein was poring over a draft analysis on North Korea. Without looking up, he welcomed his young deputy with "So I hear you got into a little contretemps with the almighty Secretary of Defense."

"Word travels fast," Rusty said, plunking down into one of the two chairs next to the desk.

"I got good sources," Rubenstein replied, coming around into the other chair. "Rosie called me from the car. She said you stood up to him, the son of a bitch. Good for you. Fuck him."

Rusty smiled at the support from his boss. "I don't believe his Defense Intelligence source about the Chinese. Selling missiles is one thing, but sending troops to prop up Islamyah, and then the nutty idea they would give them nukes. Shit, I don't believe that Islamyah would even ask for that kind of help. More infidels in their holy land?" MacIntyre said, leaning toward his boss.

"I dunno, Rusty, I dunno. Stranger things have happened. It's possible, it's possible," the Director of IAC mused. "Listen, if you were running Islamyah, wouldn't you want some protection right now? Your weapons don't work because the Americans all left and won't send parts. Secretary Conrad is giving a speech a week about how bad the people in Riyadh are. The Iranians are screwing around in Bahrain again. Tehran's got the Iraqis on their side now. Who knows?"

"I feel like there are an awful lot of moving parts right now, too many pieces on the chessboard, three-level chess," MacIntyre suggested.

"There are. Lotta balls in the air at the moment. That's when America needs really good analysis," Rubenstein said, and then he sat up straight. "Here's what I suggest you do. Fly over to London. They have smart guys there on this stuff, with good contacts, better than ours, stuff they don't share through normal liaison channels with CIA. For someone of your rank, they'll open up. Besides, it'll give you a chance to buy Sarah something nice on Portobello Road. She's into antiques, right?"

"You are well informed," Rusty said, rising out of his chair. "Does someone of my rank get to fly first class this time?"

"No, business class," Rubenstein said, going back to his papers on North Korea.

MacIntyre walked up to Rubenstein's desk and quietly placed a small blue device on it.

"What the hell is that?" Rubenstein asked.

"It's a BlackBerry. It's already programmed for you with a Yahoo account in your name. It's also programmed to send me PGP-encrypted e-mail at a Yahoo address that only you and a few others know. In short, it's our own private communications system. I'll stay in touch that way while I'm on the road." MacIntyre handed him the BlackBerry.

"I'll never figure out how to work it," Rubenstein said, holding the device as if it were some extraterrestrial artifact.

"I know. One of my new analysts will help you. Susan Connor—very tech-savvy. Unlike some." MacIntyre laughed as he walked toward the door.

Finally, Rubenstein looked up. "You don't mind, do you, going to talk to the Brits?"

"I already told Debbie to book the flight," Rusty said. "Just came in here to persuade you."

"Argh," the Director bellowed. "Get the fuck out of here!"

Salmaniyah Medical Center
Manama, Bahrain

"Dr. Rashid, I am so glad you have joined us, and I want you to know that if there is anything we can do to help you get settled, you have only to ask." The cute young Pakistani nurse was positively effusive as she said good night to the new doctor. It was the end of Ahmed's first shift and he was bone-tired, but he could not rest. He had a lot more to do tonight.

Ahmed bin Rashid walked to the nearly empty parking lot and started the battered Nissan that had been waiting for him, along with the apartment, along with the job. His brother's people had seen to everything. He drove to his apartment building on the Manama Corniche and parked on the street, near the long coastal promenade, with its sweeping views of the bay. Entering the lobby of the modern structure, he went down the stairs to the basement and exited into the alley behind the building. There he found the motorbike where someone had left it for him. He drove it three miles to an old high-rise apartment block on the al Lulu Road near the Central Market. Ahmed entered the building through the service door, conveniently left unlocked. As soon as he stepped through the portal, a pair of hands grabbed him by his shoulders and spun him around, locking him in a tight grip just above the elbows. Stunned, his eyes unfocused in the dark, Ahmed tried to pull away, but whoever was holding him was much stronger.

"A moment, please, Doctor," a voice said calmly in Arabic. An instant later, another pair of hands expertly patted him down.

The men were apparently satisfied. The lock on Ahmed's arms abruptly released, and the voice spoke again. "This way."

The two men moved ahead and, with his vision adjusting to the dark, Ahmed followed the shapes becoming clear before him. As his racing heartbeat returned to normal, he gave silent thanks that he hadn't embarrassed himself by acting like a scared little girl before what he presumed was his personal collection of spies.

Ahmed followed the man through another door and into a dimly lit basement storage room. Three more men were waiting. Now, he thought, now it begins. Suddenly, he was no longer tired.

The man who had grabbed him turned and spoke. "Welcome, brother. We are your team. My name is Saif, and we await your orders." The man had broad shoulders and the look of a bodybuilder. Ahmed guessed Saif was in his mid to late twenties, which probably made him the oldest of the group of young men.

Ahmed caught his breath, painfully aware that despite the fact that he was the amateur in the room, they were waiting for him to take charge, because he was supposed to be in charge. "Why don't we start by each of you telling me where you work and how you came to the cause."

They were all Bahraini Sunni, but not from the wealthiest families. They were from the second tier of Bahraini society, for whom good higher education was hard to come by, for whom good jobs were scarcer yet. Three had gone to religious training in Riyadh four and five years earlier. There they'd been recruited and sent back to Bahrain, where they had brought in two old friends.

"We are a small cell, but we believe there are other cells," the one who was their leader, Saif bin Razaq, said. Ahmed said nothing. "Our strength is in the nature of our penetrations," Saif continued, pointing to each man in turn. "We work at the travel office at the American Navy base, the telephone switching center for overseas calls, the Foreign Ministry, the airport, and I work at an Iranian import/export office in Sitra. It is actually a front for the Qods Force."

"But why do you run these risks for us? What do you hope for?" Ahmed asked, straining to see the faces of the five zealots in the dim light.

"Not for you, Doctor, for Allah," Fadl, the youngest-looking one, said softly. "We want Bahrain to be part of the new Islamyah. Now Bahrain is run by one family, who are Sunnis, yes, but they are threatened by the Shi'a majority here."

"Iran is helping the Shi'a," Saif joined in. "The mullahs have sworn that they will add Bahrain to Iran, just as the Shah wanted to do thirty years ago. Liberate the majority Shi'a from oppression. *Tppt.*" He spit on the floor. "From here they will move on the Eastern Province of Islamyah, where they say they will go to liberate the Shi'a majority there, too, but really they just want to seize the oil."

"If Bahrain can become part of the greater Islamyah, we Sunnis here will be part of the majority of a great new Muslim nation, which can hold back the Persian forces," Fadl finished the thought.

"The Persians have a very long memory and an equally long time horizon," Ahmed responded. "They think that if they wait, and keep their hand in, these things will fall to them like ripened figs from the trees."

"No, Doctor, they do not plan to wait." Saif was excited. "This is the news we have for you! They are working on something big in the month of first Jamada. This is why they do these bombings now in Manama and blame it on us." Saif pulled out an American newspaper. "Look at these lies that they spread, look here: 'The work of Islamyah's terrorist cells,' they say!"

"Do you know for certain the bombings were done by the Persians?" Ahmed asked, taking the copy of *USA Today*.

"As I said, Doctor, I work in the building that is the front company for al Qods, the Iranian special services. I repair their photocopier and the printers." He smiled for the first time. "And sometimes I help myself to what they print." Now Saif handed over a thick wad of paper in a red file folder. "The Qods Force here is to step up the bombing, targeting the American Navy. Then in first Jamada they plan to be ready to stage a coup, and a popular uprising, as they had planned to do in 2001. Only this time, they think the American fleet will not be here and the

Persian forces will be able to land quickly to support the uprising."

"The American fleet never really leaves Bahrain," Ahmed scoffed as he opened the red file. "It only sails nearby in the Gulf."

"Doctor, over the last several years, the Americans have pulled their soldiers and ships out of Lebanon, Somalia, Saudi Arabia, Afghanistan, and Iraq." Fadl looked up, smiling. "Maybe the Persians know when they plan to leave here, too."

Yes, Ahmed thought. Maybe they do. He turned. "Saif, your cell must find out when and how al Qods Force plans to hit the American Navy Base." He stood up to leave. "The Persians cannot be allowed to pin that attack on Islamyah. We cannot give the Americans an excuse to attack us." Ahmed bin Rashid moved to the door. "Find out, Saif." He walked down the darkened basement corridor and out to the motorbike in the alley.

Mounting the little motorbike, Ahmed was pleased by the quality of the men in his cell, and equally pleased by his inaugural performance as spymaster. He would use the contacts and abilities of his men to produce intelligence for Islamyah, to prove his worth to his brother, Abdullah. If he could prove that the Iranians were going to blame Islamyah for an attack they would make against the Americans . . . better yet, if he could stop the attack.

As he drove through the parking lot behind the high-rise apartment building, Ahmed's image appeared on a small black-and-white screen in a Bedford step van parked across the street. "Well, thank you, Dr. Rashid," an English voice whispered. "We had been wondering who was going to run that cell for Riyadh. Mr. Douglas will like this information."

FEBRUARY 1
A government guesthouse
Jamaran, Iran
(North of Tehran)

"The Elburz are beautiful in the snow," the man in the business suit said.

"Yes, they are, General. The mountains are beautiful all year round," the cleric replied. "Let's sit by the fire and have some hot chai." The two moved to large chairs by the stone fireplace. A teapot sat on the table between them.

"Phase One of Devil's Fish Tank is complete. The pro-Islamyah website has claimed the credit, but the Bahraini secret police believe it was our Shi'a brethren. They will begin to take measures against them," the General reported.

"Very good. So the Americans will think it was Riyadh that blew up the hotels in Bahrain, and the al Khalifas ruling Bahrain will crack down on the Shi'a." The cleric smiled broadly. "Nicely done. What's next?"

"We complete Devil's Fish Tank. Then the Armenian and his boss will demand action against Riyadh for the slaughter of so many brave sailors," the General said, pouring tea for himself and the cleric.

"You trust the Armenian and his boss? Completely?" the cleric asked.

"I trust no one but you completely." The General smiled. "But they are gullible and greedy. And because they must know that we have our meeting with him on videotape, they will not risk exposure by double-crossing us."

"You will use Iraqis in Phase Two?" the cleric asked, and the General nodded. "The Iraqis are proving to be useful?"

"They are, but our friends in Baghdad are having difficulties with the Kurds and Sunnis. Some of our people think it may soon be time to break off Basra."

The cleric rose, arranged his robes, and walked slowly to the window looking out on the snow-covered spruce. He turned back to the general. "You and the Qods Force have done so much for us, so well, for such a long time: chasing the Israelis out of Lebanon using the Hezbollah, the Buenos Aires bombings, all the things Mugniyah has done, merging Zawahiri's group into al Qaeda, the covert support to bin Laden, getting the Americans to back our man and throw out Saddam, then the Baghdad government . . .

"But your big plan, this is much more complicated, much riskier. There are many moving parts, including now, perhaps, the Chinese." The cleric fingered his beads.

"With respect, sir, they all know we have the nu-clears." The General rose and walked toward the fire. "They do not know how many and they do not know where. If for some reason the big plan does not go well, we are still secure. Allah will provide."

The cleric nodded. "I believe it is our destiny to be an

agent for Allah, to unite the Shiites and bring for them a golden age," the cleric said, his enthusiasm returning. He walked toward the Qods Force commander and placed his hands on the General's shoulders. "Yes, you are right. Allah will provide."

3

FEBRUARY 2

*U.S. Navy, Administrative Support Unit
Juffair, Bahrain*

Brian Douglas drove his own car, a green Jaguar, from his beach villa out of town to the Juffair district, home to ASU Bahrain, as the American Fifth Fleet headquarters was known. The sixty-acre compound was surrounded by a high sand-colored masonry wall. A Marine in combat gear stopped the Jag and directed Douglas to pull into the vehicle inspection lane.

"Please open the hood, trunk, all four doors, and back away from the car, sir," a female Marine with an M16 rifle said, as another Marine approached with a German shepherd. As he stood aside and watched the dog sniff its way through the Jaguar, Douglas heard a helicopter engine getting very close. A matte-gray Black Hawk flared down onto the heliport on the other side of the wall, kicking up a small sandstorm near the soccer field.

Cleared to proceed, Douglas drove to the stucco archway that was the main gate. It looked as though it had

been left on some Hollywood back lot from the set of
Gunga Din. Flashing his Navy-issued ID, Douglas was
directed to Building 903, with its typical U.S. Navy gob-
bledegook signage: "HQ-COMUSNAVCENT."

Douglas had no sooner been seated in the waiting
room when a large man in a Navy flight jacket bounded
into the suite and right up to Douglas. "Brian Douglas,
it's good to see you, you old bloke." His thinning straw-
berry blond hair and baby face made him look like anything other than the Fifth Fleet commander.

"Come on in, Bri. Ensign, two big mugs of coffee.
Just choppered in from two days on the *Reagan*." The
British SIS station chief followed in the admiral's wake
into the cavernous office.

"Sorry I haven't had you over since I got in last
month, but it's been a whirlwind of get-to-know-you
meetings up and down the Gulf. I've memorized more
royal family trees in the last week than I did studying European history," Admiral Adams continued, moving
across the room. "Here, let's sit at the conference table.
You know my N-2, the intel guy here, Johnny Hardy."
The three men sat at the long staff table.

"Johnny, Brian Douglas and I first got to know each
other back in twenty-oh-three in the Green Zone, chasing bad guys, when I was assigned to CENTCOM staff
in Iraq. Hangin' out together in the HVT Bar out at the
airport after hours. He has more embarrassing information on me than you guys in Naval Intelligence will ever
have, so whenever he says he needs to see me like he did
this morning, he gets right in. I'm here for you. You're

the best ally we've got left, almost the only one we got left, right, Johnny?"

"Well, Admiral, I appreciate your willingness to see me on such short notice." Douglas looked down at the giant coffee mug, to which somebody had already added a great deal of milk.

"You've been stationed in Bahrain for a while. Real expert on the region. How long you been here now, Brian? Tell Johnny your career," the admiral said as he reached for the tray of cookies.

"Well, sir, as you know, I served here as a station officer during Desert Storm, then Baghdad after the Second Gulf War, now back here as SIS station chief for Bahrain, Qatar, Oman, and the United Arab Emirates. I'm completing twelve years in the Gulf, 'fraid to say." Douglas tried to sound modest.

"You must like it here in Bahrain." Captain Hardy dunked a ladyfinger in his mug.

The admiral jumped in. "Lots of people do. "Hell, I wouldn't be an admiral without Bahrain. They came up with the word *amir*, meaning the guy in charge of the dhows. Shit, they were sailing dhows to Africa and India when we Anglo-Saxons were still painting ourselves blue and fighting the Romans." He turned to Douglas for affirmation.

"I think it may have been my people, the Picts, who painted themselves blue, but yes, this is a very ancient, well-fought-over piece of turf. Which is why I wanted to see you, sir," the station chief said, trying to get the conversation back on track.

"Yes, Brian, you're not here to discuss history. What's up?" Adams sat back in the chair at the head of the table and focused on his guest.

"I've already been on to your embassy and told my brethren from the Agency, but I wanted to pass it directly to you as well." Brian Douglas withdrew a paper from inside his suit coat and read, "'Highly reliable SIS sources have revealed that the Iranian Qods Force has designated ASU-Bahrain as a target for a terrorist-style attack, probably within the next four weeks. The sources also reveal that Iran may be planning to stimulate a Shi'a uprising in Bahrain, as it attempted to do in 1996 and 2001.'" Douglas passed the paper to Captain Hardy, thinking of how successful his monitoring of Ahmed Rashid had been.

"Interesting. You're the second group to tell me today that my little base here will be the target for an attack. That's why we are on a high force protection status, Threatcon Charlie. Of course, I did that myself after the Diplomat and Crowne Plaza attacks." Admiral Adams took the report from his intelligence officer. "But the Pentagon seems to think the attack will be carried out by agents of Islamyah."

The British spy coughed and sipped the heavily milk-laden coffee. "With all due respect to the Pentagon, the import of our report is that Tehran may be intending that you believe the attack comes from Riyadh. But Riyadh? Their lot couldn't stage a successful attack on the ASU. Al Qods is capable of it. Moreover, and this is not in what we gave Washington or the Agency here, we have reason to believe that Islamyah knows that the Iranians are setting them up to get the blame."

"Well, whoever it is, they will have a hard time. This place is buttoned up tight, Admiral," the N-2 asserted.

"Maybe, Johnny, maybe, but any place can be struck. I can step up protection, but the way to handle this is to get them before they get us." The admiral leaned across the table toward Douglas. "Can the Bahrainis do that? Can you and the Agency find these guys, whoever they are?"

"The Bahraini Security Service is very good, SIS-trained." Douglas smiled. "And we and the Agency each have our own sources as well. If we can find the attack team, the Bahrainis can wipe them up."

"I also have SEALs and a Fleet Anti-Terrorism Security Team here if they need any help." Brad Adams got up out of his chair. "They prefer the offense to sniffing around diplomats' Jags." Brian laughed; Adams had done his homework. As they walked to the door, Adams changed his tone and style. He said softly to Douglas, "We can't have another Baghdad here. I can't stand the thought of more U.S. troops KIA. I wasn't in Iraq as long as you, but you remember those nights out at the HTV, drinking away our sorrows with the Agency guys and the Special Forces. I was there two years, working the Sunni insurgency, trying to counter the Iranians."

"Bloody mess, tragedy really," Douglas said as he looked at the floor and shook his head.

"Yes, yes it was, Brian. I thought it was the right thing to do. Shit, everyone thought they had WMD. But with us gone, it's still a mess. The Shi'a aren't going to be able to put down that Sunni insurgency. It's been going on for years and no sign of letting up. The Kurds are probably going to formalize their independence and then we'll

see what Baghdad tries to do about that. They won't let
Kirkuk go. It's all been an awful waste of men and
money. And for what, so that Iran can tell the democrat-
ically elected government of Iraq what to do?" Brad
Adams was not playing the part of an American admiral
now. "Listen, Bri, I'm supposed to leave tomorrow for a
week in Tampa and Washington. Should I go or is this attack on the base here going to happen that fast?"

"I'm leaving for London tonight myself, Brad. We
think it's a couple of weeks off, but we can't find any sign
of an Iranian al Qods Force here in town yet, just reports.
If we find out otherwise, we'll shoot up a flare." Douglas
was thinking he was glad to be working again with this
big Baby Huey–looking American sailor. He was Ivy
League, not off the Annapolis cookie-cutter assembly
line, and he had proven again and again in Iraq that he
could be trusted, and could get things done.

As Brian Douglas drove out through the Hollywood
stage-set archway, a second armored Humvee was pulling
into place. The Marine sticking through the roof cocked
the M60 machine gun and pointed it down the access
road.

Capitol Hill
Washington, D.C.

Russell MacIntyre got out of the beat-up taxi on
Delaware Avenue, on the north side of Capitol Hill,
where that gentle rise falls off toward Union Station. It
was cold and damp, threatening to snow, so it did not

look unusual that he had on a hat, pulled down low. None of the staff exiting out the back doors of the Senate office buildings were looking up anyway; they were rushing to the Metro station to get home, or at least to a warm bar.

MacIntyre entered through the back door of the Hart Senate Office Building, the newest of the three edifices that housed the personal and committee offices of the one hundred United States Senators. The sign on the door said "Staff Only." MacIntyre flashed a badge to the three Capitol Hill policemen who stood around the magnetometer and X-ray machine. "It's okay, sir, just step through," the tall African-American police sergeant said, waving his arm. "Don't worry if it goes off." The value of the badge was that in some places where it was recognized, the security force expected that you were armed and didn't mind. MacIntyre was not carrying, although he was entitled to. The Intelligence Analysis Center he helped to manage was really not an operational unit, so he thought it would be a little odd and unnecessary to carry the Glock that he had been issued.

He had entered the Hart Senate Office Building through the back door into the basement level, but instead of taking the elevator up, MacIntyre opened a door and took the stairway down. At the B-2 level, he entered a corridor with a maze of pipes hanging under the low ceiling. It was not an elegant part of Capitol Hill.

Halfway down the corridor, he paused before a door with a sign that said only "SH-B2-101." He went to pick up a phone on the wall, but before he could place the receiver to his ear, the door lock buzzed and he pushed it open. Inside, a woman who looked to be in her sixties smiled at him from behind her desk and said, "Go on in, Rusty. The Senator's waiting for you."

Inside, the office was elegant: dark wood paneling, thick maroon carpeting, green leather chairs, brass fixtures. MacIntyre thought this is what Santa Claus's office would look like if Saint Nick became the CEO of the North Pole. It was, in fact, the hideaway office of the Chairman of the Senate Select Committee on Intelligence, Paul Robinson. Every senior Senator had a hideaway, an anonymous office where they could go to work without bumping into constituents and reporters. It was also a place where meetings could occur without there being records of the get-togethers, without prying eyes noticing whom the Senator was seeing. It was a good place to get campaign contributions from lobbyists with an interest in a committee's work. Robinson, however, didn't take contributions from anyone who lived outside of his native Iowa. He didn't really need to. No one had opposed him in his last reelection.

Robinson was standing by a bar trolley pouring two Wild Turkey bourbons, neat. As he handed one to MacIntyre, he said only, "Getting a little raw outside? Here, warm up."

Before he accepted the drink, MacIntyre pulled a paper out from inside his suit coat and placed it on the desk. "It's the estimate of Chinese oil consumption you asked for." He took a big gulp of the Kentucky whiskey. "You were right. They are consuming almost as much as we are. Lots of cars now. Booming industry. And they have few long-term contracts, so they often get stuck paying the higher spot market prices, like we do now.

"The Pentagon is all in a fever over China. The growth of their navy, their export of the missiles to Islamyah. And by the way, it was the Sauds who bought the missiles before they got thrown out, not the new Islamyah crowd. Defense Intel even has some uncorroborated story about a Chinese People's Liberation Army expeditionary force secretly going to Islamyah."

The Senator twisted about. "Tell me you're kidding. The PLA in Arabia?"

"Well, I think somebody is probably kidding Defense Intel, but they all believe it over at the Pentagon. And it's very hush-hush. We aren't supposed to brief you and the committees yet," MacIntyre admitted, following the Senator to the stuffed leather chairs next to the artificial fireplace.

"So what's so important that we have to do our weekly little private session tonight, when I could be enjoying a boring reception for the Future Fucking Farmers of America?" the Senator joked.

"I won't be here the rest of the week. I'm off to London to see if I can learn anything from the Cousins. I just think something's up," MacIntyre replied, sipping what was left of the Wild Turkey. "Number one, we've got our fearless Secretary of Defense talking about some bullshit Defense Intelligence source that says the Chinese Navy deployment in the Indian Ocean is cover for Beijing moving an infantry division to Saudi—ah, Islamyah."

"Well, you just said the Chinese need oil, but I can't

see the Islamyah Shura Council agreeing to let a lot of infidels into their precious desert, can you?" the Senator said, leaning back in the chair.

"No, I can't. Moreover, no other source has noticed a Chinese division moving. But there's more. Number two, Secretary Conrad is planning a gigantic amphibious and airborne exercise on the Egyptian Red Sea coast next month."

Senator Robinson arched an eyebrow.

"Number three, Senator, the British SIS just reported that it's really Iran that is staging the bombings in Bahrain, not Islamyah, that the Iranians want to bomb our base there and blame Islamyah, and that they are planning some sort of uprising among the Shi'a majority in Bahrain. The King there is Sunni, but he has been reaching out to the Shi'a and doing a good job.

"Number four, I am having a hard time believing that the new government in Islamyah is as bad as everybody else in Washington seems to think. Yes, I know some of them were al Qaeda–related at some point, but we have one source who says they're planning real national elections next year."

"And you put all this in your famous analytical blender and get what, Rusty?" Senator Robinson asked, staring into his glass.

"I don't know, and that's what bothers me. I feel like— what did they say in the *Star Wars* movie?—'there's a disturbance in the Force.'" MacIntyre waved the fingers on both hands as if conjuring up the Force.

"Well, Obi-Wan, what are you going to do about it?" the Senator said, rising and going for a refill.

"For starters I'm flying over to London tonight to see what I can stir up. They always tell us more in person, stuff they are hearing but can't put into a liaison report to us for whatever reason," MacIntyre said, waving off more bourbon. "And they just seem to have better analysts than we do. I'm trying to find out what that ingredient is that they have so I can inject it into our new little Intelligence Analysis Center."

"Good idea to go to London about now, but why not keep going and drop in on some of our friends in the Gulf? They always know more than they put in writing, too," Senator Robinson said, moving behind his desk. "Besides, there's a guy out there I want you to get to know. Brad Adams, runs the Fifth Fleet out of Bahrain. Did a year with me up here on some sort of officer development program when he was a captain. We stay in touch. He has, well, some of the same concerns we do about the civilian leadership in the Pentagon. I'll tell him you're coming."

"Okay." Rusty accepted that his trip to London just became much, much more.

"But tell me, Rusty, do you believe this Islamyah Shura Council will really give up power to freely elected officials? Hell, these are the guys who killed some of the Saudi royal family in their coup. Some of their supporters were al Qaeda, fought us in Afghanistan and Iraq."

"Senator, we have lots of reporting that there is a rift in the Shura Council between the jihadists, who want to export the revolution, and those who want to modernize and democratize Islamyah. It's always that way with a revolution. After a while there is a struggle among the revolutionaries, just like in the French Revolution, the Russian . . ."

Senator Robinson looked at the map of the Middle East on his wall and thought out loud, "Well, you're right, Rusty, it was a relatively bloodless coup, all in all. There's no line of royals at a guillotine. Most of the Sauds escaped to the U.S. on their private planes. The whole thing was over in three days because so much of the Saudi military was in on the coup, the revolution. And so far, all they have really done to piss us off is to eject our defense contractors."

"Senator, it was us, the United States, that froze their bank accounts here after the coup and then stopped shipping military spare parts for the weapons we had sold the Sauds." MacIntyre felt he could be frank with his old boss, and so continued on. "By placing a unilateral economic embargo on them, we made it illegal for U.S. companies to buy Saudi oil. It was only then that they nationalized one hundred percent of Aramco and broke the contracts to sell oil to America. We did it to ourselves.

"Besides, sir, the Saudi government was no barrel of laughs either. They beheaded people, they denied women rights, they funded all sorts of terrorist-related Wahhabi schools and charities before 9/11 and even after. There were literally several thousand royal princelings, and corruption was rampant."

"Look, I know all of that, Rusty," Paul Robinson sighed. "Now the royal Saudis have taken up residence in the finer parts of Los Angeles and Houston. They're throwing their money around, getting involved in American politics. Or should I say more involved? The Bushies were always in bed with the Sauds.

"You can't report this, Rusty," the Senator said, leaning forward and tapping with his finger like a woodpecker on MacIntyre's knee, "but I had one of those exiled royal sons of bitches in this room, this very room, two months ago saying he had twenty-five million dollars in an offshore account that he would transfer control of to me if I would back an intelligence finding to authorize covert U.S. action to topple the Islamyah regime and reinstall the Sauds."

Rusty whistled in amazement. "Shit, Senator . . . You could have him arrested for that."

"I know, but I would have had no proof," Robinson said, leaning back into his chair.

"So what'd you do?" Rusty asked. He had known Paul Robinson for sixteen years, since the now-Senator had hired him as a junior staffer for his House office right after Rusty had graduated from Brown. The Senator was as honest as any man he had ever met and hated dishonesty of any kind, intellectual, financial, political. Corruption just really pissed him off. Robinson had first risen to national attention on a subcommittee that investigated financial fraud in U.S. thrift savings banks.

Senator Paul Robinson had pushed through the creation of the Intelligence Analysis Center because, he said, he and the executive branch were not getting intellectually honest reporting. When the center came into existence and the Director of National Intelligence selected Ambassador Sol Rubenstein to run it, the Senator had told Rubenstein that his confirmation hearing would go a lot faster if he picked Rusty as the first Deputy Director of the IAC.

When Rusty learned that had happened, he'd called the Senator and thanked him, but joked, "You know I was doing well with this Beltway Bandit firm. You just cut my salary by two-thirds."

"Don't try that on me, Rusty," Robinson had replied. "It's not about the money. Not for you. Not for me. Never was. It's about honest government, and I've been feeling like Diogenes down here trying to find someone who will do some quality, honest intelligence analysis. You're it." There was no way that the Senator would let a bribery attempt go by, like the one the Saudi had tried to pull.

"Well, Russell, I did not call the FBI and report the son of a bitch. But I did slip an amendment into the Omnibus Appropriation that requires the Treasury Department to keep all royal Saudi assets in the U.S. frozen until Treasury files a detailed report with us on whether the funds are really personal or should be considered national assets of the people of their country. We then have a hundred and eighty days to review the report, and that period can be extended upon request of any chair of any committee of relevant jurisdiction in either house," the Senator replied as a Cheshire cat grin spread across his face. He really was a legislative master. "So that's how I helped them. How can I help you, Rusty, as you go gallivanting around Europe and the Middle East?"

"Not like that, Senator," Russell said, still laughing at the legislative maneuver. "I haven't been out to the Gulf region for a while. What can you do, sir? Just keep your eyes and ears open, especially with your friends on Armed Services." MacIntyre rose and went for his overcoat, which was lying on the leather couch. "And watch my back."

"Always do, Rusty, always do." The two shook hands and then embraced. "And give my best to that lovely, lefty wife of yours," the Senator said, smiling.

"I'll need to give her something. Right now she's probably sitting outside in her car waiting to take me to Dulles, and freezing," MacIntyre said, walking toward the door.

"Then get your ass in gear, boy." The chairman laughed, flicking his wrist. "Go, go. Never leave a pretty lady waiting in the cold."

Sarah Goldman was feeling cold at the moment, in more ways than one. Their drive out the Dulles Airport Access Road together was more taxing on MacIntyre than negotiating with the Brazilian intelligence service (which he had done three months before, hoping to learn what one of South America's leading spy agencies really knew about the Hezbollah presence in the "triangle area" near Uruguay).

"I don't mind that your job means you can't go to our friends' dinners or that you won't be here when my brother arrives tomorrow. I just don't like being told at the last minute, that's all," Sarah said, gripping the steering wheel a little too tightly. "I know your job means you can't always tell me why, and I accept that it's more important than my work, but . . ."

"Honey, I never said my job is more important. What you do for refugees is sometimes a matter of life and death, too," MacIntyre said, regretting he had put it that way as soon as he said it. He patted his various pockets looking for his passport. "It's just that in addition to secrecy, my job also involves a certain unpredictability, a spontaneity. And if I had remembered that your brother was coming to town tomorrow, I would have delayed a day; you know I love Danny.

"And if I knew for sure when I was coming back, I would tell you, but this trip is a little open-ended," he said, retrieving the worn black diplomatic passport from the new Coach attaché case her mother had given him for Chrismukka.

"It's all right, Rusty, seriously," she said, looking at him and not the traffic. "It's just that I leave Sunday for Somaliland. So I am giving the cat to Max and Theo and you have to remember when you get back to go and get Mr. Hobbs from them. And then you need to feed him, and not starve him like you did last summer when I was in Sudan, poor thing."

Mr. Hobbs was their cat and surrogate child, an arrangement that Sarah seemed to be perfectly happy with, most of the time. When he'd press Sarah for a decision to try to have their own human child, she would point out that both their travel schedules and his work hours meant that something would have to give. "It can't just be my job to raise our child like it is just me taking care of Mr. Hobbs. It would have to be an equally shared responsibility." He accepted that concept, but he did not see how he could walk away from his job to some thirty-hour-a-week position at a boring think tank like Brookings or RAND. There was too much going on. There were too few people who knew how to do it. And his mind would turn to mush writing think-tank monographs that no one would ever read.

Yeah, he wanted a child, their child. Sarah always ended these conversations with the same unconvincing assertion: "It's not like we're failures if we don't have a kid. I am not like my mother, and I just don't buy that I have to procreate to justify my space on the planet. Believe me, there are more than enough people doing that without us adding to it." So he had bought toys for Sarah and the cat in airport shops around the world. They were not much appreciated by either.

Sarah wove her way through the triple-parked cars, taxis, and police on the departure level of Dulles, to the Virgin Atlantic door. She threw on the emergency blinkers and got out of the car to embrace him, while the Dulles policeman yelled, "Move the car, lady."

"Be safe and be careful, wherever the hell you're going," Sarah said as the kiss ended and their breath formed two columns of hot air in the cold night.

"London has been perfectly safe since the Underground bombings in 2005, really . . ." he tried. She put her finger across his mouth to silence him, then slipped her hand inside his coat pocket. "You heard me, mister," Sarah said. She smiled warmly at the Dulles cop and got back into the car.

Rusty waved, hoping that she would be looking at him in the rearview mirror. Then he started looking for his badge to get through security. What he found first, in his coat pocket, was a card deck and a note on a yellow Post-it: "You need to practice the Ambitious Card trick for the IAC Charity Show. Have a great trip, boss, Debbie."

After bypassing the long security line, MacIntyre went to the Virgin Club to await his flight. He sat at the bar and opened up the deck of cards. Somehow, he realized, on trips he felt free of all the tension between him and Sarah. He was already feeling it, his muscles relaxing. As he shuffled the cards Debbie had sneaked into his coat, Rusty looked up at the plasma screen carrying CNN. Secretary of Defense Henry Conrad was giving a speech to the Veterans of Foreign Wars in Dallas. He asked the bartender to turn on the sound.

". . . dating from Franklin Roosevelt's meeting with the Saudi royal family aboard the cruiser the USS *Quincy*. Those who have forced the Sauds from power, for now, are al Qaeda murderers. They plan to spread their jihadist government throughout the region, threatening our allies in Egypt, Bahrain, and elsewhere. But I have a message for them. The United States of America will never permit them to harm our allies and will work for the restoration of the rule of law and order on the Saudi peninsula."

In Dallas, the crowd roared. In Dulles, Rusty MacIntyre cut the cards, and ordered a Wild Turkey.

4

FEBRUARY 4

The Burj al Arab Hotel
Dubai, United Arab Emirates

*N*ew York Journal reporter Kate Delmarco took a
taxi to the world's tallest hotel, a building shaped
like a giant dhow's sail on a man-made island a hundred
yards off the coast of Dubai. She did not enter the hotel,
but instead climbed into a golf cart that took her back
over the short causeway to the shore, past the Wild Wadi
Water Park, and then down to a dock where electrically
powered little dhows departed for the canals of the
nearby hotel and shopping complex. Alighting at the
modern air-conditioned souk, she followed the signs
through the mall to an Italian restaurant.

Although she was based in Dubai, her best source in
the region was her friend Brian Douglas, the British
diplomat stationed in the British embassy in Bahrain. She
knew he was more than the regional energy affairs section
chief, which was how he was listed in the embassy directory. But despite a few overnight sailing trips together on

his 32-foot *Bahrain Beauty*, Douglas had never broken cover. He had never admitted to his other job. Last week he had called and suggested to her, somewhat cryptically, that she should meet "another Dubai friend" of his. So that was what she was about to do.

Waiting at the bar was Jassim Nakeel, a scion of one of the families that were building the new city of Dubai, soaring office towers, offshore islands of villas and condos, tourist theme parks. He did not wear traditional Arab clothing but looked instead like a transplant from Malibu or Laguna Beach.

"You thought because my name is Delmarco I would like an Italian restaurant?" she said as he led her to a table outside on the balcony. Kate Delmarco looked as though her family came from southern Italy, with slightly olive-tinted skin and long black hair. Although she would be forty-five later in the year, Delmarco was fit and exuded a Mediterranean allure. She had managed to finagle an open invitation to go riding at the Dubai royal stables anytime she wanted. It had become her Saturday-morning ritual.

"No, actually, I thought you'd like this place because it has a great view of the sound and light show the Burj al Arab hotel does every night," Nakeel said as he seated Kate facing the giant sail-shaped hotel. "Besides, it has a great wine list."

"Wine list! Is there anything about Dubai that is still Arab? Wine lists, theme parks, high-rise condos filled with Europeans, you in Armani . . ." Kate stopped as the seventy stories of the Burj turned purple, stars sparkled up one side of the tower and then down the other, and then the building faded to pink.

"Dubai is the center of the new Arab world, Kate, cutting-edge, business-smart, and cosmopolitan," Nakeel said, taking the wine list. "For most Europeans, it's more affordable than the South of France and a lot more fun. Besides, it's cold there this time of year. The 1999 Barolo, please," he told the waiter without consulting her. "After what happened in Riyadh, most global companies moved their regional offices to Dubai. It's safe, secure, modern, and efficient. Besides, there are no taxes. They all love it here."

Kate frowned. "Yes, but isn't it a little close to the *old* Arab world? Islamyah? Iran? You can see the lights of the Iranian oil platforms from the bar on the top of the Dubai Tower." She stabbed a pepper on the antipasto plate that had appeared.

"Yes, that's why we're a little worried," Nakeel said, putting down the menu. "That's what I want to talk with you about."

"I'm all ears."

"For generations, the mullahs in Iran have wanted to unite the Shi'a world into a single power, ruled from Tehran or Qom, the seat of their religious leaders," he began. "Right after they took power in 1979, they started to stir up the Shi'a majority in Iraq. That's why Saddam attacked them in 1980."

"Yeah, maybe," Kate replied, breaking a breadstick. "Or maybe he just thought he'd grab their oil province while they were weak after the fall of the Shah."

"The point is," Nakeel continued, "that almost a million people died in that war over eight years, until both sides quit from exhaustion, and nobody won. Fifteen years later, the U.S. Army comes along and topples Saddam in three weeks. Three years later and the Shi'a are practically running Iraq under Iranian guidance. Washington did Tehran's work for them. While all the American attention was focused on car bombs in Baghdad, the Iranians secretly built nuclear weapons while denying it and tricking the Europeans and Americans into thinking that they were five years away from a bomb."

Kate looked bored. "Jassim, that's your version of history. I think we prevented Iraq from getting WMD again and we gave it democracy. Democracy means majority rule, so the Shi'a rule, but that doesn't mean Iran is in charge of Iraq. So what else is new?"

"The next steps, Kate. They are about to happen." He tasted the splash of Barolo the waiter offered for his approval and nodded for him to pour for the lady. "Now they want the Shi'a majority in Bahrain to take power and facilitate Iranian activity across the Gulf. Do you really believe that Pentagon crap that it's Islamyah behind the bombings in Bahrain?" Nakeel scoffed.

"No, I don't, but my editors seem to. They spiked my story blaming it on Tehran and ran a piece by our Pentagon reporter demonizing Riyadh," Kate admitted.

"Your Defense Secretary Conrad has been demonizing them since the day they drove the Sauds out." He paused and looked her in the eye. "We think Conrad is on the al Saud payroll," Nakeel said softly.

"'We'? The Dubai real estate development board?" Kate shot back. "Or do you have another job, too?"

He ignored her question. "If you want a story your

editors can't spike, Kate, talk with my friend in Bahrain."
As he spoke, the Burj al Arab and the hotel next to it that
was shaped like a giant wave both erupted into a galaxy
of twinkling stars, fireworks shot from their roofs, and
the speakers in the souk played "Rocket Man."

"I'm actually booked there on Gulf Air tomorrow afternoon, but I appreciate the advice, Jassim," she said flatly.

"Well then, may I suggest someone you might want
to interview there, a tip from the Dubai real estate
board?" He smiled as they brought his veal scaloppine
and her roasted pork loin. The music switched to ABBA.

FEBRUARY 5
The Ritz-Carlton Hotel
Manama, Bahrain

"You're not afraid to be in a hotel lobby in Bahrain,
Ms. Delmarco?" Ahmed said as he sat in the chair
opposite her in the coffee shop. He was wearing a blue
blazer and khakis, and looked like a thin, young American assistant professor.

"Should I be, Doctor?" she asked as she extended her
hand, testing to see if he would take it. He did.

"Perhaps. Many people died in the Diplomat and
Crowne Plaza, but not, as your paper claims, at the hands
of Islamyah," he said quickly, settling into his seat.

"Thank you for seeing me, Dr. Rashid. I know you
are a busy man at the hospital and . . . everything else,"
she said, lighting a cigarette. "I met an American naval

intelligence officer today at the base, who told me that Riyadh was definitely behind the terrorism, part of a plan to push the Navy out of Bahrain."

"We have to ban smoking in Bahrain," Ahmed joked. "And lies. You should have better sources than this Navy intelligence man."

"I guess everyone has their vices," she said, snubbing out the Kent after two puffs. "That captain's vices apparently include trying to pick up female reporters. We're having dinner tonight. What are your vices, Doctor?"

"I have an addiction to American television comedies." He smiled. "My family would never understand. Do you know *Frasier*?"

Kate thought Ahmed had a warm, genuine smile, and that the spy business was definitely a second career for him. As much as she liked Brian Douglas, it was going to be a lot easier getting information out of the good doctor. "*Frasier*? But you're not a psychologist, you're a cardiologist. You worry about hearts." She signaled for the waiter. "And minds?"

"Some people are trying to sow fear in the minds of Americans, Ms. Delmarco, but America does not need to fear the new government in Islamyah. We have replaced a corrupt, undemocratic government with one more in line with our traditions and beliefs as a people. We still sell oil on the world market. We do not attack Americans. Why not let us alone?" Again, he flashed the charming, boyish smile.

"'We,' Doctor? I thought you were a physician who just happened to have a highly placed brother in Riyadh, a brother from whom the Islamyah embassy press attaché assures me you are estranged. What does that mean, 'estranged'?" she said, taking out her digital recorder.

"May I call you Kate?" he asked. She nodded. "Then, Kate, let's stop the dance. I was told I could trust you, and you were told the same about me. I have known the Nakeels for twenty years. My parents have owned a vacation house next to theirs in Spain forever. Yes, many people in our new government would not talk to an American reporter, a woman reporter, but because I support that government, I will. I will try to help you see the truth, assuming you will report it." Ahmed stopped abruptly and touched his cell phone's Bluetooth earpiece. "Excuse me. I have to take this."

Kate sipped her coffee, trying to hear something of what was being said into Ahmed's ear. His face had changed; he looked concerned, almost afraid.

"I apologize. I have to get back to the intensive care unit. May we meet tomorrow? May I call you?" he said, placing Bahrain dinars on the table.

She smiled and handed him her card, with the Dubai cell phone number. "Anytime, Doctor."

In a moment, he was gone. Kate Delmarco turned off the recorder and wondered what could happen at the ICU to put fear into such a pleasant young man.

The beat-up Nissan was no more. He had ditched what the cell had given him and purchased something more to his liking. Ahmed Rashid's new BMW 325 was supposed to be parked at the hotel door, thanks to a small contribution he had made to the doorman, but it was nowhere in sight. A young man in a valet's uniform ran over, key in hand.

"Excuse me, sir, but we had to move your car. It's just around the corner. Should I bring it or would you like to follow me?"

Impatient, Ahmed waved him forward. "Let's go."

The valet nodded and stepped smartly, Ahmed behind. The valet turned the corner and disappeared. Ahmed could see the front of his BMW as he moved past the building's edge. He vaguely wondered where the valet had gone when he spotted something moving to his right. As he turned his head, he saw the valet, hand out in front. But instead of car keys in his hand, the valet held something large and metal and black. As Ahmed realized it was a gun, the valet suddenly lurched and fell to his knees and then on his face. Ahmed now faced Saif, breathing rapidly, eyes narrow and dark.

Ahmed looked down at the valet. A knife was sticking out of the base of his head, blood gurgling out from the wound and onto his uniform and on the concrete. The thought floated through Ahmed's mind that Saif knew his business: the valet, or whoever he was, had been half dead before he had hit the ground.

"Iranian," Saif said. "Qods. He's been shadowing you for a couple of days. Waiting for the right opportunity."

And you've been shadowing him, Ahmed thought. Or me.

"Thank you," Ahmed said simply, hoping his voice didn't sound as shaky as he felt.

Saif nodded. "Go. I'll clean up and follow."

Ahmed got into his BMW and drove quickly through the Manama traffic, fighting his shock, increasingly feeling a sense of vulnerability and dread. What if Saif hadn't been there? How long had the Iranians been planning to kill him? Would they try again? He had been so stupid: the amateur spymaster. Ahmed violently shook his head, refusing to give in to fear. There was no time. Not now. So this was what his brother dealt with every day of his life. So now it was his turn. Good.

He wove rapidly through the late-afternoon flow, south toward Sitra, the industrial area near the refinery. Fifteen minutes later, he pulled another cell phone from the console between the front seats and hit a speed-dial number. "Two blocks out," he said and disconnected.

As the blue BMW approached the faded warehouse, a metal door rolled up. It closed again after Rashid was inside. He took the stairs inside the warehouse two at a time to an office looking down on the darkened interior.

"You used the emergency code phrase, Fadl," Ahmed said as he came through the office door. "What is your definition of an emergency?"

"Saif's device in the Qods Force office . . . he put it in their printer, we downloaded it . . . two hours ago and it . . ." Fadl was flustered, stammering. He handed a paper to Ahmed bin Rashid.

Ahmed took the paper and studied Fadl. He was certain that the young man's distress had nothing to do with what had happened at the hotel. Fadl didn't know. Ahmed decided to keep it that way. He looked at the paper.

"This is incomprehensible, Fadl. What am I supposed to . . ." Ahmed said, squinting at what looked like some sort of message format. Fadl stood next to him and pointed at a paragraph toward the bottom of the page and read aloud, "'Karbala team to move to site by 16 this day, board and take down without alarm, and set sail no later than 1730. Jamal 2157 will proceed out as normal to marker red twelve, then turn north with maximum speed to ASU. Ram DD if possible or drive on to land, then ignition.'"

The doctor stared at the earnest young man in front of him. "What is that supposed to mean, Fadl? Who is Jamal 2157? Do you even know him? And Karbala, why do I care what happens at some Shi'a shrine in Iraq?"

The door opened and Saif joined them. "*Jamal* is not a person, brother Ahmed. It is a Japanese ship with 2157 painted on its side. The Qods drove two trucks to a pier here in Sitra this afternoon. Taha, from our group, followed them. He said the Qods had Iraqis with them. He said they took two harbor service boats out to the ship an hour ago. He is on a roof near the dock now, keeping watch."

Ahmed swallowed. "Let me see the message again. What kind of a ship is this? What are they smuggling into Bahrain, explosives?"

"Type? Taha said it is very large . . ." Saif responded.

Ahmed looked anxiously around the office, filled with books, boxes, and papers. "The computer, is it connected to the Internet?" He typed "www.google.com" and then "Jamal 2157." In twenty seconds, the screen changed and a list of Internet pages appeared. Ahmed clicked on the first listing. Another screen appeared with a picture of a large ship with five spheres protruding from the deck. On the side of the red ship were the white letters "LNG *Jamal*."

"Allah help me," Ahmed gasped. "Liquid natural gas! Where is this ship now?"

"Taha said it is offshore, tied up to a special floating dock or point of some kind. I will call him." Saif quickly changed the SIM chip in the back of his phone and punched in a number. He mumbled a few words into the mouthpiece, listened for a minute, then quickly disconnected. "They are beginning to move the ship, to untie lines. They did not unload explosives into Bahrain. Taha . . . Taha thinks they brought explosives *out* to the ship. Some of the Qods people left the ship, left the Iraqis on board."

Fadl had taken a maritime map down from the office wall and was laying it out on the table in front of Ahmed. "Here is where they are now," Fadl said, pointing to a channel off the Sitra oil and gas facility.

Ahmed looked at the navigation chart and saw a red triangle with the notation "R-12" east of the ship's location. From there the channel went east to the Persian Gulf. Directly north of that buoy, however, was a notation, "NOMAR: Permanently Restricted Military Area." Above the Notice to Mariners notation was Juffair, and the American naval base called the ASU.

"Who do we know in the harbormaster's office, the port police?" Ahmed asked, moving to the door.

"We have a source in the traffic police . . ." Saif was saying.

Ahmed bin Rashid stood in the office door at the top of the stairs. "Send out the emergency signal to all of your people, tell them go to ground, disappear, no communication for five days. And get out of here, drive inland, to the west coast. Now!" He ran down the stairs and searched frantically in the BMW's console for the card that Kate Delmarco had given him.

As the metal door lifted and he backed the BMW out of the warehouse, he punched in her Dubai number. It took what seemed a long time and many clicks before it rang. She answered on the fifth ring. "Kate Delmarco."

"Kate, don't say anything, just listen. I am the man you had coffee with an hour ago. Don't speak my name. Are you with your dinner date yet, just yes or no."

"Yes, yes, we are having cocktails, yes . . ." she answered uncertainly.

"Listen to me. You must persuade him that at this minute a liquid natural gas tanker in the harbor, the LNG *Jamal*, has been seized by Iranian commandos and is about to sail into the Americans' base and explode the liquid natural gas. The blast will go for miles, like a mini-Hiroshima. There is no time to ask questions. Don't hang up, just put down the phone on the table so I can hear him."

There was a long pause. He heard music and clinking. Then he heard Delmarco's voice, made out some of what she said: "Good source, Johnny . . . intelligence . . . right now a gas tanker which has been seized could be, no is, is actually . . . right now . . . driving toward ASU. . . . I am serious, very. . . . Look, just check, call, you can call . . . what do you have to lose?"

He was driving erratically, with one hand holding the phone, speeding toward the hospital. If his call failed to persuade them, as he thought it would, there would be thousands of people in need of emergency medical attention shortly. There was only music and noise coming over the phone.

He ran a red light and sped into the traffic circle, almost getting hit by a bus. He dropped the phone onto the floor. On the other side of the circle, he pulled into a parking lane and stopped, searching for the phone. He put it to his ear in time to hear a man's voice say in American-accented English, ". . . may be something wrong . . . be right or regret . . . going to Threatcon Delta . . . my word . . . drill . . . SEAL . . . you stay put . . . be back . . ."

Then he heard Kate clearly; she was speaking to him. "He just left. He's pissed as hell, but his duty officer seemed to think something was wrong, so he has ordered something. He thinks I set him up. Did I?"

"No. You didn't. I didn't. You'll see now. If you can see the harbor from where you are, go look." He disconnected and began driving again, more carefully, to the hospital.

Kate was at a bar on the Corniche. She looked around. Across the street and a block away was the Banc Bahrain Tower office block. She ran for it. Darting across the street, she walked into the lobby and noticed a sign for an express elevator to the "Top of the Corniche." Minutes later, stepping out of the elevator fifty-three stories up, Kate Delmarco ran into the rooftop bar, walked to a window, and scanned the horizon.

"Wanna borra dees, miss?" the bartender said in some version of English as he thrust a pair of Nokia binoculars across the counter. "Your ship coming, yes?"

Administrative Support Unit,
Southwest Asia (U.S. Navy Base)
Juffair, Bahrain

The klaxon finally stopped.

". . . assume Force Protection Condition Threatcon Delta, repeat, Threatcon Delta . . ." a voice of God said from seemingly everywhere on base. Marines poured out of the security barracks, throwing on flak jackets and carrying M16s. Humvees with blue lights blinking moved down the middle of the street toward the main gate.

At the SEAL dock, Lieutenant Shane Buford was on the red Alert Phone to the COMNAVCENT Operations Center on the other side of the base. "It will be hard to coordinate with the Marines' helos, Commander, if we move this fast. . . . Aye, aye, sir." Buford looked at his chief, a seasoned, gnarled enlisted man with twice as many years in as Buford. "Chief, launch all three boats. We are to marry up with the duty boat and move toward the channel and . . . get this . . . board the LNG tanker *Jamal* near the R-12 buoy.

"We are to presume the LNG may have been seized by heavily armed men who may have explosives. The Marine FAST, if it can get going, may rappel from Black Hawks onto the deck, simultaneously with our assault if possible. And"—the young SEAL shook his head—"this is no drill."

Eighteen SEALs ran down the dock into the Zodiacs. Each boat was rigged with three heavy machine guns. The lines were untied and the boats away in seconds. Moving abreast, the Zodiacs cut through the water off the Navy base into the channel. Buford looked back at the gray hulls tied up in the main dock area. He saw the tower of an Aegis-class destroyer, the masts of two minesweepers, the big mass of a munitions resupply and under-way replenishment ship. Three littoral patrol craft were tied up to one another at the end of one pier.

It was dinnertime and many of the base personnel who lived "on the economy" were in private apartments nearby, but at least four thousand Americans were in the ASU at the moment. Another two thousand were probably within a few kilometers, within the blast radius if the LNG tanker went up.

The Zodiacs were speeding through the main shipping channel now, and Buford was monitoring several frequencies on his headset. His call sign was Alpha Three One.

"Alpha Three One, be advised harbormaster reports suspicious responses to his hails to LNG *Jamal*. Bahraini navy patrol craft is getting under way from Juffair East."

And another voice: "ASU Ops, this is Coast Guard D342. We are about three klicks from R-12, have subject vessel in sight. She is proceeding east at eight knots." Years ago the Coast Guard had sent a maritime safety and security team to help the Navy patrol Bahrain harbor. They were still there and drove 25-foot Defender-class boats designed for harbor-security missions.

In each of the three Zodiacs, the chiefs were going over the rules of engagement with the teams: "Possibly heavily armed men, possibly explosives, but we are not sure, so do not pop some Japanese merchant marine guy without identifying him hostile."

The fourth SEAL Zodiac, the duty boat, had been patrolling to the west of the ASU and could now be seen speeding to rendezvous with the three alert boats. Buford hailed it on a tactical frequency: "Alpha Three Four, you will team with Alpha Three Three and move down the port side of the target vessel." As he said that, he realized that they would have none of the tactical surprise that they normally counted on when storming a ship. The sun had just set, but there was still enough ambient light from the city and the refinery that they were not exactly operating in the dark that they normally used to protect them. Buford's laptop, which he had strapped to the deck, beeped, and he looked down to see a new PDF file with the deck plans of the LNG *Jamal*. They had just been sent to him from the N-2 at the base.

"ASU Ops, this is Coast Guard Delta 342, subject vessel is turning toward the Juffair Channel and making wake. We will close in three mikes. What are our orders?"

There was a pause before the ASU Operations Center answered the Coast Guard Defender boat. Then, "Roger, 342, you are to hail the target ship on radio, with lights, flares, and loudspeakers. Advise them they are entering into a restricted area and must reverse at full speed. After they clear the zone, tell them that you want to board. Do you have a Bahraini officer for boarding?"

The Defender, like all the Coast Guard boats and ships in the region, typically carried a host country rider, who had the legal authority of the sovereign state in whose waters they sailed. With him on board, they could enforce local laws and come aboard any vessel without permission from the ship's master.

Buford could now see the orange Coast Guard Defender boat two kilometers out ahead, but the tanker had to be running with few lights. He could not make out the huge ship with his binoculars, so he raised the night-vision glasses from his belt. In the green light of the glasses, at the distant setting, the big LNG tanker, with its spherical containers, was clear. It was now heading straight up the Juffair Channel toward the ASU. A bright light erupting in the night-vision glasses forced him to pull them quickly away from his eyes.

"Coasties are shooting up flares at her," the chief said. "She has stopped talking to the harbormaster, ignoring his hails."

Buford switched to the Coast Guard frequency and heard in English, "LNG *Jamal,* LNG *Jamal,* this is the United States Coast Guard. You are entering a restricted area. Switch to reverse full power. Repeat . . ."

He saw it come from the bow of the tanker, a flash there and then a line of light shooting forward in front of the tanker, then . . . a ball of fire where the Coast Guard Defender had been and a thud and a crackling sound moving across the water. Someone on the *Jamal* had fired a heavy, man-portable antitank weapon at the Defender, which had exploded, sending flaming pieces up into the sky and sideways to the right and left.

"Alpha Three One to all Alpha patrol boats, target is hostile, repeat, target is hostile," Buford called into his headset. "Change of plans. Implement Redskins Blue Two, repeat Redskins Blue Two. Alpha Three, join me at point; Two and Four, play stopper." Buford called out a prearranged maneuver from the SEALs' playbook, just as he had called plays as the Springfield High quarterback seven years earlier.

The Zodiacs were running full out, without lights, changing their patterns repeatedly to avoid being targeted the way the Coasties had been, by a gunner with night-vision devices on the bow of the *Jamal*.

Buford heard the Marines' Fleet Anti-Terrorism Security team commander on another frequency. "Where the fuck are the Black Hawks? My team is ready for pickup." Probably as many as thirty-six Marines were suited up in body armor and waiting at the ASU landing zone for the ride that would take them to points above the deck of the target ship. The plan was that, as the helicopters hovered in the dark, the Marines would rope down onto the ship. It was only slightly more crazy than what Buford planned to do with the SEALs at some point tonight, which was to launch rope rockets onto the ship and then climb up special ladders onto the deck, 200 feet above the sea.

Another voice on the headset: "This is Bahraini Navy patrol craft to LNG *Jamal*. We are proceeding to your location. Come to full stop. Prepare to be boarded." Buford checked the tactical plot on his secure wireless laptop. The Bahrainis were about twelve minutes away. Buford was now about two minutes from executing his play.

"Brrrt. . . . Brrrt. . . ." Buford could hear arms fire and he saw flashes from the *Jamal*'s bow and port side, but not another antitank missile. Whoever was on board the *Jamal*, they were firing automatic weapons, trying to keep away frogmen who they assumed would be there. If there had been time, the SEALs would have, in fact, approached the target ship on diver sleds. The shooters seemed to know that.

A starburst flare overhead lit up the night sky, followed by another off the starboard side. The Zodiacs would be clearly seen now, without night-vision devices. Another missile could be coming from the *Jamal* any moment. The ship seemed huge now as she plowed up the channel toward the Zodiacs at full speed.

"Alpha Three Three, fire at will, repeat, fire at will," Buford said, and he gave the go sign to his chief. A second later there was a crack, a whoosh of air, a shock of light. The Zodiac bucked like a horse hearing a cherry bomb go off. Then, half a kilometer away, another Zodiac also let loose with a Javelin antitank missile. As soon as they fired, the two Zodiacs began evasive action before anyone on the bow could fire at them. Buford's Javelin hit the tower of the ship and it lit up like a dry Christmas tree. Then the second Javelin hit and the flames on the conning tower shot higher. If anyone was steering the ship and controlling the speed from the tower, they were now toast. If the SEALs had missed and hit one of the five round gas tanks protruding from the deck, the entire harbor would have been on fire. If the fire on the tower spread, that might still happen. But the book said it wouldn't spread.

The *Jamal* continued to move closer and farther up the channel toward the base at high speed. Buford saw the Black Hawk in his peripheral vision and switched to the FAST frequency. "FAST one moving into position for stern assault. Where are my other three birds?"

"Oh Christ," Buford mouthed over the roar of the Zodiac. His chief signaled back, "What's wrong?"

Buford yelled into the chief's ear above the din of the motors. "The Marine FAST Commander seems to have gotten frustrated waiting for his rides and launched only one squad with the first chopper he could get. Worse yet, he's going to do a stern rappel just when Alpha Three Two and Three Four are about to shoot out the props on the tanker."

Buford was only a Navy lieutenant, and the FAST commander was a Marine major, but Buford was going to have to tell his superior officer up there in the Black Hawk that the SEALs, on the Zodiacs coming around behind the tanker, were about to fire rockets at its propellers. If done properly, there was no danger of the ship's fuel igniting, but there might be a problem for Marines roping down onto the deck above the props.

"FAST-One, this is Alpha Three . . . " Buford began, when he saw the light jump up from the ship's deck. Then the Black Hawk exploded into an orange-yellow burst and he could see the fuselage buckle in the middle while the rotors still turned. The men on the *Jamal* had fired a Stinger missile or Russian SA-14 at the Marines, twelve of whom were now aflame as the Black Hawk fell to the sea.

Buford now heard the thuds from his two Zodiacs attacking the propellers. If they had succeeded in hitting the large propellers, the ship would slow, but its forward momentum would continue to push it up-channel toward the Navy base. He yelled to the chief, "If they are going to blow the LNG, now's the time they will try to do it. We got to get on board now and stop them."

"Boarding party, aye, sir," the chief screamed back.

Buford coordinated with the other Zodiacs so that all four would launch their climbers up different parts of the ship, then pull back to give the climbers covering fire from the machine guns.

As his boat pulled up next to the tanker, that 200 feet to the deck seemed like a mile of steel looming above them, and moving ahead. Buford yelled to three SEALs in his Zodiac, "Pull out the beanstalk." They brought out a titanium device that looked only 6 feet high, but its two thick poles contained extensions. Buford pressed the launch button, and the poles shot 75 feet into the air. Between the poles, thin, narrow steps made a ladder. Suction cups and magnets on the sides of the poles attached themselves to the tanker. They moved their Jack and the Beanstalk tower so that it hooked onto a scupper on the side of the tanker, then started to ascend, Buford first.

The Zodiac pulled back out, to get an angle where they could take any people on the deck under fire. Normally, the SEALs would have had their own helicopters, Little Birds, with SEALs sitting outside on the landing gear, providing covering fire. Unfortunately, the Little Birds were training on barges out in the Gulf with most of the SEAL team. Buford was left at home to guard the fort, literally.

As the Zodiac moved off from the tanker, Buford was startled by a noise and a motion above. He looked up from the water to see flames from the tails of two Bahraini F-16s as they shot by 500 feet above the sea. He hoped they knew they should do nothing but look good. Then he heard another, more familiar sound: Black Hawks. The rest of the FAST had arrived on three or four more birds, and so far they were not being targeted with Stingers.

Buford quickly switched to the FAST frequency. "FAST Commander, this is Alpha Three One. I have a dozen men climbing up the sides at positions one, two, and six. I need covering fire from your helos. Suggest we put all men on board on one tactical freq. Over."

"Roger, Alpha, we will rope down into positions three, four, and five. We will fire at the deck near your positions until you get topside," the Marine in the lead chopper responded, using the numbers that the SEALs and Marines both employed to designate locations on a ship being assaulted from the air or from the sea's surface. "Alpha, have your men switch to tac freq 198.22, over."

Buford and his team had climbed the beanstalk, hooked onto the side, and pulled the ladder up behind them. They then fired it up another 75 feet and hooked on. After the second climb of the tower, they shot ropes onto the deck. When the ropes seemed to be securely caught on something on the deck, the SEALs began climbing the last stretch of the steel behemoth.

Buford could hear small-arms fire now. He imagined some terrorist leader inside the ship lighting charges that would explode the five gigantic gas-carrying spheres. Even from here the explosion would create a blast wave and fireball that would kill hundreds at the ASU. Any moment now . . .

Above it all, Buford heard a siren. Turning, he saw the Bahraini patrol craft charging at full speed up the channel, all lit up and with a blue bubble-gum light blinking on its tower like a highway patrol car. Then he heard someone on the headset saying, "Hovering above the debris of the Defender . . . No joy . . . No joy." They weren't seeing survivors of the Coast Guard boat.

Machine guns on the Zodiacs and the Black Hawks

were now ripping at parts of the deck area of the *Jamal* where someone might try to shoot at the SEALs as they climbed up the sides or at the Marines, who were about to rappel down ropes onto the ship. "Keep your fire away from the spheres," Buford heard someone say on his headset.

Then, as the SEALs neared the deck, he heard, "Cease fire, cease fire, only targeted fire on hostiles." Finally, he was on the deck. The muscles in his forearms burned, his biceps and back throbbed. He had designated the four SEAL assault units of four men each red, blue, green, and gold. He and the three other SEALs from his Zodiac were gold. "This is Gold One. We are on deck," Buford said, swinging his assault weapon from his back to his right hand. The other SEAL squads soon confirmed that they, too, had made it on deck. Sixteen SEALs were aboard the *Jamal*. None had been lost in the perilous climb up the side of the ship.

The SEALs assumed positions behind objects on deck to provide covering fire as the FAST Marines now fell onto the deck on the port and starboard sides. Another FAST squad was, Buford knew, hitting the bow. Buford was on the stern deck. His view of the bow was obscured by the smoke from the smoldering conning tower of the tanker. The Javelins had done a good job.

"Blue squad, join up with Gold. We'll go below to find the auxiliary controls in the engine room," he yelled into his headset. "Green, Red, join up with the FAST and go down amidships, look for booby traps and timers, any sign that someone is trying to blow up the ship." Then he transferred all tactical control to the FAST team leader, a Marine captain. Once he went below, there was little probability that his radio would be able to transmit more than a few feet.

He pulled open a hatch and realized that the lights were out inside the ship. He pulled down his night-scope, and using hand signs, Buford and his squad entered the ship. He tried to remember the deck plans from his laptop. The two squads moved below down a darkened companionway. They descended three decks, providing cover for one another as they moved, just as they had drilled so many times.

He opened the hatch into the corridor. If he remembered correctly, the second door on the left would be the auxiliary helm control room, and from there the ship could be steered. According to the data he had read on the laptop as the Zodiac bounced out to the *Jamal,* this ship also had two emergency mini-propellers amidships. He wanted to deploy them and throw them to full throttle in reverse.

Buford and the rest of Gold squad found the door and assumed their positions to go through it together, high and low, covering one another. He pulled down the latch handle, and in a second they were in. "No shoot, no shoot," an Asian man in a T-shirt screamed. Buford saw no one else in the room through his night-vision goggles.

"Are you from the *Jamal*'s crew?" Buford yelled as he placed his weapon to the Asian's chest. The terrified man nodded affirmatively. "Where are the midship props and rudder controls?" Buford barked.

The Asian's hand went out to a switch. "No!" Buford screamed, and knocked him away. The SEAL wanted to see the controls for himself. It looked fairly user-friendly and intuitive. Everything was marked in Japanese and English.

"This should do it," he said to the rest of his squad as he hit a button that deployed the mini-props. Then he dialed in full reverse. "It will at least stop what's left of the forward motion and in a few minutes it'll start slipping her backwards. Now let's start looking for explosives."

The young SEAL lieutenant grabbed the quivering Asian ship's crewman by the T-shirt and threw him back into the chair in front of the console, exactly where he had been sitting when the SEALs burst in. "Where are they? Where are the terrorists?" Buford screamed at the frightened sailor. "Tell me now!"

Almost in answer, a shape moved in the dark. From behind a file cabinet the sound of gunfire exploded in the little control room. Above it, Buford heard a shout: *"Allah ahkbar!"* He swung to his right, beginning to raise his weapon as he took three rounds into his body armor, one above the other. Then one pierced the skin at the top of his nose and his head exploded as his body fell backward onto the control panel.

Fire from two SEALs in the control room cut the gunman in two. With the sound of the weapons exchange causing his ears to ring and his nostrils to fill with acrid smoke, a SEAL hit the transmit button on his chin microphone. "Gold One is down. KIA, repeat Gold One KIA." No one on deck could hear the signal through the steel of the hull.

• • •

Still hogging the bartender's binoculars and juggling them with her cell phone, pressed against the window glass at the Top of the Corniche, Kate Delmarco was dictating to a CNN news anchor in Atlanta. She had been at it for half an hour, her reports also turning into bulletins that the Associated Press was running on its global network.

"The helicopters are still hovering above the deck and are scanning below with really bright spotlights. The troops from the helicopters have been on the deck now for almost ten minutes, but I can't make them out. The fire seems to have gone out in the tower thing." She squinted. "And I'd say the ship is definitely dead in the water. A lot of little ships are now around it and I can see the lights of more on the way. One has a blue, like a police light, spinning. . . . The fighter planes are still circling higher up. I can't confirm the report that the American base was evacuated, but this huge liquid natural gas tanker definitely was headed that way, and had it been exploded by terrorists, thousands would have died, Americans and Bahrainis. I must stress that we do not know the identity of the terrorist group yet, despite rumors that may have appeared."

The bartender, who had never before had such a high tipper as this American woman, hung up his telephone behind the bar and wrote a note on a napkin. He walked around the bar to the window and placed the napkin in front of Delmarco. It read, "Man from hospital call you. He say *shokran jazeelan*. Just tell you *shokran*."

No, Kate thought, as tears welled up in her eyes. Thank you very much, Doctor, thank you.

• • •

Across town, in a small office on the intensive care ward at the Salmaniyah Medical Center, Dr. Rashid was composing an encrypted e-mail to his brother, Abdullah, in Riyadh.

. . . although the Iranians may try to manufacture evidence. Those the Americans captured on the tanker are Iraqi Shiites, who should lead them to the Iranian Qods Force involvement.

The American newspaper reporter I met at Nakeel's suggestion, she was how I told the Americans about the attack in time for them to stop it. She will say Islamyah was not involved in the attack, in fact helped to stop it.

I think they will believe her. Nakeel said she has good sources in the military and intelligence. I must ask Nakeel how he knows her. Sometimes, Abdullah, I wonder about our friend Nakeel and how he knows so much if he just develops real estate. For now, at least, we have stopped Tehran from staging a major massacre of Americans and blaming it on us. But, I am sure, they will not stop. There will be more. In your service, Ahmed.

5

FEBRUARY 5

"It gives me the willies just to be in this place, Pammy," Brian Douglas confided to Pamela Braithwaite, executive assistant to the Director of SIS. "I'd be afraid to work in a glass palace like this, it's just too vulnerable."

"Yes, well, you'll recall, or maybe you won't, Brian, you were in the Dhofar with the Omanis, I do believe, running ops into the Yemen looking for al Qaeda back in 2000 when it happened"—Pamela shut her eyes to remember the scene—"when a Russian antitank missile came crashing into the eighth floor here. The Irish. Made a terrible mess, we moved everyone off the floor for three months. Now, of course, we have surveillance cameras throughout the neighborhood and police boats on the Thames. . . ."

Barbara Currier, Director of SIS, strode in carrying a stack of papers, followed by Middle East Division Chief Roddy Touraine. "Well, Brian, you leave Bahrain for a day and the place goes to hell in a handbasket," she said, thrusting out her hand to Douglas.

"I was surprised by the timing of it, Director, but we *had* just told the Americans it was coming relatively soon," Brian said defensively.

"Sit, sit," the Director urged. "Yes, I made a point of that to their Director of National Intelligence this morning on the vid link. And he acknowledged it, more's the wonder."

"My station staff have done great work in the last twenty-four hours finding out more about the details, if you'd like to hear them, Director," Brian offered, pulling out his notes. Currier nodded enthusiastically while pouring herself a cup of Earl Grey.

"Those the Americans found on board were Iraqis, maybe Sunni, maybe Shi'a. Don't know yet. Most of them got killed by the Marines in the firefight, but the SEALs captured one alive who said they were ordered not to detonate the ship until they had rammed a U.S. destroyer or run aground on the base. They had rigged two of the five natural gas spheres with enough RDX to set off a firestorm that would have lashed out almost three kilometers.

"Our traces as to how they got into Bahrain, where they stayed, et cetera, indicate that they were facilitated by a front company called Medkefdar Trading, which we link back through Hezbollah to the Iranian Qods Force.

"The Americans were alerted just before the attack by an American newspaper reporter, who in turn claims to have been warned by what she describes as an Islamyah source; we're checking on who that may be. I can find out. This does, however, confirm my earlier reporting that the terrorism in Bahrain is from Iran and not from Islamyah," he said, folding the notes back up.

"Not what I'm hearing from across the pond," Roddy Touraine piped up. "A ruse, they say. The Yanks are still keen that it's the al Qaeda regime in Riyadh." Roddy Touraine had once used the commercial cover of an accountant, and he looked the part.

"It's not an al Qaeda regime, although there may be some ex–al Qaeda in it," Douglas shot back.

"*Ex*–al Qaeda? Can one be *ex*–al Qaeda, Director?" Roddy Touraine asked rhetorically to Barbara Currier. "I would have thought once one, always one. Can a camel change its spots?"

"You mean like once a Pentagon liaison always a Pentagon toady?" Brian flashed.

"Children, children, enough," the Director asserted, chopping the air with her hand. "What's next, that's what I want to know. How do we stop these attacks? How do we prove—*prove*—whose hand is behind them?"

"Director, if I may," Brian began. "As you know, I ran a small but highly effective network in Tehran several years back. I met them outside of the country, but from time to time I went in under commercial cover. My successor shut down the network because one of the group was caught and killed by VEVAK in Baku. Rather than risk the rest, we put the net into hibernation.

"As far as we know, the rest of the group were never revealed and are still in positions to know much of what we need now. I'd like to go back in, activate one of them, and see what we can find out about the Iranian role in

Bahrain and what they are up to in general, in Iraq, with the nuclears, the whole ball of wax."

The room was quiet for a moment. Brian heard a siren going by on the embankment below.

"Personally? You want to activate them by going in country, personally?" Touraine asked incredulously. "Don't they know you by now? Haven't you been made by VEVAK?"

"If I stayed there any length of time, they would have time to match photographs, but that will take a few days, and that's all I need," Douglas insisted. "There is no way to contact this source or the others in the cell remotely, and I am the only one left here that our network know, will recognize. Yes, there is some danger, but it's moderate, and I am prepared to accept it."

"Danger to you, fine. Accept away," Touraine shot back, "but it's a danger to the Director, the Service, and HMG if the Iranians announce to the world that they've captured a senior SIS officer traipsing about the whorehouses of Tehran with secret Iranian government documents!"

Now there was only the noise of the heating system. SIS Director Barbara Currier was sketching butterflies on her notepad.

"We do need to take risks. We are not the Girl Guides," she said finally, standing to shake Brian's hand, indicating that their meeting was over. "Just don't get caught, Brian, will you, now?"

Pamela Braithwaite walked Brian to the elevators. "There's being a field man, Brian, and then there's being a cowboy."

He shot her a glance. "I thought you were a friend."

"I am. Why do you think she approved this little adventure of yours? I told her this morning she could trust you." Pamela smiled. "Don't prove me wrong and Roddy right."

Brian smiled back. "Thank you. Without you I'm sure Roddy would have torpedoed the whole thing. I just don't trust that man. Always running to Grosvenor Square, telling all to Uncle Sam. I'll tell you one thing, I'm not going to run the operational details about this mission through that bastard."

Pamela walked back toward the Director's suite. "No, I will do the needful with Ops, get you cover, backup, emergency egress plans . . . make sure you're authorized all the little bits that you will need . . . TTFN."

Office of the Intelligence Coordinator and
Chairman,
Joint Intelligence Committee
The Cabinet Office
Whitehall, London

"Delighted you could come over, Russell. Always willing to return a favor for Sol, work my way a little out of his debt. We've been wondering how this new analysis agency has been coming along, hoping we could learn a thing or two from you." Sir Dennis Penning-Smith was in his late sixties, with a full head of thick white hair, and, in his three-piece suit and wire-rim glasses, looked somehow appropriate in this old government office building on Whitehall. He looked beaked, birdlike; he could have been a senior don at Cambridge, Rusty thought. But he was anything but that.

"Sir Dennis, as Intelligence Coordinator and Chairman of the Joint Intelligence Committee, you know far more about analysis than we could aspire to for years. Your track record here at JIC is better than anything Washington's produced over the last twenty years," Rusty replied.

"Very kind of you, Russell, very kind. We've had our share of mistakes, though. We didn't get Iraqi WMD right either, although we did call the insurgency and the civil war. And Washington isn't always off the mark. Occasionally, INR, the State Department's little intelligence analysis branch, is spot-on. Little, that's the common theme. In the analysis business, smaller is better. Fewer people, higher quality."

He continued, "Most of the fancy technologically based information, from satellites and whatnot, is American in origin, but thankfully, you share almost all of it with us. We contribute some code-breaking and listening, but mainly our side of the bargain is what the boys and girls over at Vauxhall Cross provide, the good spy work, and we share almost all of that with you. For some reason CIA has just never done very well at the spying bit. When they get one, it's usually a walk-in, a voluntary, not a recruit.

"But whoever gets it, it all comes here and to you—all the spy reports, the intercepted communications, the satellite pictures, and the publicly available information. That's the open source. Often the very best material is the open source, but Washington hasn't liked it, you know, believes it's disinformation unless they stole it, bought it, or picked it up in the ether.

"We have a small in-house assessments staff who see everything that comes in and then draft our estimates— or analyses, as you call them. We often call on someone from the Foreign Office to do the first draft. Depending upon the topic, we even ask a don or two from Oxbridge— all perfectly vetted, of course. Then it's a free-for-all, with the Defense Ministry, Foreign Office, Home Office, SIS, et cetera, all having their whack at it. Finally, it comes before the JIC, and we polish it off and send it through the wall."

Rusty frowned at the last part. "Through the wall?"

"Oh, yes, literally." Sir Dennis stood and walked toward the back of his long, thin office. "I am not high-powered like your Director of National Intelligence, but when I wear the hat of Intelligence Coordinator, my number-one client is the Prime Minister." He pulled a key from his vest and gave a shove to a bookcase on rollers. Behind it was a door, which he proceeded to un-lock and throw open. "Ta da!" Sir Dennis exclaimed. "Number Ten." He then disappeared through the door and could be heard saying, "Penning-Smith here. Clos-ing back up." No alarms seemed to have gone off, no electronics appeared to be involved.

When Sir Dennis Penning-Smith reappeared, MacIn-tyre was still laughing, "You mean you have a secret door that brings you around the corner to Downing Street? What if the Prime Minister is in his silk pajamas?"

"Not to worry," Sir Dennis assured him while locking the door and easily moving the bookcase back into place.

"They live on the upper floors. The point of this little magic trick, however, Russell, is to be seen by the others around town as having direct access to the PM whenever I want it. I have done that act for every member of the JIC, one at a time." He clapped his hands to shed any dust and sat back down in the Queen Anne–style reading chair.

"I do a little magic myself," Rusty said, smiling. "But it's strictly on a more amateur level. I do agree with you about the value of open-source intelligence," he went on, trying to get the conversation back on track. "In fact, we've just given out a major contract for an automated system of collection, web-crawling, and cataloguing. If that works, we'll be glad to share it with you, of course."

"Automated crawlers, well . . . We may have different views of open source, Russell. Tell you a story about our mutual friends, the Israelis. They had a problem once with Libya. Haven't we all? Seems old Muammar was planning to buy missiles or something from Korea or somewhere, doesn't matter, and the Israeli Prime Minister wanted to know right away when the bloody things arrived." Sir Dennis was warming to his own tale.

"So they assemble their Israeli version of the JIC and task each agency to find out. Next week the Air Force reports that it has flown reconnaissance flights over Tripoli harbor and seen nothing new. The Navy intelligence people have stationed a submarine off the coast and have slipped into the port for a peep, and nothing. Mossad suborned Qaddafi's tailor, some queen from the Via Veneto, and lined one of Muammar's flashy robe things with a transmitter, but all they heard was Beatles music. The *White Album,* by the by.

"Finally, Russell, the little man from the Foreign Office intelligence staff, Avi something, says, 'The ship from Pyongyang arrived last Wednesday, unloaded at Pier Twelve, and set sail Saturday.' How do you know, they all ask. 'I called the harbormaster and asked him,' the little bugger says. That, you see, is open source, no crawly worms involved." Penning-Smith smiled and sat back.

MacIntyre was chuckling. "You may have a point there, Sir Dennis. So what concerns you now? What are you looking at?"

The Joint Intelligence Committee Chair stood again and opened doors that revealed a blackboard, on which he, or someone, had written the plan for the first quarter in red, green, and white chalk. "Next up is 'Whither Islamyah?' Who is going to emerge from the Shura Council to run the place, and what will he want to do?

"Then, staying in the region, what's the latest in 'Iran-Iraq Relations'? Can we figure out seams and pressure points so that we can rend apart this entente cordiale between the two great Shiite nations?

"Moving east, the ever-popular 'Heroin Production in Afghanistan,' which is way up again. How do we stop it from showing up in Brixton?

"To the Orient, 'Chinese Economic Trends.' Can they continue to plow money into military modernization and keep every little Chan happy with modern gizmos?

"Then, oops, you shouldn't have seen this one, 'America's Next Steps: Learning from Failures?'—an examination of how policy problems with Iraq, Afghanistan, Pakistan, Iran, and Saudi will affect near- to midterm decision making in Washington. I should, of course, ask *you* that," Penning-Smith said, shutting the doors to the blackboard.

"Seriously? I don't know if we are learning from failure," MacIntyre said, not contesting the premise. "Yes, we have had a bad start to the twenty-first century. The Iraq War did not result in the people there loving us and did produce this continuing low-grade Sunni insurgency against the Shi'a government, which does seem more and more aligned with Tehran. At least we are finally out of there.

"On Tehran, we could never tell when they went nuclear or where they store them, but we are pretty confident now that they slipped that past us successfully while we perseverated in Baghdad.

"Afghanistan is probably best described as again a borderline failed state, decentralized, but the regime in Kabul is clearly toeing the line of the fundamentalist coalition in Pakistan, which in turn is overtly nuclear-armed. It's that coalition of military and clergy in Islamabad that worries me most. They've stopped hunting al Qaeda, won't talk to India, and seem to be in bed with that new gang in Saudi Arabia.

"And then there is Saudi Arabia. We rode that horse too long. Didn't have our own sources in the country to tell us that the opposition to the Sauds had grown, organized, and coalesced. So now it's Islamyah, its future too early to tell. I am convinced that if we are not hostile to them, we can still keep them from becoming a threat. Their revolution is still young, malleable. I would love to see what your estimate ends up saying about who will emerge from the pack to lead it," MacIntyre concluded, holding his two palms open. "Some of these guys were once al Qaeda, or clergy, but most were reformers, democrats, or just disgruntled bureaucrats and military fed up with the stagnation and inbreeding of the House of Saud.

"Yes," Sir Dennis said, checking his red Economist Diary appointment book. "Yes, indeed, lots of policy problems. You know, Russell, you are my last scheduled thing today. What do you say we discuss this over a wee dram?"

The Travellers Club
Pall Mall, London

After a short ride through the traffic of Trafalgar Square, the Cabinet Office driver dropped them off at what looked like a Florentine palace on a quiet dead-end street.

After depositing their overcoats, they ascended the Grand Staircase together, MacIntyre trying not to appear a country rube as he gaped at the portraits, the chandeliers, and the Greek frieze in the library. "Yes, stole it from the Temple of Apollo. The Greeks want it back, the buggers." As they sat down in armchairs by a window, Sir Dennis touched a large red button. "Will you do with a Balvenie, Russell?" he asked as a bookcase slid aside, revealing a butler's pantry and a butler, carrying six glasses on a tray. Three of them had water. None of them had ice.

Smiling at another door pretending to be a bookcase, MacIntyre said, "Next time you're in the States, Sir Dennis, I'll have to take you to a castle I belong to in Los Angeles. It has a number of false doors, too."

"Really, a castle? What kind of people belong?" Sir Dennis asked, sniffing the aroma of the single malt.

"You have to be a magician," MacIntyre replied.

"Well, then, Sir Dennis certainly qualifies," said a man MacIntyre had not noticed approaching.

"Russell MacIntyre, may I present the scoundrel Brian Douglas, from another clan, the SIS. Our man in Bahrain, on a brief trip home, is Brian," Sir Dennis said, shaking hands and handing a glass to a man who looked twenty years younger and tanned. "I asked young Brian to drop by to meet you, as, from what Sol Rubenstein tells me about you, Russell, you and Brian have similar interests, including the three I's—Iraq, Iran, and Islamyah. And Brian is about to become a traveler; I can say that to Russell, Brian, and he will not report it back to Langley or Foggy Bottom, will you, Russell?"

"He means I'm flying to Tehran under alias," Douglas said softly over his Balvenie, looking uneasy.

"And who is it this time, just in case I read about you in the papers?" Sir Dennis persisted in pressing the younger man to reveal more than he appeared to be comfortable discussing.

"Ian Stuart, a South African rug dealer from Joburg. It's a new legend, but well supported by our office there," Douglas vamped, not wanting to tell the American the true cover, "and let's hope you won't be reading about me, at least not in the press."

"Russell, Brian asked me something this morning that I couldn't answer and thought you might," Sir Dennis said, crossing his legs and turning toward the American. His manner was different now, brisker. "What was the

Pentagon Under Secretary, Kashigian, doing at Christmas, meeting with the Rev Guards in Tehran? That's not on the approved travel list for Defense officials, I would have thought. His legend was credible, Brian—an Armenian diplomat, was it not?"

Now Russell MacIntyre understood this meeting a bit more. It was a test on several levels. Could he be trusted not to report back to Washington that SIS was sending a senior officer into Iran under cover? Would he prove his bona fides by explaining a recent secret mission by a senior U.S. official, also to Tehran? The problem was, MacIntyre had not known about Ronald Kashigian's going to Iran. Now he had to persuade his hosts of that without immediately appearing to be inconsequential.

"If Kashigian was in Iran at Christmas, I will tell you truthfully, I was not cleared to know that. Nor was Sol Rubenstein, I'm confident. Are you sure it was Kashigian and not really an Armenian diplomat?" MacIntyre said, trying to sound as honest as possible.

The two Brits looked at each other for a second. Sir Dennis nodded to Brian Douglas. "He flew in on a Pentagon Gulfstream, without markings," Douglas said flatly. "His trip was arranged and coordinated by the U.S. defense attaché in Ankara."

"Shit," MacIntyre said, furrowing his brow. "Why would they—we—do that?"

"Precisely what we were wondering, Russell. Odd time to be doing an opening with the Persians, after forcing Old Europe to join in antinuclear sanctions just a few years ago," Sir Dennis almost mumbled as he pushed back in his chair.

MacIntyre quickly replayed what had been said. "Wait a minute. The only way you could know this is if you're tapping or spying on the U.S. defense attaché in Turkey. I thought we had an agreement in place that the U.K. and the U.S. didn't spy on each other."

"We don't spy on America, Russell," Sir Dennis said slowly. "As you do, we listen to others who sometimes report on what America is doing. Some such NSA reports do not always leave Fort Meade," he added, referring to the Maryland headquarters of U.S. signals intelligence, the National Security Agency, "but they do get distributed to a few of us by our signals intelligence unit, GCHQ, which sees everything NSA sees. It's been that way since 1943." Russell wondered who had the authority to tell NSA to sit on a report. Somebody evidently did.

"We're convinced Iran is behind the hotel bombings in Bahrain, maybe even the hijacking of this LNG tanker, although those found on board were Iraqi of some sort," Brian said quickly to MacIntyre. "I'm going back in there to rekindle a few embers quickly, because every bone in my body tells me the Iranians are up to something.

"The point is, MacIntyre, that if some people in Washington are talking to some people in Tehran, I would be at risk if anyone in Washington knew I was going in clandestinely." Douglas spoke with his hand covering half of his mouth.

"So why tell me?" MacIntyre said, shaking his head. "I don't get it."

"We're telling you this, Russell," said Sir Dennis, "because Sol Rubenstein and I have been exchanging thoughts these last few months—very securely, of course—about our mutual concern that the Iranians are getting too assertive, exercising their mobile nuclear missile launchers, conducting amphibious maneuvers with tanks, enforcing their way in Baghdad, even inserting their people into the Iraqi government there under thin cover.

"And the situation in the Gulf is very fluid right now. Sol says you believe that we should not yet write off Islamyah, says you're one of the only people in Washington to believe that, forcing old Sol to defend you with the Director of National Intelligence, SECDEF, and the White House crowd," Sir Dennis went on, telling MacIntyre things that he had never heard from his boss.

"Well, we happen to agree with you, you see, despite some lower levels in Vauxhall Cross and elsewhere who may not. So this coincidental bumping into Mr. Douglas in the library at the Travellers is really an agent recruitment attempt of a sort.

"While Sol has you out of town cooling off, as it were, we thought we would place some intelligence collection requirements with you as a traveler. See if any of the U.S. diplomats or spooks or sailors in the Gulf will tell you more than we are getting out of them. See if some of the Bahrainis will open up to you, since your lot is paying much of their tab these days, not us anymore."

Sir Dennis was no longer a pleasant, slightly distracted don. He had just revealed a personal transatlantic alliance with MacIntyre's boss, Sol Rubenstein, that MacIntyre had not even guessed existed. He had also revealed that Rubenstein was spending time deflecting criticism of

MacIntyre, without even letting the object of that criticism know about it.

Now Sir Dennis Penning-Smith revealed himself as a Brahmin executive, a tough, realistic British intellocrat. "What are the Iranians up to? Not that I doubt for a minute that Brian will reveal all upon his return from the Persian carpet stalls. How stable is Bahrain if the Iranian Rev Guards want to topple the King? If you're right about the window of opportunity in Islamyah, what do we do with it? With whom do we speak? Who exactly is the Dr. Castro of this revolution in Islamyah? What do we say or do to prevent this Castro from becoming a nuisance now that his revolution has just succeeded, as it were? I don't think we have much time before the window closes in Islamyah. If Douglas is right, we may not have time before the Iranians try something across the Gulf in Bahrain." Sir Dennis rose and pulled a book off a shelf labeled only "By Members" and gave it to MacIntyre.

"It's called *Arabian Sands,* written by a Traveller named Thesiger over half a century ago. Dressed up like a Bedouin, lived with them, loved the place. Laments the discovery of oil, says it ruined everything," the JIC chairman said, apparently preparing to leave. "And I guess it did, too, unless, of course, you like to drive automobiles, fly aircraft, et cetera, et cetera.

"You two have a good bonding dinner downstairs. I am off to a dreadful dinner for my visiting Australian counterpart. Don't worry about the book. I shall replace it." With that, and with quick handshakes, he was gone, leaving the newly introduced Brian Douglas, Britain's top spy in the Gulf, and Russell MacIntyre, the apparently controversial deputy director of America's fledgling intelligence analysis agency, sitting amid the bookshelves with empty glasses.

As the waiter appeared from the butler's closet with another round, Douglas seemed somewhat less gung-ho than he had in the presence of Sir Dennis. "These trips don't always work, of course. There was another Travellers Club member, fellow named Tomkison, went to Socotra, island off the Yemen, to do research for a treatise on the strange accent and ancient version of Arabic he was told was spoken on that lovely isle."

"What happened?" MacIntyre asked. "They behead him?"

"No." Douglas smiled, tasting the Scotch. "None of them said anything—not one single word—till he left."

"Something tells me you will do better than Tomwhatever," MacIntyre said, toasting his new acquaintance's prospective travel.

"It will be a quick trip. Has to be. Can't give them time to recall my face from dusty bins. And the source will either talk or not. Either be alive or not. No need to wait around a week to find out," Douglas said, more to himself than to MacIntyre. "I'm coming back through Dubai, allegedly to change planes for Durban. Could we meet there to compare notes on the tenth at eight, in the old city? It's a very small curry place," Douglas said, passing a small card across the table. "I will have to prepare a report for Sir Dennis and Sol on what I found and what you were able to pick up."

"Of course I'll be there. I go to Kuwait first, but by then I will just have wrapped up in Bahrain and need to stop in the Emirates anyway," MacIntyre said, and then he paused, picking up on what had just been said. "You report directly to Sir Dennis? You're an SIS station chief; he's Cabinet Office. And you say your report isn't just going to be for Sir Dennis but for my boss as well? What gives?"

Brian Douglas rose and emptied his glass. "Well, SIS has its wiring diagrams and Sir Dennis has his. As you might suspect from looking around this place, there are old-boy networks. Dennis and Sol are two of a loose club of intellocrats. Despite his bitching, Sir Dennis has just eagerly gone off to meet one of the better members of that club at the Australian ambassador's house. He's supposed to get a report on planned Chinese naval activities in the Indian Ocean, a gem that Canberra collected from a source so good that they are unwilling to risk it by sharing the information with London. But tonight they'll give it to Dennis," Brian said, replacing the empty glass on the tray. "Shall we go down for dinner? There's a lot I want to go over with you."

Looking up at a bust of the Greek god Hermes, Russell MacIntyre was feeling the way he had the first night he'd applied for membership at the Magic Castle. He had thought he knew something about prestidigitation, until he had seen the members there perform for one another. And here . . . He shook his head.

As MacIntyre and Douglas left the library, the false bookcase slid back into place. The Balvenie and the empty glasses had disappeared.

6

FEBRUARY 8

Causeway to Islamyah

"Dr. Ahmed bin Rashid," the Bahraini border police officer said, reading Ahmed's new Islamyah passport at the entrance to the causeway leading from Bahrain. Ahmed remembered when there had hardly been any formalities at the causeway at all. The revolution that had thrown out the al Sauds had changed all of that.

"How long will you be gone, Doctor, and what is the purpose of your trip?" the border guard asked in Arabic while eyeing the dashboard computer screen on the new BMW.

"Back tomorrow. Family emergency, Officer," Ahmed replied courteously. The officer scanned the passport into a computer. Ahmed noticed in his rearview mirror that a television camera was pivoting to image the rear license plate of the BMW. Another camera was looking at him through the windshield. The officer waited a moment. The computer in the gatehouse booth beeped, and the officer then pressed a button on a handheld device. The

V barrier, a metal plate that had been raised in front of the car, dropped, a green light flashed on, and Ahmed was on his way for the 16-mile drive across the causeway.

Border control at the Islamyah checkpoint was much swifter. Here he flashed the special green-and-gold passport that his brother had given him and was waved through. After arriving back on dry land, he turned east and drove fifteen minutes to the al Khobar Corniche and the Golden Tulip, the hotel next to the Aramco building.

Aramco, the largest oil company in the world, now totally owned by the Islamyah government, had not changed its name. Everything else, he noticed, seemed to have new designations. The signs saying King Fahd Causeway, King Khalid Street, Prince Turki Street, had all been removed or painted over. He could see the new pattern. They were being named after the early caliphs, who had succeeded one another as leader of the Umma after the death of the Prophet. It was now the Abu Bakr Khalifa Causeway, Umar I Street, Muawiyah Abu Sufyan Street, and Yazid I Street. There would be no roads named after the early Shi'a caliphs, like al Hasan and al Husayn, he thought, even though the local residents here in the Eastern Province were overwhelmingly Shiites.

The encrypted e-mail from his brother had said that he would be at Aramco most of the day, reviewing security for the massive oil infrastructure, but would join him at the Golden Tulip for an early dinner. At six o'clock, one of Abdullah's bodyguards came to Ahmed's room to escort him to a private patio off the pool barbecue area.

As the waiters were setting a small mezza for two, Abdullah strode in. "My heroic doctor," he said, grabbing his younger brother. Ahmed lightly kissed each of his brother's cheeks in a sign of friendship and respect. Four of Abdullah's bodyguards moved into positions around the patio, their backs to Abdullah, looking out.

"Even the troublesome ones on the Shura Council agreed that I should congratulate you for your hand in uncovering the Persian plot to blow up the American base. We would certainly have been blamed. Now even the White House spokesman admits that those on board were Iraqis." Abdullah scooped up some baba ghanouj. "So which Iraqis were these, do you know yet?"

"What I think and what I can prove are two different things," Ahmed began. "The instinct in me says they were from the martyr brigade that the Iranian Rev Guards have been training, but we do not yet have the proof. The Iranians involved left Bahrain on several small boats and left no trace that they had ever been there. Abdullah, these Iranian Qods Force people are very good at what they do."

"Yes, yes, they are. And for now it is in our interest to make sure they do not succeed. We must keep the King on the throne in Bahrain," Abdullah confided. "Yes, yes, I know he is from a royal house, but he has been fighting corruption, bringing the people into the decision making. If he were thrown off the throne, what would replace him, Ahmed? Just another Iranian puppet government like Baghdad, no friends of ours," the Islamyah security chief said, jabbing the table with his index finger. "We voted this morning to resume secret funds transfers to the Bahraini government, for social projects and jobs in the poorest Shi'a communities."

The sun had set and a slight cool breeze blew in from the north. Two waiters lit heating lamps and then withdrew to leave the sheik alone with his guest. "Then the Shura is better behaved than last we talked?" Ahmed asked.

"Seldom." The waiters now brought the entrée of grilled *hammour,* grouper fish. Abdullah slowly cut the fillet with a fork. "There is a strong faction, led by Zubair bin Tayer, who want strict enforcement of Sharia rules, and to keep all women in their homes, you know the list, and then," Abdullah said, throwing his fork on the table, "then they also want us to export the revolution, bring Wahhabism to all Islam, grow strong enough to confront the infidels. These are the ones who pushed to complete the Chinese missile project. Now they say we should have nuclears for the missiles. From China, Korea, or Pakistan, or build our own."

Ahmed was aghast. He put both hands on the table, almost as if to steady himself. "Brother, these were all mistakes of the Sauds. That way leads to stagnation or worse. Surely the people will not support this in the election."

Abdullah said nothing, then looked into Ahmed's eyes. "They also do not want to *have* the election, or perhaps only one election ever, to approve their rule. Only approved Islamic scholars would be allowed to vote after that."

"One man, one vote, one time," Ahmed said softly, almost to himself.

"What?" his brother asked.

"It is what the Americans said about the elections in

Algeria: only men could vote, and they would only be allowed to vote once—they would give up their right to ever vote again. That cannot happen here!" Ahmed said.

"The Americans!" Abdullah spit. "The Americans think democracy solves everything. It took them over a hundred years to allow all their people to vote, the poor, women, the blacks. Has it solved their problems? They waste so much time and fortune in their elections. It is a game to them and they never stop playing at it. And are their results so different? We overthrew hereditary rule here. They still have it: fathers followed by sons, wives seeking to replace husbands.

"They have three hundred twenty-five million people and how many ruling families?" Abdullah asked, waving his hand. "Do they not have poverty, do they not make their people pay for doctors, for university, in the supposedly richest country in the world?

"Then they think they are so superior that they must reshape the Arab world in their ghastly image. How? By bombing our cities, killing our women and children? Locking up our people forever? Raping them?" Abdullah said, repeating a rant Ahmed had heard before.

"With respect, it is not about our becoming like the Americans," Ahmed responded. "It is about what was promised to our people: more freedom, more progress, more opportunity, participation, ownership of their country." Ahmed was using phrases that he had heard his brother use before the revolution. "It is about not being like the Sauds. They held back our people by spending the people's oil money exporting their Wahhabist view of Islam, which many of our own people do not follow. They spent it buying expensive arms from the Americans, the British, the French, the Chinese. They threw away our sisters' skills and closed the doors to their secret family meetings.

"Did you, brother, fight, and did you take lives, so that some new Sauds could arise to keep our people as second-class citizens?"

Abdullah was staring at him, but Ahmed could not stop. He had wanted to say things like this to him for so long. "Yes, I have lived in North America, but I have also been to Germany and Singapore, to medical conferences in China and Britain. Things are invented there. Technology and pharmaceuticals. What have we invented in the last thousand years? The world is leaving us behind because we have tied this Wahhabist *brick* around our ankles. Our scholars study only the Koran, which is good, but we need only so many Koranic scholars in a generation."

Ahmed pulled a blue book from beneath his robe. "This UN report is by Arabs. It is about how we measure up to the rest of the world. Not well. The winners in the modern world are knowledge societies, countries that put an emphasis on learning, sharing information, doing research.

"Look at these numbers," he said, paging rapidly. "Two percent of our people have Internet access, compared with ninety-eight percent in Korea. Five books are translated into Arabic a year per million people, compared with nine hundred translated into Spanish. Even in our own language, we publish only one percent of the world's books. One out of five books published in Arabic is on religion. We spend less than one-third of one percent of our GNP on research. Maybe this explains why one out of four of our university graduates leave the Arab world as soon as they can. We do not create knowledge; we do not import knowledge. We import finished goods. This is not the way of the modern world, which is leaving us in the dust.

"You can be modern and Islamic. The Islamic scientists I met in Canada, Germany, and America are devout. Islam is the fastest-growing religion in America! No one prevents Muslims there from following the teachings of the Prophet, blessings and peace be upon him. Besides, the Prophet never taught that we should convert or kill the Christians and Jews. And if we tried, even if we took centuries, we would only devastate this little planet in the process. Does Allah want that? The nuclears, if we get them, will cause the ruin of our country.

"If you let these people on the council have their way, we will continue to be slaves of our own oil, able to do nothing but watch as what Allah put in the ground comes out of it. And the money we get from it will continue to be wasted in supposedly 'religious' follies. We are not a country, we are an oil deposit! And if that is all we are, others will come, the scorpions will come for their food, their precious black liquid. They will keep us enslaved, buying everything we need from them, including weapons which we do not need.

"We could instead use our wealth to join the twenty-first century, to revive the time of greatness when Arabs invented mathematics, astronomy, pharmacy, and the other sciences. *You* could do that, brother." Afraid he had gone too far, Ahmed stopped abruptly and hung his head, averting his eyes from the continued silent stare from Abdullah.

Somewhere in the hotel, a television was on. Ahmed could hear a news program and also the roar of the gas flame in the heater above his head.

"Do you think, little brother, that while you were skiing in the snows, dancing in the clubs, that I was risking my life, hiding in basements, killing men I had never met, to create a society in which our people would waste their lives? Do you?" Abdullah's voice rose with the question, then sank to a whisper. "I did terrible things, for which I pray Allah will forgive me, but when I read the Koran I am not sure he will. Right here in Khobar in 1996, while you were almost still a baby, I was in a cell that helped the Hezbollah and the Iranian Qods attack the U.S. Air Force base here."

This was the first time Ahmed was hearing this story, the first time that his brother had lifted the curtain on his vague, earlier terrorist life. "Qods," Ahmed asked, "these are the men who were trying to blow up the American Navy base in Bahrain. You worked with them?"

"No, I worked for Khalid Sheik Muhammad, who was bin Laden's operations man. Because I thought that he wanted to kick the foreign troops out of our country," Abdullah admitted, reluctantly. "Khalid was asked by the Qods people to have some of us lend a hand with an operation that they were planning in Khobar, against the foreign base. So I helped them set up at a farm not far from here. Khalid said we owed the Qods a lot, so I helped."

Ahmed was afraid to say anything that would stop his brother from continuing. Nonetheless, he had to ask, "What did al Qaeda owe Qods?"

Abdullah was quiet, as though he was calling up the memories from a corner of his brain that he had not recently visited. "I met bin Laden, met with his brains, Dr. Zawahiri, and his muscle, Khalid Sheik Muhammad. Osama himself was not as important to operations as those two. They used him as the symbol, the unifier. I went to Afghanistan to see them. Why? Because they were the only ones really opposing the al Saud monarchy. No one else was doing anything to get these leeches off our people. I was not opposed to monarchy. I know England and the small Gulf states have good monarchies, but we did not! The Sauds were stealing, holding our people back. They let foreigners set up their own military bases in the land of the Two Holy Mosques, not to help us but to protect the oil for themselves!"

Ahmed sensed there was guilt in Abdullah about this past. His tone was the one he had used when explaining to their father that he had dented the car. Ahmed tried to shift the conversation from his brother's role to his own current interest, the Iranians. "And you met Qods people in bin Laden's camps?"

"No, no. They were never visible. If you were good at something special and they trusted you, Khalid would send you to Iran for advanced training with Qods or with Mugniyah's Hezbollah people. Dr. Zawahiri had an office in Tehran and went there a lot, from the days when he ran Egyptian Islamic Jihad. Many of the brothers came to the Afghan camps by flying to Tehran, where the

Qods people got them through immigration and sent them on their way by bus to the border," Abdullah recalled. "But the fact that Qods was helping al Qaeda with money and training was never to be spoken about, because even the President of Iran did not know. And, of course, the Americans did not."

Ahmed shook his head in amazement. The Revolutionary Guards' Qods Force really was a service within a service, reporting only to the big ayatollah, the Iranian supreme leader. "What happened, Abdullah, between you and al Qaeda? Why did you break with them and start your own movement inside our country?"

Abdullah shrugged, as if to say that the answer to that question was well known, or should be obvious. "After 9/11, I broke off from bin Laden. I thought they had gone too far, killing innocent people. Then, after the Americans invaded Iraq, I went to Iraq and worked with that crazy man Zarqawi for a short time. Why? For the same reason our uncle fought in Afghanistan. For the same reason I opposed the al Sauds. To get the foreign troops out. I participated, I learned, and then I led so that we could be our own nation, a great nation, not an American military base, not one family's money machine."

Ahmed was so proud of his brother, who had seen the excesses and mistakes of the others and forged his own movement to free his homeland. There was also something of a parallel with al Qaeda in what Abdullah had done, because Abdullah had done the hard work of operations and let theoreticians like Zubair bin Tayer be the public face of the movement. "And you succeeded," Ahmed added.

"Yes, but right now we are weak. The Sauds took our money." Abdullah returned to one of his current themes, financing. "The Americans have frozen most of it, probably so they can claim it for themselves. But with what they have, the Sauds are buying trouble for us. They want to come back and rule again, and kill me and all the council. I don't know how much time I have before they do that. Every day I get reports." Ahmed looked up and their eyes met. Abdullah pointed with his head toward one of the bodyguards.

Abdullah continued, "I accept many things in the Shura that I do not personally agree with, things I do not think will be good for the future of our people. I accept them for now because we are weak and cannot have internal divisions that our enemies, what you call your scorpions, will exploit."

Ahmed thought for a moment and then replied, humbly, "I know the only right I have to speak on these issues is that our father's blood flows in both of us. I have not earned a say, as you have.

"But I do love this land and I do love you and I do not want to see your efforts go to waste. If you do not stop your enemies on the council now, they will shape Islamyah in a mold that will harden fast. Then they will come after you, because you are not part of what they want to build. And what they want to build will weaken Islamyah and attract my scorpions in droves, especially if they try to get the nuclears." Ahmed reached across the table and squeezed his brother's forearm. "If you think you are going to get killed, die for something *you* believe in, not for what *they* believe in."

Abdullah put his right hand gently on top of the vise grip that Ahmed had placed on his left forearm. "So is that your prescription, Doctor, that I should get killed?"

"No, my care is seldom that lethal to my patients." Ahmed smiled. "My prescription is early prevention. The new army would follow you, and you already run all of the police. Use that power while you have it. Use it for the good of our people. They have not yet been fully liberated. If the people are with you, really with you, they will keep the scorpions away."

"*Inshallah,*" Abdullah said as he embraced his brother. The two men walked back into the Golden Tulip, holding hands. The bodyguards went with them, in front and behind. On the table in the patio, they left the remnants of the mezza and the *hammour*. Abdullah had placed the blue UN report inside his robe.

"Come upstairs with me and meet my team that has been spending all day looking at the Aramco books. Tell them some of your theories." Abdullah guided them toward the elevator. Off the main dining area of the rooftop restaurant was a private room with a floor covered in carpets and pillows. An incense burner in the corner let off a sweet smell. When Abdullah entered the room, the men who had been sitting in a circle on the floor smoking water pipes all rose to their feet.

Abdullah walked the circle formed by his men, shaking hands and kissing cheeks, introducing them one by one to his brother, the doctor-spy. "So you have examined the security of our oil company and you have examined its books," he said, seating himself on the floor amid a pile of pillows. "What have you found? Did the Sauds

suck all the oil out and take it with them to California?"
A servant brought Abdullah a fresh water pipe and
helped him light it.

"No, Sheik, even the Sauds could not steal it all,"
Muhammad bin Hassan replied, evoking the laughter of
the men. He had been a partner in a major accounting
and consulting firm in London, and had returned after
the revolution at the request of the man with whom he
had played football as a boy in Riyadh, Abdullah bin
Rashid. "Our declared reserves are 290 billion barrels.
Another 150,000 to 200,000 lie in the fallow fields."

"I'm sure that's a lot, 'Hammad, but what does that
mean? How does it compare with everyone else?" Abdullah asked as he exhaled the apple-flavored tobacco
smoke.

"It means we have over one-third of the world's remaining oil, another third is elsewhere in the Gulf, and
the final third is spread around Russia, Venezuela, Nige-
ria. But ours is the cheapest to produce. It just comes
bubbling up from right below the sand. Russia and
America have to spend huge amounts to find it in their
countries and raise it from under the ice or on the bottom of the sea. It is their demand and their cost of extraction that has driven the price to ninety euros a barrel.
Our oil is also cheap to refine, whereas so much of the
rest of the world's needs costly refinement.

"The current rates of consumption are also in our favor. China and America each import over ten billion barrels a year and climbing. Here is the key: almost every
other oil producer has pumped all the cheaply extracted
oil and can see the day when they will have pumped it all.

At our current rate of production, we have over another hundred years of oil. When everyone else has run out, we will still have plenty for ourselves and plenty to sell."

There were smiles around the room, except for Ahmed, who looked to his brother for permission to speak. "Ahmed, what do you think of this good news?" Abdullah asked.

"With respect to Muhammad, I am not sure that it is actually good news," he said tentatively. The smiles froze.

"Let's not talk of today and tomorrow," he went on. "Let's imagine us back in our grandfather's time. Let's say he was a camel dealer, which he actually was, Abdullah's and my grandfather. If there had been a pestilence among the camels elsewhere and they had all died, and he still had his camels in good health, would he not fear that the other tribes would come to steal them?" There were nods around the circle.

Ahmed warmed to his tale. "And unknown to our grandfather, there would also be those abroad who would see this as an opportunity to import Land Rovers and teach the other tribes to drive them instead of camels. So even if Grandfather fought hard and spent a lot of money defending his camels, in a little while no one would want them because they would all have Land Rovers and Mercedes." The men laughed.

"So what is your point, Ahmed, you who drive a BMW these days, I am told?" Muhammad asked, looking at Abdullah.

"Your scorpion fears: go ahead, brother, explain them to us," Abdullah encouraged.

"My point is that the remaining oil will attract all sorts

of scorpions, like America and China. We will be a target and a pawn in many games. Meanwhile, some of the other countries will finally be developing alternatives to oil, and after they have waged war in our land to get their oil, they will not need the last fifty years' supply. It will be worthless, like camels."

"Camels are not worthless!" one man called out in protest.

"Ahmed, I respect you as a doctor but not as an economist," Muhammad shot back. "They have been fooling around with alternatives for years. Their hydrogen fuel cells for cars take more energy to make the same power than gasoline-burning cars. They can't fly their planes or sail their ships on hydrogen or solar power. Nuclear power creates radioactive waste that is dangerous. The American oil imports have gone up at almost two percent a year and the Chinese at over ten percent a year."

"Perhaps, 'Hammad, but Ahmed is right that if we end up being the only country with a large amount of oil, the scorpions will come for it," Abdullah said slowly as he stirred the ash of his tobacco.

"But that is where you come in," Khaleed said. "You are now in charge of our defenses and I have complete faith in you. As a defender at football, I could never get by you to shoot on goal," Khaleed teased, sensing that the conversation had grown too serious for this time and place.

"If only our enemies were as easy to block as you were, Muhammad," Abdullah joked back. "But maybe we should ask the doctor to develop a new scorpion trap like that American thing for the roaches—what is it?"

"The Roach Motel," one man offered in English. "They check in, but they don't check out."

"Yes, but we don't *want* them to get in, Jassim, that's the point," Abdullah replied, laughing. "Ahmed, what we need you to develop is a gate to keep them out, a scorpion's gate." All the room laughed at the sheik's humor, and as they did, Abdullah playfully threw his arm around his brother and whispered to him. "Think about it. I will think about what you said, about the UN report. You give me a plan."

The room settled down. "Now, Jassim, let's hear your report on the security of the oil infrastructure and then we'll talk about the workers who have replaced the Americans," Abdullah said, laying out the rest of the night's agenda.

U.S. Central Command Headquarters
MacDill Air Force Base
Tampa, Florida

"Attention on deck," the sergeant barked as the CinC, the Commander in Chief of U.S. Central Command, entered the darkened war room. Forty-two officers, including admirals and generals, stood up from their seats in the little amphitheater. On the twelve large flat screens in front of them, computer displays showed the current status of forces in the Indian Ocean, the Red Sea, the Persian Gulf, from the top of the world in the Hindu Kush Mountains to the bottom at the Dead Sea.

"Be seated," U.S. Army four-star general Nathan

Moore mumbled as he dropped down into the oversized chair reserved for the CinC. There was a shuffling and scraping sound as the officers were seated and pulled their chairs forward to the desklike countertops in front of each row. "We are delighted to be joined today by the deputy chief of staff of the Egyptian Armed Forces, Marshal Fahmi. Welcome, sir. We look forward to this week's Combined Planning Conference and, more important, to the largest Bright Star exercise yet. Please, begin."

The basement Command Center of the United States Central Command was in a nondescript office building on an Air Force base sticking out into Tampa Bay. When Central Command was formed in 1981 to coordinate the few U.S. forces in the Middle East, no country in the region would permit America to create a headquarters for the command. In frustration, the Pentagon had temporarily placed the headquarters at an F-16 base in Florida. Special Operations Command had also moved its headquarters onto the base. Now, three or four wars later, the F-16s and other flight activity at MacDill AFB had gone, but CENTCOM was still there. It also now had a sophisticated "forward" headquarters in Qatar and a naval headquarters in Bahrain, in the Persian Gulf (or, as the Pentagon calls it, the Arabian Gulf).

As a young Air Force officer walked to the podium, the CENTCOM logo (an American eagle flying over the Arabian peninsula) faded from the main screen and was replaced by a large weather map. What followed was a lot like the weather report on the International Edition of CNN. "Heavy rains continue in Mumbai . . . Six inches of snow in Kabul . . . Eighty-two and sunny in Dubai . . .

Five-foot seas off Alexandria . . ." The audience, heads down, were examining their briefing books.

Next up was an Army one-star general, the J-2, head of CENTCOM's intelligence branch. Because of the presence of the Egyptians, the intelligence briefing was short, devoid of the usual close-up satellite pictures the J-2 called "Happy Snaps" or the juicy intercepted messages with which he liked to punctuate his morning briefings. "And now to Bahrain," the J-2 said as a picture of the ornamental main gate of Brad Adams's headquarters flashed onto the main screen. Adams thought he could hear eyeballs click as, he was sure, everyone in the darkened theater looked at him. "Investigation continues into the identity of the terrorists who hijacked the liquid natural gas tanker *Jamal* in an apparent attempt to explode the ship inside the CENTNAV Administrative Support Unit, Fifth Fleet Headquarters. Initial reports indicate the hijackers were Iraqis, otherwise unidentified. Defense Intelligence in the Pentagon speculates that they were working for the Riyadh regime called Islamyah. . . ."

Sensing the tension in the room, the CinC interrupted. "Let me just say this about that, ah, episode: Admiral Adams's team did an outstanding job stopping this attack, outstanding. Those SEALs and Marines . . . and, ah, of course, the Coasties who died, Captain Barlow, where is he?" The CinC looked around in the dark for the Coast Guard liaison officer. "Tremendous job. Thousands of lives saved. This is how to do force protection. Admiral," he said, looking down the row of seats to where Adams sat with an Egyptian navy officer on his left, "you should be proud of how you trained your forces, drilled them, planned, so that you could get that sort of outcome without you even being there. Well done."

Adams swallowed. "Thank you, sir." As the director of operations, the J-3, an Army two-star general walked to the podium to begin the Bright Star Exercise briefing, the officer on Adams's right slipped a folded note under the Fifth Fleet commander's briefing book. Unfolding it, Adams read, "Was that a compliment or a reprimand?" The author, Marine Major General Bobby Doyle, was the new director of policy and plans, the J-5. He had also gone to the National War College with Adams five years earlier, where the two had competed for the class tennis trophy. Doyle had won.

"As you know, sir, the Bright Star series of U.S.-Egyptian exercises began in the early 1980s. . . ." The J-3 was proudly showing a short documentary film of the early exercises. He finally moved on to the plans for the up-coming operation. "Largest ever, incorporating amphibious and airborne insertions of multiple brigade-size American units, supported by bombers from CONUS and tacair from the carriers," he said, pointing to symbols that were appearing on the large map of the Red Sea on center screen, "marrying up with Egyptian armor divisions and moving inland. . . ."

Adams had scribbled on Doyle's note and passed it back: "And the horse you rode in on."

Reading the reply, Doyle peeled another page off the CENTCOM notepad on his desk and scribbled for what Adams thought was a long time. The J-3's briefing was now diving down into details no one needed to hear:

". . . sustained desert operations . . . two hundred and forty thousand tons . . ."

Finally, Adams discreetly opened Doyle's second volley, "U/me, Dinner, 2100, Colombia restaurant, Ybor City, already made resev. Civvies. Meet there." Adams chuckled, thinking what the night would be like and whether his liver was up to it.

". . . Stryker armored vehicles, which will be offloaded from roll-on/roll-off ships . . . " the J-3 droned on.

A shaft of light stabbed into the theater command center as a door was opened from the basement corridor in the rear of the complex. Adams craned his neck to see who had shown up late, because whoever that was would certainly get the CinC's wrath now or later. "Right this way, Mr. Secretary . . . " a young woman from Protocol was saying. A civilian picked his way down the row to an empty seat at the CinC's left. No one stood, and the briefing was not interrupted, until the CinC realized that his guest had shown up. "Ah, Mr. Secretary, ah, let me introduce you to Marshal Fahmi here, who . . ." The J-3 halted while the VIPs in the room chatted.

Adams turned to Doyle and mouthed the words, "Why is he here?"

Doyle responded with a quick note reading, "Under Secretary of Defense Ronald Kashigian = Dr. Evil."

"Okay, okay," the CinC said, hitting the microphone in front of his seat with his index finger, "let's resume. General, you were saying that that fuel . . ." Adams felt an overwhelming wave of jet-lag fatigue and wondered how he would make it until a nine o'clock liquid dinner

with Doyle. To stay awake, he stabbed his left palm with
a pencil with the CENTCOM logo on it.

Colombia Restaurant
Ybor City, Tampa

Climbing out of the taxi on 21st Street a little before
nine o'clock, the commander of the Fifth Fleet
could have been a vice president for sales, in town for a
convention downtown. He was alone and in a polo shirt
that revealed a paunch. Usually he traveled with aides
and bodyguards. Back in the States and in civilian
clothes, he could be just like anyone else, not a three-star
admiral.

In the lobby, the maître d' spotted Adams as soon as
he came through the door. "Admiral, thank you for join-
ing us. Right this way. General Doyle is already here in
the Patio Room."

Adams was trying to figure out how he had been iden-
tified by someone who had never seen him before, but
the host gave him no opening to ask. "Not busy this early
in the week, so some of the rooms are closed, but you'll
have a very private table just behind the Dolphin." They
entered a bright Spanish-styled courtyard with a skylight
roof as he continued, "A copy of a fountain found in the
ruins of Pompeii. If you've never had it here before, I
highly recommend our paella Valencia . . ." Adams spotted Doyle seated, chomping on a cigar.

"I think you're in violation of the smoking regulations,

Dr. Evil, is it?" Adams kidded the trim Marine and gave him a fake punch as he sat down.

"You kiddin' me, boy? Ybor City is the home of cigars. They used to make a quarter billion a year here. Billion. Rolled on the thighs of virgins," Doyle said, producing a Cohiba from a leather cigar holder for Adams. "For after dinner. Smuggled from behind the lines in Cuba. You know last time we really invaded Cuba, this was where the U.S. Army massed. Rough Riders and all, here in Ybor City, where the rail line from the north stopped."

"Illegal cigars. Now I really will have to put you on report," Adams replied, taking the cigar. "Shall we try the paella? I hear it's good here."

Forty minutes later, Adams was feeling full, but the wine had given him a second wind. Suddenly, there was music, and flamenco dancers came in through three of the four doors into the Patio Room. Doyle moved his chair around to sit next to Adams, apparently so he could watch the dancers, but as the music covered their conversation, the Marine asked, "You see anything odd about this Bright Star?"

"Well, I gather it's blowing the entire CENTCOM exercise budget for the year, plus some extra money from the Joint Chiefs," Adams replied, watching the lead dancer. "Why?"

"Why? 'Cuz it's like my cock, it's real goddamn big, that's why." Doyle chuckled. "No, really. This exercise is too big, too unnecessary, too real."

Adams took his eyes off the dancer for a moment and glanced at the Marine, who continued, "While you were snoozing during the briefing today, swabbie, General Ballsucker was ticking off some very interesting data. They're bringing enough shit with them to conduct two weeks of sustained combat operations. Why the hell they doin' that shit? You know how much it will cost to lift all of that out there?"

Adams stopped looking at the dancer altogether. "You tell me."

"I got the questions, boyo," Doyle said, leaning in closer to Adams. "Why do we and the Gypoes need to do a combined op? We expecting Libya to come across the Sahara to steal the fuckin' Sphinx?

"Why on the double-secret-handshake map of the exercise I saw yesterday is your battle group not gonna be in the Red Sea at all and instead is fanned out like a picket line in the Indian Ocean, huh, buddy?

"Why is Dr. Evil down here for this exercise-planning conference this week instead of up in D.C. polishing the SECDEF's shoes, or whatever he usually strokes for him? I'll tell yah: because Dr. Evil and his friends from these think tanks believe the U.S. military are just a bunch of chess pieces that they can move around to implement their globaloney theories. They don't understand that we chess pieces bleed, while they're yukking it up on some bullshit Fox talk show.

"And get this: why are my friends in SEAL Team Six playing the role of the reconnaissance force in the exercise and why does the team chief have detailed maps of the coast around Jeddah and Yanbu in his room at the BOQ? Got it now, Einstein?"

Adams was trying to find his way through General

Doyle's logic. "SEAL Team Six is a national asset. It shouldn't be in some regional exercise like this." The admiral squinted at his old friend. "Jeddah and Yanbu are in the Red Sea, but that's the wrong side of the Red Sea, that's . . ." Now he realized what the Marine was saying. The flamenco dancers ended their number with a flourish. "Oh my God!" Adams let loose, just as the music ended.

"Jes, jes. Dey are bedy good," a waiter replied.

After paying the check, the two flag officers walked down 7th Avenue, in civilian clothes, smoking their Cohibas. "You really think they're going to invade Saudi Arabia? Home of the Two Holy Mosques?" Adams asked. "The Islamic world will go nuts!"

"I do. I think Secretary Conrad really thinks we can reinstall the House of Saud. They've had us going over the Lessons Learned from the Iraqi Occupation. Why? So we don't make them again when we occupy Islamyah?" General Doyle asked, chomping on the cigar.

"Bobby, the Iraq occupation almost ruined the Army and Marines. It stretched them thin and it totally busted the National Guard and Reserves. Recruitment has never come back. We got seven thousand kids who are now veterans without legs or with missing eyes and we got nothin' for it," Adams said, feeling the anger rising in him. "I served there. So did you. I had buddies killed, and for what? Because we had a SECDEF then who didn't think it out, had no plan, put in too few troops. You think the American people are going to stand for that again? No way."

Doyle stepped off the sidewalk, into the doorway of a

store that had closed. "Why do you think they're doin' it this way? You think if Conrad or the President went to the Congress and said let's invade and occupy another Arab country, they'd get one vote for it? Shit, they'd more likely be impeached." The Marine spat out a piece of the cigar. "That's why all the cloak-and-dagger stuff. We will just happen to have an invasion force off the Saudi coast when, hell, I dunno, somethin' gonna happen. Maybe the Gypoes are in on it, too. Maybe they're comin' with us like in '90, got me?

"But I do know this. I went into Fallujah with my brigade in '04 and I saw what we did. You know the three-star Marine in charge of all of us jarheads in Iraq recommended against assaulting the city, ju' know that? They didn't have no WMD there. They weren't hiding Saddam or Osama. When we went inta Fallujah the second time, we fuckin' leveled the place. City a quarter million people, gone-ski. Did we fuckin' think that would make us popular? No wonder you got Iraqis still trying to blow up your headquarters in Bahrain.

"You know, we were gonna pay for that whole little escapade by getting some deal for their oil. Wha'd they do? Blew up their own pipelines, storage tanks, the whole infrastructure. We go into Saudi, they'll self-immolate, too. Then no one will have any fuckin' oil. Move to Florida, that's what I say. It's nice here, in the winter."

Doyle moved close to Adams and placed a finger on the admiral's chest. "I still remember Dorian Dale, my G-3. His mom worked herself almost to death putting that man through Howard, her and ROTC. He coulda been the next Colin Powell, 'cept he got his head blown right off his shoulders in Fallujah, right off. Blood squirted all over. Why? Because some set of lunatics from a think tank escaped and took over the Pentagon, that's fuckin' why." Doyle exhaled. "We can't let that happen again. We gotta stop this shit, Adams. It's our duty. It's our duty to our troops. It's our duty to our country as military men."

Adams looked away, then back at his friend. "Bobby, all my life since I was seventeen I have saluted and followed orders, including some pretty stupid fucking orders. At this point in my life, if I tried to step out of line I would probably seize up," he whispered. "We have a system in this country. The military is under civilian control. Maybe they make mistakes sometimes, but they get paid for looking at the big picture and some of them get elected. Nobody elected us.

"The President, Secretary Conrad, these are smart guys who see a lot more info than we do. Having a big exercise in Islamyah right now to scare them into not messing with us, that makes sense to me.

"Besides, Bobby, what you're talking about sounds like doing something, I don't know what, but something that violates the UCMJ. That's not just giving up the next promotion, it's giving up everything, not just for us but for our wives, family. I got both kids into Penn because of the legacy thing. That's a hundred thousand a year worth of scholarships and loans."

They stepped back out onto the sidewalk. Adams talked with his head down as they moved down 7th. He sensed Doyle was feeling let down. "Okay, Bobby, supposing you're right about this invasion?" The admiral spoke carefully. "Does the CinC know? What could we do to stop it if you wanted to? You can't even prove they're gonna do it."

"The CinC? Nathan Bedford Moore?" Doyle said sarcastically. "I don't know what he knows or doesn't know. But his number-one priority is number one. He sees Secretary Conrad making him the next Chairman of the Joint Chiefs. He ain't gonna buck the tide. Hell, he's invited Conrad out to see the so-called exercise, be on the USS *George H. W. Bush* bobbing up and down in the Red Sea with the troops.

"I don't know what to do, Adams. I plumb don't know," the Marine said, looking up at the admiral. "That's why I had to talk to you: because you're the only one I can trust about this, and I thought you'd know what to do."

The admiral stared at Doyle without knowing what to say. Then he pulled out his half-finished Cohiba and threw it onto the brick street and ground it under his heel. He looked back at Doyle. "There was a motto over the gate at college. I think it was from Hannibal, the general with the elephants who almost beat the Romans. It said 'Inveniemus Viam aut Faciemus.' We will find a way, or we will make one."

Doyle put his hand on his friend's shoulder. "Well, buddy, you faciemus better."

Across 7th Avenue, a civilian-looking couple kissed on the sidewalk. They were actually both master sergeants assigned to a little-known unit from Fort Belvoir in northern Virginia, the 504th Counterintelligence Battalion.

Upper Pepper Street
Cape Town, South Africa

"Well, I can see why they call it Table Mountain—it's flatter than a flounder," Brian Douglas mused aloud, looking out the top-floor window and stretching after the long flight from London. "Magnificently beautiful city."

"That's why I love this location, it has such a nice view," Jeannie Enbemeena replied as she came back into the room with a handful of papers. She was a thirty-something, short, and highly attractive black woman from Natal who had been with SIS for six years. For two years she had been running the small South Africa regional services and support office for British intelligence, out of a Cape Town property with no obvious connection to the embassy in Johannesburg. "Never been here before, Mr. Douglas?"

"First time. I'm an Arabist, you know," he said, taking the false documents that Jeannie handed him. "What do you do, Ms. Enbemeena, may I ask, when you are not creating legends and playing hostess for wandering Arabists?"

"I keep an eye on the Malay mosque down the street. We've tied some of the regulars there to an al Qaeda spin-off that was plotting to blow things up in KL and Singapore. The lot here did a small bombing spree two years ago at the American Express and Barclays"—she smiled—"but I went to school in Durban, and our boys there did a good job on your papers and back story. I would believe it. You are now Simon Manley, recently in the fruit-and-nut business and seeking a reliable and cheap source of pistachios. Where else but Iran, pistachio capital of the world?"

"And how does Simon the nutter get from here to there?" Brian chuckled.

"We fly you to just outside Durban on an air taxi we own, no questions asked. Then you will be driven to the main Durban airport, where you catch the once-a-week flight on Emirates to Dubai, have a two-hour layover in the duty-free, and then Iran Air to Tehran, where Marty Bowers meets you on the other side of Customs," Jeannie said, reading from her notes.

"Marty who? Meets me? I am operating solo on this— no one from the Tehran station is even to know I'm in country!" Brian exploded at her.

"Cease fire!" she shot back. "Jesus, mate, don't kill the waitress for the chef's faux pas. London told us to send someone from Durban base who could be part of your cover story, to be there just in case, precisely because you won't be going into the embassy or seeing any one of the boys and girls who work at the station there.

"Marty Bowers's regular cover is that he runs an import warehouse in Durban. We've made him one of the investors and partners in Manley Fruits and Nuts. He will not get in your hair at all. He'll probably spend most of his time as a tourist. London orders." Her smile returned.

"London." Brian Douglas sighed. "Only London could come up with Manley Fruits and Nuts, the perfect oxymoron. Is Simon Manley's passport and picture in the South African government's database?"

"Of course, we have hacked all of their databases and inserted your life story. Now, then, Simon Manley, you are bald with a monk's collar of gray hair and you have brown eyes and glasses," Jeannie said, walking into the next room. "So if you will follow me, Mr. Manley . . ."

Two hours later, the full head of sandy hair was gone, the newly exposed scalp was tanned, the blue eyes had become brown, with tortoiseshell frames for the glasses, and slight bits of flesh-colored material had been attached to the nose and ears with a powerful epoxy resin glue. When Brian Douglas emerged from the back room where the disguise technician had worked wonders, Jeannie Enbemeena was startled. "Goodness, why it truly is Simon the nutter," she said. "I don't have a need to know, but may I ask why we had to do all of this to you? You were, if I may say so, a rather good-looking man."

"You're right. About the part that you don't have a need to know," Brian said while rubbing his suddenly bald head. "But there is some chance that Tehran has my face on file, and with the new face-matching software that's commercially available, they just might figure out who I really am before I depart. That would be bad for the nuts, in more ways than one."

7

FEBRUARY 11

U.S. Navy Base
ASU—Bahrain

"That's the LNG tanker over there, Mr. MacIntyre. The Japanese are flying in a new crew and hiring some heavy-duty tugs to pull her out. That's pretty shallow water where she ended up." Captain John Hardy, NAVCENT J-2, was talking into the headset mike and pointing at the LNG *Jamal* as the Osprey, the Navy's V-22 tilt-rotor, lifted off from the ASU helipad. The two enormous rotors were facing straight up, making the aircraft operate like a helicopter. It moved out over the water, shuddering as it transitioned from helo to aircraft, the giant rotors turning 90 degrees to a horizontal position. "The Pentagon tried to kill the Osprey program so often they ought to have renamed it the Phoenix," Hardy joked, "but don't worry, we've had thousands of hours of successful operations now and only six or eight crashes."

"This is one hell of a windshield tour, Captain. Many thanks."

"Well, the admiral said you come highly recommended, Mr. MacIntyre, and he said to tell you he was sorry he couldn't be here when you arrived. He left you this personal note. I think it says he wants to see you when he gets back from CONUS, if you can wait around a couple days."

The Osprey circled around the LNG. "She looks very well guarded," Rusty MacIntyre said, hitting his push-to-talk button, which was dangling on the cord below his helmet.

"She is. Two Bahraini patrol boats and three of ours, plus divers, plus helos, plus a Bahraini army detachment on the shoreside approach. We're not taking any chances. She's still loaded with frozen gas." Hardy seemed to shake as he mentioned the gas. "If they had blown her, the fireball would have taken out most of the base."

"So who were 'they,' Captain? I've heard a few different theories," Rusty said as the Osprey flew over the line of U.S. ships tied up at the dock below.

"The SEALs captured some of the terrorists alive. They were Iraqis, apparently seeking belated revenge for the U.S. occupation. Anyway, that's what the Pentagon thinks," Hardy replied carefully.

"But I hear they were Shiites, so they weren't likely to be retaliating for Fallujah. Possibly working for the secret police, the new Iraqi Muhabarat?" Rusty suggested.

"Could be," the captain said, looking over his sunglasses, which had slipped down his nose. "That's what my source believes, the one who tipped me to the terrorist attack. She says it was definitely not Islamyah. In fact, she says it was Islamyah that *told* her about the attack. All I know is, the guys we caught were Iraqis."

"Iraqi Muhabarat, which is under the tutelage of the Iranian Revolutionary Guard and its Qods Force . . ." MacIntyre said, looking down on the LNG tanker, now directly below the helo.

"Like I said, Mr. MacIntyre, could be, but the Pentagon thinks that they are Iraqis related to al Qaeda, related to Islamyah, even if you and I know there *are* no Shiites in al Qaeda of Iraq." Hardy pushed his sunglasses back up.

MacIntyre looked straight at his tour guide. "Whoever it was, I suspect they will try again. Are you planning any new security measures?"

"Of course," Hardy said, smiling. "We are also planning to put most of the force to sea soon for a major exercise. With the base pretty empty, they may hold off for a while."

"Yeah, Bright Star, coming up this month," MacIntyre said, letting the Navy intelligence officer know that he was privy to the plan. "Doesn't it seem a little unusual to strip the Gulf of assets for an exercise in the Red Sea, especially if it's the Iranians who are stirring things up here?"

"Above my pay grade, sir. Or, at least not my area of specialization," Captain Hardy answered as the Osprey got up speed and headed out into the Gulf. Hardy stared out the side window of the V-22. "On the other hand, that ship out there in the haze is my area of specialization. She's the *Zagros*, the Iranian navy's big destroyer, Sovremenny II–class, made in Petersburg. Rigged out with antiship and antiair missiles, and all sorts of listening devices." Hardy handed the pair of 7×35 binoculars to MacIntyre.

"That is a big ship," MacIntyre said, focusing the glasses. "What's she doing so close to Bahrain?"

"My educated guess is that she's monitoring our communications, visually checking out the movement of our ships as they come out of port, and probably putting a few divers over the side with undersea sleds to check out the coast. Our SEALs chased a few away last week."

"Checking out the Bahraini coast, Captain, underwater? Now, why would they be doing that, do you suppose?" MacIntyre asked, handing back the glasses.

"I hear we got SEAL Team Six doing the same thing over in the Red Sea for Bright Star. It's what you do before you conduct amphibious landings. Make sure there's nothing underwater that will hang up your landing craft."

"The Iranians got any landing craft?" MacIntyre asked casually as the Osprey flew down the side of the *Zagros* and Iranian sailors on deck waved up at the funny-looking U.S. aircraft.

"Shitload of them. Karbala-class LSTs, homemade. Hovercraft. Semisubmersible gunboats. You name it." Hardy smiled at MacIntyre. "They exercised all of them at once a few months back, successfully invading themselves. Their landings in Iran were unopposed."

"So you're saying they're planning for landings in Bahrain? Any idea when?" Macintyre asked.

"I do intelligence, Mr. MacIntyre. That means I do capabilities, not intentions. Everybody wants Intelligence to be fortunetellers, but that's not our job. But in terms of their capabilities, I'd say they should be at maximum readiness in a week or two." Hardy let his words hang for a minute and then added, "But I don't know what they have in their sights, sir." The V-22 banked and headed toward the Qatari shoreline. "Off to our left is the world's largest source of liquid natural gas, Qatar, also home to U.S. Central Command's forward headquarters. It's a lot more valuable than Bahrain, but who knows, the Iranians may just be doing a drill, just like us."

Rooftop Restaurant
The Ritz-Carlton Hotel
Manama, Bahrain

"Ms. Delmarco? Rusty MacIntyre. Sorry to be late," he said, holding out his hand. "I was getting a little aerial sightseeing tour and kind of lost track of time."

Kate was waiting at the bar. "That's all right," she said, closing a book. "It gave me a chance to finish. Here, you might want to read it, *The World at Night,* by Alan Furst. All of his books are about Europe in the late 1930s, about how average people, little people, know that a war is coming but they can't do anything about it. They all get swept up in it. Pretty convincing stuff."

"Maybe I should read it," Rusty said, accepting the book. He tried to guess her age and thought she was about his own age, give or take a couple of years. She had a presence, style.

"So that was you in the Jules Verne contraption thing that landed at the Navy base a little while back? You do have courage. Yes, you can see a lot from up here." Delmarco slipped off her stool. "I'm starving. Let's get a table."

The maître d', who seemed to know Delmarco, seated the two at a corner table, where they could see in two directions out to the Gulf. "I understand you did see quite a lot up here recently," Rusty said as the waiter appeared with menus.

"Yes, just lucky, I guess," Kate said, smiling innocently.

"It was one hell of a story. You must have been on live with CNN for over an hour. But it wasn't just luck, was it, and you didn't just happen to be at the bar here. You were the one who called Captain Hardy with word that the attack was under way." Rusty put down the menu and stared at Delmarco.

"Johnny has a big mouth. That sort of talk could get me killed, Mr. MacIntyre." Delmarco's voice had dropped an octave.

"Don't blame Captain Hardy. I just guessed and happened to be right," Rusty almost whispered across the table. "When Brian Douglas suggested you were someone I should see while I was out here, I figured you were more than the usual American foreign correspondent. And I was right about that, too."

The waiter brought a small mezza of tabouli, hummus, olives, feta, and baba ghanouj to start. A U.S.

minesweeper made smoke and pushed off from a dock below.

"Well, I figure Brian Douglas is more than the usual British Embassy petroleum whatsit himself, especially if he knows the deputy director of . . . What is your title again, Rusty?"

"Intelligence Analysis Center. We're the writers, the sifters, not the spooks. Brian and I met at a petroleum research conference in Houston last year," MacIntyre tried lamely.

"Right," she said sarcastically. "Where is he, by the way? He hasn't returned my calls in days. I need to return something to him." As she spoke, Kate Delmarco took a small reporter's notepad from her bag and placed it on the table next to her.

"Well, since you've already seen through Brian's intentionally thin cover, he's in London for a week or so. So what is it you were hoping to tell someone in a Western intelligence agency?" MacIntyre saw no point in continuing the charade and hoped his candor would buy him some credit with a reporter who appeared to have very good sources.

"Well, that was frank. Which is more than I can say for Brian when it comes to his job. Thank you, Rusty." She wondered whether she had given away too much about her friendship with Brian. She wondered how much he had told the American. "The reason I knew the attack was under way was that I was told so by someone tied to Islamyah intelligence. And the reason I knew *him* was that I was introduced to him by a Dubai real estate mogul, whom Brian Douglas suggested I should get to know. In short, our mutual friend Brian must know that Dr. Ahmed bin Rashid over at the Salmaniyah Medical Center here is the brother of the head of Islamyah intelligence. So why couldn't he just tell me that straight out?"

MacIntyre paused, trying to follow the connections. "As I said, I am not an operational type. I write analyses, or rather, I have a bunch of really smart people who write analyses based on the things that people like Brian collect. So I can only assume . . . But I think it has something to do with deniability. What would Dr. Rashid have done if you called up and said, 'Can I interview you? You were just outed as a spy by the British'?"

"He would have freaked." Kate laughed. "You're right. Instead, with the Dubai guy as our mutual friend, he has become quite a source for me. I've seen him a couple of times since the tanker hijacking. He's worried. That's what I would tell the mysterious Brian Douglas if he weren't off in London."

"Worried about what? That the Brits and the Bahrainis know who he is and what he's doing here?" Rusty asked.

"Lots of things," Delmarco said, looking at her notes. "That the Shura Council in Islamyah may do something soon, something really stupid that will provoke the Americans. That it's dominated by fundamentalists who will continue some of the mistakes made by the Sauds. That his sources that keep tabs on the Iranians here think something big is about to happen. He's a very nervous man, our doctor. I wouldn't want him keeping an eye on me in the intensive care unit."

"I'd like to meet him," MacIntyre said.

"No way. Do you want to get me killed? 'Excuse me, Ahmed, meet my spy buddy from Washington.' I'd never hear from him again," Kate said, closing her notebook and placing her napkin on the table.

Rusty MacIntyre took the napkin. "It's amazing they use paper napkins in a high-class place like this," he said, and tore it into four pieces.

"What . . . what are you doing?" Kate stammered.

MacIntyre held the pieces of the napkin in his right hand, moved his left above it, and then, looking straight at Kate, said, "I must see Ahmed." He then pulled the napkin from his right hand and handed it back to Kate in one piece. She gasped. He grabbed the napkin back, ran it through his hands, and repeated, "I must see Ahmed." What appeared from his right hand was a napkin in the shape of a rose.

"I don't believe it," the reporter said, accepting the paper rose.

"Excuse the parlor tricks," MacIntyre said. "I just wanted to get your attention. Kate, if Ahmed's right and things are about to happen in Islamyah and Iran, there may be no more time for niceties. Besides, Brian isn't coming back for a few days. I need to do this now. Tell Rashid that I'm your editor from New York, tell him I'm your older brother, tell him—"

"Nice try. Older brother. I like that. I have you by five years at a minimum." Kate thought for a moment. "If I do this and lose him as a source, you'll have to do some other magic trick to make it up to me, with material at least as good as I got from Ahmed. Deal?"

"Deal. See if you can get him to meet me tonight," MacIntyre urged.

"I'll try, but he works late at the hospital." She took out her mobile. "Are you staying here at the Ritz?"

"No. I have the guesthouse at the American ambassador's residence. It's . . . safer," Rusty admitted, blushing slightly.

As Kate Delmarco called Dr. Rashid and left a voice mail for him, saying that they needed to get together tonight if possible, Rusty MacIntyre checked the PGP-encrypted e-mail on his BlackBerry. There were three messages and only four people knew the account. One was from Sarah. She had to go to Somaliland to do a refugee survey and would be back in D.C. in ten days. The neighbor kid would look in on the cat. One was from Brian Douglas, suggesting they meet at Jaipur, a "dive curry house" on Dubai Creek in three days, when he would be on his way back from his "shopping holiday," meaning his trip to Tehran. Even using encrypted e-mail, Brian was careful.

The third message caused him to focus:

Rusty, All right so I had to handwrite this and give it to Ms. Connor to send to you. The keyboard on this thing is too small. Anyway, here's the story. Secretary Conrad's DIA source in China now says that the Chinese troops will fly into Islamyah on the 28th, a day after the Chinese fleet arrives in several Islamyah ports. We still cannot confirm this with any other source, so Conrad may be making it up. Separately, one of the military

guys on our staff says he learned from a friend in
CENTCOM that the date for the Bright Star Exercise
with the Egyptians has suddenly been moved up from
March 15th to February 25th. I have no idea why. Be
careful out there, but find out what you can and get your
ass back here pronto. We may not have a lot of time. R.

"Hello? Sorry to interrupt . . . " Kate was saying. And
then as Rusty looked up from the BlackBerry: "I left a
message. If he calls back and agrees to meet my editor,
I'll call you."

"What's today's date?" Rusty asked, distracted.

"February eleventh, here on earth," Delmarco needled.

"Right. Sorry. So—tonight. I really need to see him
tonight." A three-ship flight of Bahraini F-16s swept low
over the port, headed out to the Gulf, out toward the
Zagros.

Imam Khomeini International Airport
Tehran, Iran

"Simon, old boy. How was the flight? Bloody cold here
compared to back home, i'n' it?" a tall, broad man in
a heavy overcoat said loudly as he approached Brian in
the sparkling, high-vaulted glass cathedral that was the
international arrivals hall. "Did Limpopo really beat us?
God, you know, I leave Durban for a little bit and our
team starts losing to the likes of Limpopo. Next we'll be
going down to the likes of Mpumalanga. Here, let me

take that," he continued boisterously. This, apparently, was Martin Bowers, of the SIS Durban base, playing the nut importer and partner of fellow South African Simon Manley.

Brian Douglas let his newfound friend take his bag. He looked about in amazement at the modern airport.

"Yes, it is a wonder, isn't it, Simon? They tell me the old airport was a proper dump, Mehrabad with emphasis on the 'bad.' Glad we never had to use it," Bowers continued as they pressed through the mob by the Customs door. "This is only about forty-five kilometers south of the city, so at this time of day less than two hours' drive. After the traffic here, I'll never complain again about Durban. That's why I splurged and got us a driver for the run in: I couldn't navigate us safely with these crazy drivers."

Good, Brian thought, a hired driver taking two foreigners in from the international airport is likely to be on the hook to report to VEVAK, the Ministry of Intelligence Service. Let VEVAK know that the two white South Africans were not afraid to get a hired driver and that they spoke only about traffic, football, rugger, and pistachios. Someone trying to avoid VEVAK attention might take the crowded bus downtown; Simon Manley and Marty Bowers would never even think of VEVAK. Maybe Bowers is more than the oversized blowhard he played.

When they got in the car, Bowers started, "We're staying at the Homa Hotel, which they say was once a Sheraton. Very nice and on the high street, or what passes for one—Valiasr, I think they call it. Now, let me tell you about Tehran . . ." Brian Douglas, now Simon

Manley, tuned out of the explanation that was meant mainly for the driver to overhear. He thought instead of the Tehran he knew so well, the back alleys off the bazaar, the poor streets in the south of the city, the dead-letter drops in the mountain parks an hour north of the sprawling, polluted jumble that was now the capital of Persia, or the Islamic Republic of Iran.

He thought of the network of Iranian sources that he had run successfully until, after he had moved on to the station chief Bahrain job, his best source in the Iran network had been shot dead on the street by VEVAK. Shot dead after depositing the plans for Iran's new air defense system in a dead-letter drop in Baku two days before. Until then it had worked well, largely because it had not involved the British Embassy in Tehran. VEVAK kept close track of the entire embassy staff. His network of Iranian spies had survived because only Brian and a few in Vauxhall knew who they were and the meets were almost always out of the country: Ankara, Istanbul, Dubai, and, of course, Baku.

After the hit, London had ordered all contact broken until an assessment could be made of how the source had been compromised. They never had figured it out. Months went by and Brian had been posted to Bahrain as chief of station for the lower Gulf, including the posts in Doha, Dubai, and Muscat. Downsizing had forced SIS into having one senior officer for all four posts. Now, three years on, he did not even know if the members of the network were still alive, still at their old addresses, still in the jobs that had made them so valuable. Most important, he could not know whether they would still recognize the invitation to a meet. He thought of the cameras in the Border Control booth at the airport and subconsciously wiggled his newly shaped nose.

"So here we are, the Homa," Bower said, breaking Brian's reverie. "Owned by the airline, this chain is. Not really what we would call a five-star, but Iranian five-stars are the best they have. What we would think of as two-star."

The room was simple and relatively clean. His window looked down on Vanak Square and did little to stop the noise of the incessant Tehran traffic below. He gave it a quick check for audio and video surveillance, without being too obvious about what he was doing. If they already knew who he was, the surveillance devices would be too good to detect. If they thought he was a South African nut buyer, there might be some lower-quality devices placed there on a purely random basis. The fact that he could not see anything told him he was either clean or under sophisticated monitoring.

He dined that night with Bowers at a place near Vanak Square, a place with a mix of locals and some foreign businessmen. The hotel doorman had recommended it. When they returned to the Homa, they approached the front desk. "Could you give me a wake-up call at eight o'clock tomorrow?" Brian asked in English. He turned to Bowers. "I'll see you downstairs for breakfast at nine, since our first meeting isn't until eleven." Bowers had arranged to visit a pistachio exporter near the bazaar.

As he got into bed, Brian Douglas set the alarm on his wristwatch for 0530.

The Gulf Café
The Corniche
Manama, Bahrain

Russell MacIntyre looked at his watch again, impatiently. "I thought you said he would show up around eleven. It's almost eleven-thirty."

Kate Delmarco sipped her Tanqueray and tonic. "I said he gets off shift at eleven, assuming no one is dying on him. Chill. Anyway, people here work on a different rhythm of time. This isn't Washington."

"Miss Delmarco, my name is Fadl." The young man had appeared out of nowhere. He wore jeans and a T-shirt that said "California University" with a map of California below it. "Dr. Rashid would like your guest to come with me. I will take you to him, sir."

"Well, we both want to . . ." Rusty began.

"Just you, sir. Dr. Rashid was very specific," Fadl insisted. "Not the woman."

"Okay. Well, Kate, I'll meet you at the Ritz later. I'll call your room and we can meet at the roof bar." Rusty wanted to make sure that somebody actually saw him later that night to know that he was all right. He hoped she understood what he was doing.

"And if I don't hear from you by last call?" Kate asked, smiling. She was enjoying seeing MacIntyre squirm. She was actually surprised that he'd agreed to go with the young man he had never seen before.

"Call the place where I'm staying. Tell them to leave a light on for me."

MacIntyre followed Fadl and climbed into a minivan,

which pulled up as they made it to the curb. There were two more men inside. Fadl introduced them. "This is Jassim. He will pat you down. No guns, cameras, recording devices. You understand."

Jassim looked closely at the BlackBerry and then removed its battery. "You will get it back when we return you to your ambassador's residence, Mr. MacIntyre." So much for being Delmarco's editor from the *New York Journal*, thought MacIntyre.

His efforts to engage the three young men in conversation failed totally, even though at least two of them were apparently fluent in English. At least, he thought, there is no blindfold involved yet. Despite his ability to watch where they were going, Russell MacIntyre doubted he could reconstruct the route down alleys and side streets without street signs. Finally, the minivan stopped on a dusty back street lined with run-down apartment buildings. "He's waiting for you," Fadl said, pulling back the door.

"Where?" MacIntyre asked, looking down a barely lit pedestrian passage between the buildings directly in front of the van door.

"Over there. In the Mustafa Café," Fadl said, pointing across the street in the other direction, where a storefront was lit and a small Pepsi sign glowed dimly, with the name of the shop written in Arabic below. MacIntyre got out and walked across the little three-way intersection to the store. One street was unpaved, dirt. On the others, the curbing was intermittent. The parked cars were old and beat-up. The street lighting was occasional. This was not the high-rent district. As he pushed open the door, a little bell overhead rang to let the owner know someone had come in. It was a combination convenience store and café. Not the kind of place that would be open at midnight.

"Mr. MacIntyre, over here," a man said from the farthest of the four tables along the wall. He rose and walked toward the American, holding out his hand. "Thanks for coming to my part of town. Hope you don't mind. I am Dr. Ahmed bin Rashid. I understand you wanted to see me."

They shook hands and sat down at the little table. Rashid was drinking a Pepsi and had a second bottle opened and a glass waiting for his guest. MacIntyre noticed there was no one else in the shop.

"Dr. Rashid, America has many intelligence organizations. I am from one of them," MacIntyre said as he placed his business card on the table. He doubted many recruitments had been done quite this way. "Our job is not to run operations but to interpret information that others collect. Sometimes, however, when we are not getting the information we need, we go to the field ourselves to learn. I am here to learn, from you."

Ahmed examined the business card and then dug out one of his own. It said he was "Attending Physician, Cardiology, Intensive Care Unit, Salmaniyah Medical Center." Noticing Rusty's smile as he read the card, Ahmed added, "And, as you know, my brother is Abdullah bin Rashid, a member of the Islamyah Shura. What would you like to learn about, Mr. MacIntyre?"

"About the Shura and how America could deal with it in a way that prevents a long period of hostility. I personally—and I stress this is just my belief—I personally think that our two countries could be reconciled. Unless, of course, the Shura is intent on adopting policies that will make it impossible for us."

"What would those policies be, Mr. MacIntyre?" Ahmed asked stiffly, formally.

"Policies that enforce a strict Wahhabist approach, denying human rights, exporting terrorism. Policies that might involve the introduction of weapons of mass destruction, or restricting the export of oil to one market. But I am not here as a policy maker or negotiator. As I said, I am here to learn, Dr. Rashid."

"You must come to a café on a dirty back street in Manama to learn about Islamyah because you cannot learn from your embassy in Riyadh. You closed it, out of fear and lack of understanding." Ahmed shifted in his chair. "Very well. Here is what you must learn. The pronouncements of your government, particularly the Pentagon, make it sound as though you have not accepted what has happened in my country. The Sauds are gone from power, Mr. MacIntyre, and they took the people's money with them. And your ministers consort with them to bring them back to the throne. This drives some on the Shura to look for ways to protect our country from America. It strengthens the hands of the faction who also want the Wahhabist policies you object to."

MacIntyre spoke slowly, softly. "Dr. Rashid, I am not too sure I know all the factions in the Shura, but I do know that your brother, Abdullah, was a member of al Qaeda. I don't know whether he personally killed any of my fellow Americans, but I can tell you that the presence of people in your government who are or have been terrorists makes it very difficult for our two countries to have normal relations."

Ahmed stood up abruptly, his white robe swirling after him. He stood by the empty halal meat display container, folded his arms across his narrow chest, and looked down at the American. "You deal with Israeli prime ministers who were terrorist fighters, who killed British troops. You deal with Palestinian leaders whom you called terrorists earlier. You talk to the Irish terrorists in the White House. Let me ask you, was Samuel Adams, the man they named the *beer* after, was he a terrorist? My brother acted to free his country from an oppressive, illegitimate regime that was stealing the people's patrimony. Yes, he had to associate with some unsavory people in the process. Have you never associated with unsavory people, Mr. MacIntyre?"

"I am sure the American government, which is now well into its third century, has made a lot of mistakes. It has also done more to promote democracy and human rights than any other world power since the dawn of time," Rusty said, reflexively. "And Sam Adams was a patriot."

Ahmed continued on. "My brother, sir, is a patriot. Abdullah saw the U.S. troops after your first war with Saddam, how the troops stayed in our country against your promise to leave after the war. He saw that the al Sauds were being propped up by America so that you could get access to the oil. You waste the oil, worse than anyone. You could do so many other things with all your technology, but you don't really try, you give lip service to other energy sources. Why? Because you think you have special access to the biggest oil supply in the world. Let everyone else be efficient. Who cares what the al Sauds do with the money? Who cares if they mismanage the kingdom?"

MacIntyre turned to face Rashid and crossed his legs to appear relaxed, trying to defuse the tension. "There have been times when terrorists have renounced terrorism, particularly after they came to power or entered into peace talks. We would welcome that from the leaders of Islamyah. But I am also serious when I say that we do not know about factions and we may be doing things that help the wrong faction, precisely because we do not know who is who or what is going on in the Shura. Its meetings are not exactly broadcast on C-Span or al Jazeera. Maybe if we can open a way for us to talk, we will be better informed."

Rashid unfolded his arms and walked over to the small table. "All right, Russell. Let's talk." He sat down and took a swig of Pepsi. "Because America acts as if it will subvert our regime to have a countercoup and Saud restoration, my brother's opponents are talking with the Chinese. I noticed in the *Washington Post* last week that you have discovered the new Chinese missiles in my country. There are no nuclear warheads on them. But there are those in the Shura who might decide to get some, if they are pushed.

"Because America seized the al Saud assets but will not give them back to us, it is harder for my brother when he argues that imposing Sharia law and other Wahhabist acts will cause us to be rejected by the rest of the modern world. His opponents point out that we are already rejected, and unable to benefit fully from the technological revolutions. America keeps pressure on the Europeans to maintain economic sanctions on us."

Rusty found the young doctor to be a strange mix, a highly Westernized doctor but also a spokesman for a radical Islamic government that had come to power by killing. He wanted to know more about him. "So, Dr. Rashid, are you telling me that your brother opposes using the Sharia religious law as the basis of the Islamyah legal system? That he opposes exporting the Wahhabist philosophy of hating non-Muslims?"

Dr. Rashid stood again and walked in a tight circle, thinking or trying to calm down before he spoke again. "So you don't want us exporting Wahhabism? You mean like your friends the al Sauds did? What do you know about Wahhabism? Just that it's linked in your mind to al Qaeda? Do you know that your so-called Wahhabists don't even use that name, that phrase?"

"No, I didn't know that," Rusty admitted, "but I did know the Saudis paid for building and operating mosques and madrassas—schools—in sixty countries, but made sure they all taught hatred of non-Muslims, death to Israel, death to America."

Ahmed laughed. "Not just hatred of *non*-Muslims. They teach hatred of *Shi'a* Muslims and even of the major schools of Sunni thought, because the Saudis consider them polytheists."

Rusty was confused and it showed on his face. "Muslim polytheists? What do you mean? I thought monotheism was a central tenet of Islam."

Dr. Rashid did not respond. He shook his head in disgust. Finally, he told Rusty why. "You haven't a clue, do you? You come to our world and make demands about how we live, how our governments act, and yet you know nothing about our culture, our religion, our history."

Rusty pushed back. "Listen, Doctor, I don't have to be a historian of thousand-year-old religious disputes and trivia to know that it's considered noble to kill Americans. Become a suicide bomber and you'll have seventy-two virgins waiting for you in heaven. That's not religion, that's crap!" He heard his own voice, too loud, too confrontational. "Okay, so what more is it that you think I don't know and should?"

Ahmed smiled. "Let's start with the relations between the Sauds and Wahhabism. It's not just that some of their kings took to it. Without Wahhab there might not even have been a Saudi Arabia."

"You're right. I would like to hear that story," Rusty admitted, "and, yes, I probably should already know it."

Dr. Rashid began slowly, as if teaching a child. "Almost three hundred years ago, the al Sauds were the largest family in an area around the little town of Diriyah in the Najd region, not far from Mecca. From a nearby town came Muhammad ibn Abdul Wahhab. He preached a version of the teachings of Ahmed ibn Taymiyyah, a radical from five hundred years earlier. They both had what they called a pure Koranic interpretation, rejected by all four schools of Muslim thought.

"Wahhab convinced the al Sauds of his beliefs and that they should sally forth killing those who opposed those beliefs. They did, and consolidated power in their region, eventually taking Riyadh and slaughtering many.

"Wahhab's daughter then married Saud's son. The crossed swords in the Saudi royal seal belong to Sauds and Wahhabs. The Sauds have funded Wahhabist evangelism ever since."

Rusty suddenly saw the pieces coming together. Why had no one in Washington ever told him this background? Wahhabism was as important to the Sauds as the Declaration of Independence or the Constitution was to some Americans, and about as recent. It was not some thousand-year-old dispute.

"Now, Russell, here is the great irony. Ibn Taymiyyah and the Salafis, including Wahhab, taught that it was the duty of Muslims to overthrow corrupt or irreligious governments. So bin Laden used a Salafist or Wahhabist theory to justify overthrowing the al Sauds, who had so promoted Wahhabism. Get it now?" Ahmed asked.

"I think I'm beginning to," Rusty answered, carefully. "But your brother and his buddies who overthrew the al Sauds, and who worked with al Qaeda, aren't they Salafis or Wahhabists?"

"Some of those in the anti-Saud movement are. Some are secularists. Some are what you would think of as mainstream Sunnis."

Rusty had begun to realize that the Islamyah Shura Council was more riven than Washington had imagined. The differences in the anti-Saud coalition were profound.

Finished with his lecture, Dr. Rashid sat again near Rusty. "Okay, Ahmed. May I call you that?" MacIntyre said, sensing that the ice had been broken between them.

Rashid nodded. "Ahmed, you're right. We don't know what we should. But we do understand international security, and you have people in your government who would lead you to ruin. And, yes, probably so do we. It's up to people like us to help our two governments do the right thing. We have a lot of damage to repair, but first we have to stop any more from happening. If nuclear warheads show up in Islamyah, all bets are off. I know you know that. So if you think that is about to happen at any point, then we will need to think together about how we can prevent it from happening."

There was a long pause. Rashid did not seem to be embarrassed that he was taking his time to consider how to reply. MacIntyre heard the old refrigerator's motor clunk. Finally, the young doctor looked up. "If the Shura believed that Iran was about to do something against our country, they might reach out to Pakistan, or North Korea, or China, to get nuclear warheads for the missiles. They would do that only to checkmate Iran's nuclear weapons. Is Iran about to do something, Russell?"

Now it was MacIntyre's turn to consider his answer carefully. "We see signs that Iran's military is exercising its intervention capabilities, but we do not know that they intend to use them. We exercise all the time, too. Nor do we know where Iran might act, if they do. Some of our analysts think that the Iranians might try again to go after Bahrain. Truth is, we don't know." As he said that, he thought about Kashigian. If the British knew that Kashigian had been in Tehran, maybe Islamyah did, too. Maybe Ahmed knew. He added, "At least, I don't know."

"You guys are in this mess because you still need our

oil, after all these years," Ahmed said, shaking his head in disbelief. "And because you haven't come up with alternatives, you put my country more at risk, with everyone fighting over its oil. It's your failure that's causing this, you know that."

"Maybe," Rusty replied.

"I assume Ms. Delmarco told you it was my people who penetrated the Iranians here. That's how we learned about their plan to hijack the LNG," Rashid continued matter-of-factly. "From the penetrations we still have, we think they are planning an across-the-Gulf strike at the end of this month. We have to assume it is a strike on us, since an overt move against Bahrain would be an attack on the United States Navy."

"And if the Shura believes that will happen, they will try to get nuclear warheads?" MacIntyre asked.

"Some would, yes," Rashid replied. "And if the Americans think that Islamyah is about to get nuclear weapons, they would strike us?"

"Some would, yes," Rusty echoed.

The two men in the dingy store-café stared at each other.

"Then we must stay closely in touch and think of ways we could stop these things if they were about to happen, perhaps later this month," Ahmed said.

"Yes. We have also heard that something may happen this month. And on our calendar it is February, a very short month that is almost half over."

They shook hands, almost warmly. Rusty emerged from the store to find the minivan gone and a Mercedes taxi waiting. He got in. "To the Ritz Hotel, sir, or the Ambassadors?" the driver asked in English.

As Ahmed bin Rashid emerged from the store into the dimly lit square, he was filmed by two men lying in the trunk of an old Chevrolet Impala across the street. They were U.S. military counterintelligence.

8

FEBRUARY 12

The Homa Hotel
Tehran, Iran

Brian Douglas woke to his wristwatch alarm at five-thirty. He dressed quickly in a set of old clothes he had bought years ago in Tehran. He had removed the labels, in case anyone asked how a first-time visitor had such clothing. On top of them, he donned a worn overcoat and a hat typical of the Tehran street in winter. He walked down the stairs from his fourth-floor room and exited by the door near the kitchen, avoiding anyone monitoring the lobby.

The traffic had already started up, even before six o'clock, even before the sun. The green buses and orange taxis coughed their contribution to the day's smog. The sky was low, heavy, and gray. The snow from three days before had turned to brown slush or short whitish walls where the plows had pushed it up. The air smelled wet and of diesel.

He walked quickly, checking discreetly to see if he had a tail, past the Brazilian Embassy. Then he turned and headed toward Park Mellat and the Metro. The park dated from the 1960s, when it was begun as an English garden. Now its evergreen trees were a rare, pleasant sign of life in midwinter.

The Metro station looked like a concrete bunker from outside, but inside it was bright, clean, and filled with color. Modern art covered the walls in the ticket hall. The escalator down to the platform was enclosed in a brushed-steel tube, and the platform itself was broad and well lit. Few people were waiting for the train, but it came quickly. Douglas smiled as the cars' arrival reminded him that the Metro trains in Tehran were emblazoned in red, white, and blue.

He went only one stop and got off at the major switching point for the three subway lines, Imam Khomeini Station. Its grandeur reminded him of Moscow's palacelike subway. The magnificent new airport and the sparkling Metro were certainly unlike the beleaguered Tehran of the eighties and nineties. The oil wealth of the twenty-first century was beginning to be invested in modern infrastructure.

Now the morning rush was beginning in earnest. People moved quickly and in growing numbers. Douglas went up a stair to the main level. Shop stalls lined the hallway, selling flowers, pastries, tobacco, and magazines. He went to the last stall. As he bought a newspaper, he discreetly looked up at the men who ran the newsstand. The father was there. Still there.

Brian waited to pay the older of the two men behind the counter. With his head down, looking at the magazines, Brian Douglas asked in Farsi, "Do you have the *Baghiatollah Azam* medical journal?"

After a moment, the older man behind the counter spoke softly as he placed the change on the countertop. "No. For that you have to go to the university bookstore. Do you know where it is?"

"Yes, thank you, it's on Mollasadra," Douglas said in a Tehran accent, and was quickly gone down the corridor and into the enormous crowd now filling the main hall of the terminal. A gray man among so many, he blended immediately and disappeared.

At eight o'clock, a groggy-sounding Brian Douglas answered the hotel's wake-up call on the third ring and asked, in English, what the weather was like. At nine, he joined Bowers in the breakfast room.

Office of the Secretary of Defense
The Pentagon, Suite E-389
Arlington, Virginia

"Ever been in there before, Admiral?" the sergeant asked.

Adams shook his head no.

"Biggest desk in Washington, maybe in the world. Goes back to the first SECDEF in the 1940s. Job got to him. Went loony, they say. Checked into Bethesda and didn't check out. Jumped out the window from his room on the top floor of the tower. At least that's what I heard."

Adams was not really listening to the receptionist in the Secretary's outer office. He was wondering why he was there. After the Bright Star planning conference in Tampa, he had flown to Washington to check in with friends in Navy Headquarters. It was always good to show your face there once in a while, to learn the corridor gossip, who was going to be promoted, who was getting what assignment. Now that he was a three-star admiral, his promotion options had narrowed. There was a chance that he would make it to four-star, to head up one of the Unified Combatant Commands like Pacific Command, PACOM. The Commander in Chief Pacific, CinCPAC, was nicknamed the Viceroy because he was Washington's proconsul in the Pacific. You needed to be more visible in Washington than he had been, however, to have a real shot at that job. You needed to have spent time on the Joint Chiefs of Staff, on . . .

"Admiral Adams?" an Air Force officer asked, breaking Brad Adams's self-assessment. "Major Chun, sir. Sorry to keep you waiting, sir. Please come with me."

Adams followed the young officer to a small, windowless office in what was apparently the second layer in the enormous suite that housed Secretary of Defense Henry Conrad and his immediate staff. Adams knew that the full Office of the Secretary was a small agency with over two thousand employees. They sat on top of a pyramid of over a million civilians and almost two million military personnel in the department. At the base of that pyramid were over five million "private sector" employees of defense contractors. The man inside these walls made decisions that affected every one of those eight million people, and many more beyond.

"Admiral, I am awfully sorry, sir, but it does not look like the Secretary will be able to see you this afternoon, sir. There has been a last-minute change in his schedule, happens all the time, he had to go to the White House this morning, and then his hearing with Appropriations got shifted . . ." Major Chun babbled from behind a small desk piled high with folders and stacks of papers.

"Major, stop," Adams said softly, raising his right palm. "Back up, son. Why was I asked here in the first place? I was up the hill at Navy Headquarters at BUPERS when I get a call from an aide in the CNO's office, all excited, saying I need to get my ass over here ASAP. Major, I have never even met the Secretary before or even been on the third deck of the E Ring."

Major Chun rolled his eyes and laughed. "Admiral, I am just a butt boy around here. I do what the colonel tells me. He does what the milaide, General Patterson, tells him. And the general, sir, he does what SECDEF or Secretary Kashigian tells him. It all flows downhill, sir, if you will excuse my French."

"Major, I haven't always been an admiral. In another lifetime, when I was younger than you are now, I was flag aide to CinCPAC in Honolulu. Never saw the sun. Never went to the beach. Might as well have been in Kansas." Adams smiled, remembering why he had always tried for ship assignments after that.

"Yes, sir, Admiral. Well, sir, all I know is that you were

on the first schedule this morning, supposed to have an audience—I mean, a meeting with SECDEF. Just you two and Mr. Kashigian. But now there is no time left because he is flying out of here tonight for the NATO ministerial meeting in Turkey. So instead, I am supposed to take you downstairs to get a briefing and then manifest you for the flight to Turkey tonight. Guess you'll talk on the plane."

Adams's mind raced. A private meeting with the Secretary of Defense could mean an interview for a four-star job, but the Navy had not nominated anyone yet. It was too early in the year. "Turkey, huh? Well, I was going to fly commercial back to Bahrain tonight, so I guess at least Turkey is in the right direction. What's the briefing?"

"Not for me to know, sir, but it's in a SCIF, in the bowels," the major said, checking an e-mail on his computer screen. Special compartmented information facilities were vaults protected from physical or electronic intrusion. They were where extremely sensitive information was stored and where "you never heard this" briefings were given. "I'd better take you down there, Admiral. It gets a little scrungy once you go below the first floor."

Major Chun escorted Adams down three flights on escalators. No one they passed seemed impressed to see a vice admiral. In Bahrain, he was a god on base and aboard his ships, but here he was just another three-star. They descended the next two flights by a dimly lit stair, reminding Adams that whatever flashy displays were in the corridors, this was still a building that had been quickly thrown up at the start of World War II.

On the mezzanine level, Chun maneuvered quickly through a maze of narrow corridors. The five concentric rings that gave some logic to room numbers on the Pentagon's aboveground floors all disappeared in the dingy subterranean complex. "I see why you call it the bowels, Major. Tell me, what's it like working for the top dog? Lotta guys your rank would give their eyeteeth for a chance like you've got," the admiral asked, trying to be informal with the junior officer.

"Well, sir, between you and me, they can have it. Only time I ever see the top dog lately is after eleven at night, when he sends all the other aides home and I get to hang around to close up after him. Sometimes he works till one A.M., making calls all over the country, all over the world. It's gotten real crazy around here last few months. He's driven, sir, but I don't know by what. You can see it in his eyes. There's a fire. He never relaxes. Even when he went golfing down in Houston last month with these big oil company execs, he was having me place secure calls on the satphone for him almost every other hole."

They arrived in front of a metal door. A camera looked down on them from the right of the door. On the left was a phone and a small aluminum box attached to the wall. The box had no top, and Major Chun placed his hand inside it and punched numbers onto a keypad hidden from the eyes of passersby. The door clicked open.

"Admiral, I will leave you here, sir, with Dr. Wallace, to get the briefing. If you could, sir, come by when you are done and I'll have your orders and schedule ready for you to get on the plane tonight and be billeted in Turkey tomorrow," the major explained, handing Adams off to a civilian who looked to be in his late fifties, with curly gray hair, rimless glasses, and an ill-fitting brown suit. Adams wondered if he would ever be able to retrace his route to the Secretary's office, many stories above.

Dr. Wallace asked Adams to sign a paper in a folder with a cover sheet that read "Special Access Program, Eyes Only, Opal." The paper had been prepared with Adams's name, rank, service number, and date of birth already entered. "Now I can give you the briefing," Wallace said, walking into a small theaterlike room off the vault's foyer. There were three rows of cinema-style seating, but no audience. Adams chose the aisle seat in the second row.

Dr. Wallace walked to a podium and pressed a button, and the large screen came alive with an image of a yellow dragon on the deck of a Chinese junk. The dragon and the boat were set on a backdrop of loud red. The words "Special Access Program" and "Top Secret Opal" appeared. The civilian suddenly became animated, too, walking in front of the podium, folding his fingers into a pyramid. "We will now tell you everything we know about the Chinese fleet. And that is quite a lot."

The screen showed video of a large aircraft carrier slowly moving in what appeared to be Sydney Harbor. The video was clearly filmed from a helicopter. "The *Zhou Man* arriving for a friendly port call last year in Australia. She was stripped down. Only a few aircraft on board for the visit. No nukes. A few antennae missing. Most of the electronics off. Nonetheless, a most impressive ship, wouldn't you say, Admiral?"

"I'd say she looks as big as the *Stennis, Reagan,* or

Bush. Only newer. Sleeker," Adams offered, beginning to understand what he was doing there. "As commander Fifth Fleet, I have not had to keep up with the Chinese fleet modernization, Dr. Wallace, but I do already know that it surprised us."

Wallace sat down in the chair in front of Adams and turned sideways to face him. "Surprised some in our Navy, Admiral. Not me. I told them it was coming. You could see it. The Chinese bought the HMAS *Melbourne*, a steam catapult carrier, from the Aussies. Said it was for a maritime theme park. Then they got the *Varyag*, a sixty-seven-thousand-ton aircraft carrier, from Ukraine and made it into a casino." A glint shone in the civilian's eyes. "Our Navy experts said that Russia would never sell carrier technology to a competing Pacific fleet. Well, they didn't. Ukraine did.

"Ukraine had all the carrier expertise and all the fighter aircraft development skills needed. And Ukraine has no Pacific fleet to worry about! Do they?

"So, in four years, the People's Liberation Army's navy, the PLAN, put to sea three full-sized, conventionally powered aircraft carriers from Delian Shipyard, not with jump jets like our Navy experts supposed, but with catapult-launched fighters, Sukois and Yaks, from Ukraine."

Adams had the feeling he had been locked in a darkened room with a mad scientist. He leaned back in the rocking-chair cinema seat. "But a carrier is just a supertanker with a flat deck. It's about her electronics, her aircraft's electronics, and her escorts."

"*Zhou Man*'s escorts were visiting Brisbane, Melbourne, and Perth at the same time she was in Sydney," Wallace said, jumping up and hitting the clicker to pull up another image. "Here is the *Ping Yuen*. Looks just like a Burke-class Aegis air defense destroyer, doesn't it? Vertical launch tubes for supersonic missiles, phased array radar. Jiangnan shipyard has built six so far."

Adams was impressed.

Wallace was not done. "Here coming into Brisbane harbor is the *Fu Po*, an eight-thousand-ton nuclear-powered attack submarine every bit as good as the Russians' Victor III. Long-range cruise missiles that would sink a carrier. They have two already in operation."

All this information was what he would have known had he been reading his *Jane's Intelligence Report*, Adams thought. So why am I locked up with Doctor Science in a vault, having signed my life away to be let in to some special secret club? "Okay, they have made great progress, more than some expected in such a short time frame, but what is so secret about . . . ?" Adams asked.

"I was wondering when you would ask," Wallace said, resuming his place behind the podium. On-screen was a picture of a PLAN officer posing with the Sydney Opera House in the background. "What we tell people is that DIA has great sources inside China. Well, that's not really true. Admiral Fei Tianbao, commander of the *Zhou Man* battle group. He loved Australia when they went there on that courtesy diplomatic port call. Had a great time. Met distant cousins who live there. The Aussies ended up loving him, too."

Pictures flashed of Tianbao at dinners, bars, sporting events. "I am not supposed to tell you his name, Admiral, but you might meet him someday, so I thought you should know." Adams noticed that in the bottom right of every picture there was a designation ASIS-C-0091N. The Australian Secret Intelligence Service. They had turned the Chinese admiral.

"Only a dozen people in the building have been cleared by DIA to get this compartment, plus a few at the White House and the intel community. No one on the Hill. What I was supposed to tell you is only that we have a highly placed source in the PLA, with proven access, with a record of reliable reporting, who has told us the following." A new slide showed south China at the top right and Iran at the top left, and the Indian Ocean at the bottom.

"The Huang Hai shipyard has not been building warships. It's built roll-on/roll-off vessels to move cars and trucks. Here's one." A long, blue-and-white, boxlike ship appeared on-screen. "They are almost five hundred feet long and carry two thousand cars and berths for thirteen hundred people. China Shipping Group owns eight. All eight are scheduled to sail this month from Zhanjiang in south China to Karachi in Pakistan and Port Sudan. Carrying Chinese cars, being exported.

"Except our friend Admiral Tianbao says they will be loaded with PLA light tanks, trucks, and troops headed for Jizan and Jubail in Islamyah." Red arrows shot across the map of the Indian Ocean to the Red Sea and Persian Gulf ports.

"Where they will marry up with more troops flown in

on China Air. And it gets better." Wallace was almost bouncing on the soles of his shoes.

"The two simultaneous friendship port calls the PLAN are scheduled to do later this month and next—the *Zhou Man* carrier battle group to Karachi and the *Zheng He* carrier battle group to Durban and Cape Town. The real ports of call, says our Tianbao, will be Dammam and Jeddah." Blue arrows appeared on the map and moved rapidly to the Gulf and Red Sea ports of Islamyah.

"Admiral Tianbao doesn't know why all of this is being done, but he does know that the two battle groups are sailing with aircraft and missiles on board, full combat load.

"Accompanied by two nuclear subs."

The Ritz Hotel
Manama, Bahrain

The Mercedes taxi had dropped him off at the Ritz the night before. When he made it to the rooftop bar, no one was still there, except for the bartender, who was closing up. "Mr. Rusty?" he asked. "Ms. Delmarco said if you return to give you note."

It was scribbled on a *New York Journal* note pad: "If you get this, you're safe. Good. You forgot the book I gave you. Drop down and pick it up. I'll be up till about two, filing a rewrite with New York. Come by and tell me what happened. #1922. KD."

Rusty was surprised to find that the note gave him a thrill, the sort of thrill he hadn't felt in quite a while. Had things with Sarah really gotten that bad? Had it been that long since it had been fun, since they had been fun, that long since he had felt the kind of anticipation he was feeling now?

"I know you're closing, he said to the bartender, needing a second, "but any chance I can get a Balvenie?"

He downed the single malt in a hurry, too rushed to do justice to the fine Scotch whiskey. Still, he was glad for the drink, for the warmth he felt.

"Can I borrow the phone?" he asked, trying to sound casual.

He felt like an idiot.

Kate answered the phone.

Rusty self-consciously cleared his throat. "It's Rusty. Rusty MacIntyre."

"Yes," Kate said. In his slightly fevered state, Rusty could have sworn that Kate was smiling. "Successful evening?"

"Well," Rusty replied, "it was interesting."

"Why don't you come up and tell me about it?" Kate offered. "Or come up and don't tell me about it."

Rusty paused, if only for a moment. "Why don't I?"

He had been exhausted, jet-lagged, weak—or so he told himself. Sitting on the balcony of her room, having breakfast with Delmarco, he felt a little guilt, but mainly confusion.

"Kate, sometimes I just think there's so much going on in my job, in my life, that I can't structure it, I can't see what's important. I make mistakes," Rusty stammered.

"Is that what last night was? A mistake?" Delmarco asked, letting her sunglasses slip down her nose.

"No. Maybe. Who knows? Anyway, I wasn't talking about that. I meant everything else is a mistake. There are people in Washington who are out to get me, and what the hell have I done to deserve that? My job, that's what I have done, that's what I am doing. I could still be back on the Beltway making three times as much money for half the work," Rusty said, running his fingers through his unkempt auburn hair.

"Then why don't you go back?" Kate asked as she stared out over the harbor.

"'Cuz I'm trying to help make things better after the screwups, after 9/11, after Iraqi WMD, after the Islamyah coup. We have to get better intelligence analysis or we will keep making painful, costly mistakes. I just thought I could help get us on the right track. Sound arrogant?"

Delmarco shook her head no.

"Why don't *you* go back?" Rusty repeated her question back at Kate. "To the States. Why be out here in Dubai still reporting when you should be running reporters from New York?"

Kate laughed. "You sound like my brother: 'What's a girl like you doing all alone in some Arab flytrap when you should be an executive?' Well, first of all, Dubai is a marvelous place to live. Second, I have a lot of friends here and up and down the Gulf. But mainly because this is where the story is. America and the Arab world is the story of this part of the century, Rusty, in case you hadn't noticed. And you can't understand what's really going on by reading wire copy in Manhattan. I am a reporter. I don't want to be a manager. Besides, how many women international news editors have you seen lately? In some places, journalism is still a boys' club with a heavy plate-glass ceiling. But you have to understand, my dear, I am professionally and personally very satisfied. Who wants the nightmares of drug-addicted kids and drunken, disappointed middle-aged husbands? Is that arrogant, or selfish?"

Rusty thought a moment. "No, I'd say it's free will, a choice, an informed choice. Just make sure you're not fooling yourself into believing a justification you developed to use on others. And frankly, it doesn't sound as though you are. Not arrogant, not selfish."

Kate raised a glass in toast. "To two not-arrogant smart-asses."

Rusty toasted, then added, "But I still think it's arrogant to think that one guy can derail a locomotive that's barreling down the tracks the way I feel it is now. I feel a war coming, Kate, and it's not going to be a good one for the red, white, and blue. Meanwhile, I'm here. Sarah is God knows where . . ."

"Rusty, we're all human, not saints." Kate leaned across the breakfast table and placed her hand on his.

"I have to stop worrying about me right now, Kate, and figure out what's going on. Despite last night, I'm not here on a vacation. My boss and a few others expect me to fill in the blanks for them by coming out here and snooping around before something happens. But I get the feeling all sorts of things *are* about to happen, and I can't quite make all the pieces fit, let alone stop them."

Kate Delmarco reached down into her large straw bag and withdrew a yellow legal pad. It was covered with notes and circles, arrows connecting thoughts. "This is what I do: free-flow the factoids. Then, as they say, connect the dots."

"So have you connected them all into a neat picture yet?"

"Not yet, but what Ahmed told you helped. Things are still up in the air in Riyadh. No faction has yet solidified control."

"Yeah, maybe, but things could force their hand." Rusty stood up and leaned on the railing, looking out at the water. "I'm due to fly up to Dubai today. I have to meet someone there tonight."

"What a coincidence. I'm flying back there, too. My office there misses me. Are we on the same flight, Gulf Air at two?" Kate looked for the ticket in the straw bag.

"No. The Navy is flying me up on a little prop job, and you are not flying with me on it. No need to give them ammunition." Standing behind her, he kissed her hair lightly, smelling the citrus shampoo. "I'll call your office tomorrow."

Coming out of the hotel, he bypassed the taxi rank and walked across the street to the Corniche. He walked along the tiled pathway for two blocks, then sat down on a concrete bench with a high curved back. He withdrew the BlackBerry from his jacket, turned on the PGP encryption, and typed quickly using only his thumbs on the little keyboard:

To Rubenstein
Subject: Update

1. US military here is concerned Iran has been exercising intervention forces and may plan an incursion in Bahrain, or possibly gas-rich Qatar. But I still have a problem thinking that Iran would pick a fight with us. They must know we will come to the rescue, even if Iran does now have nukes.

2. Bigger problem may be Islamyah-China connection. The leadership in Riyadh still has not jelled, but if they see Iran being aggressive nearby, those in the Shura who want to put nukes on the top of their new Chinese missiles will win out. Even if that doesn't happen, the DIA report on China planning to send more military advisers or whatever they are to Islamyah increases the chances of an exclusive oil deal with Beijing. If that oil is taken out of the market, prices will go even higher than the $85 a barrel that they are now. Conrad's idea of scaring them with a big Bright Star off their coast may have the opposite effect of what we want. It may get a consensus in the Shura for even more Chinese presence to protect them from us.

3. Speaking of Secretary Conrad, if it's true, as I learned in London, that his henchman Kashigian has been secretly in Tehran, presumably trying to scare them straight, we have a problem in our own gov-

ernment of who is supposed to do what, and with whose approval.

4. I still have a feeling that we're not putting all the pieces together and I have this dread, this sense of impending something. Sorry to ramble. Jet lag. On to Dubai today. Hope to learn more about what Iran is up to from a Traveller, who is due in tonight from Tehran. By the way, thanks for not telling me all about your buddy, Sir Dennis. Anything else you're not telling me?

Rusty

After he hit Send, he checked his in-box for new messages. There was one. It was from Sarah. "Arrived Berbera. Boy, do they need help here. The project site manager has already asked me to stay for at least a month. Will let you know."

Rusty didn't have to wait to know. He had no doubt that Sarah would stay as long as she was wanted. His wife was more interested in saving the world than in saving their marriage. It was an ungenerous thought, Rusty recognized, and maybe the same could be said about him, but that was how he felt.

His head ached. His back hurt. He hailed a taxi.

9

FEBRUARY 13

The Grand Bazaar
Tehran, Iran

"I've never smelled so many different aromas at once," Bowers said as he and Brian Douglas walked down the packed, narrow aisle between two rows of stalls. "Jasmine, cumin, roasting nuts, incense, coffee—it's overwhelming."

"Yes, it certainly is," Douglas replied, filling his lungs. "I think we need a good supply relationship with someone here. Look at all the pistachios. They'd love this in Joburg." Douglas had not noticed surveillance when they had left the hotel, or in the Metro, but the Ministry of Intelligence and Security (MOIS)—or VEVAK, as they were known in Persian—was very good, and the fact that he could not see a tail did not mean there was not one.

They wandered up and down aisles, asking questions in English, sampling foods, examining prints. At the end of one aisle they noticed a sign pointing to toilets. "You go on a bit," Douglas urged Bowers. "My gut is about to erupt. Something we ate last night. Or the water. I'll catch up." Passing down the side aisle toward the toilets, Douglas moved quickly, stepped behind a high pile of boxes, and opened a back door into the rear of a carpet stall. The older man from the Metro newsstand was sitting on a pile of carpets, sipping tea. A pipe sat next to the tea. The room was barely lit by the single bare lightbulb that hung from the canvas ceiling. A radio played loudly. Douglas locked the door behind him.

"So you return" was the older man's greeting. He did not move from the carpets.

"Thank you for meeting me, Heydar. It has been too long," Douglas said, moving to sit on the lower pile of carpets opposite the man.

"A long time in which many were killed. Tortured first. Praise Allah, they did not give up my son's name. But if they had, how would you have helped us get out, when you had already severed all contact?" Heydar Khodadad had aged. The lines in his face were etched. His eyes were deep in their sockets.

"They did not give you up, Heydar, because they did not know your name, or your son's." Douglas was speaking Farsi, quickly, fluently. "I compartmented things precisely so that if this sort of thing happened, if some of you were discovered, the others would be safe. You were safer here, acting innocent, than if we had tried an extraction. I severed all contacts so that the VEVAK could not connect you to me, to the network. But you did get the money, yes?"

The older man nodded, yes. *"Moteshakkeram."* Thank you.

"How is Soheil?" Brian asked, helping himself to a glass of tea from the pot sitting on an electric coil.

"My son is safe. He hates what he does, the people he works for, but what else can he do? If he quits, they will suspect him, think him disloyal." Heydar was opening up. Brian refilled the older man's glass and listened as he went on. "They are so cynical, these people. They loosen up a little to let off steam, make it look a little more free, pretend to have elections. Still it is all run by those you do not see and their mullahs. They line their pockets. They play their games, in Lebanon, in Iraq. They build their bombs, while the people have to pay a treasure to live, for housing, for hospitals. Without your money, my wife might have died. The public medical care is a joke."

Douglas was pleased to see that Heydar's attitude toward the Iranian government had not changed. He hoped the same would be true of his son's.

"So, Soheil. You will want to see him again, yes? Not an old newspaper seller. You would put his life in danger again? And if they are following you or Soheil, will you be able to do more to rescue us than you did for Ebrahim, or Yaghoub, or Cirrus?" Heydar ticked off the names of British assets who had disappeared into VEVAK detention cells, men who no doubt had died painful deaths.

"Heydar, the VEVAK never found me. They penetrated because one of the circle was sloppy, not me. I have been doing this for twenty years in Lebanon, Iraq, Bosnia. I am not still alive because I am careless. I am still alive because I am good at this. Soheil can pick the place he thinks is safest." Brian was not the polite diplomat here, or the diffident South African. This was a man who had recruited agents in dangerous places and gotten them to do risky things.

"Tomorrow night," the news seller said flatly. "I told him you were here, that you had given me the meet signal. I told him not to see you. No good can come of it. But he insisted to see you. Here is the address. Ten tomorrow night." He handed Brian a slip of paper. "Now go."

Brian read the address, then took a match from the box sitting by the older man's pipe. He lit the piece of paper and dropped it on the concrete floor. *"Moteshakkeram,"* he said, and left.

Not until tomorrow night. He had wanted to be gone by then. He thought again about the cameras at the airport and brushed both hands across his bald head. Then he felt the modification to his nose. It was warm inside the bazaar.

Aboard United States Air Force Tail Number 3676
The National Airborne Command Post (E-4B)
38,000 Feet above the North Atlantic

"Brad Adams, it's great to see you, buddy. I just heard you were on board back here." The Air Force one-star was dressed in a tight-fitting green jumpsuit. "Congratulations on the career, man. You can see mine has stalled out a little. Got to brigadier, but it looks like I'm going out that way. But this is my plane, so let me show you around. Sorry we don't have better accommodations for a vice admiral, but the boss has taken the suite up front."

Adams had quickly checked the officer's name tag, stitched onto the flight suit, and remembered George Duke from the year Adams had spent as an exchange student at the Air University in Alabama. They had both been on their way then, he to being a Navy captain and Duke to being an Air Force colonel. Their on-base houses had been back-to-back.

"Don't I remember your little girl was Shawndra? My Jackie had a big crush on her," Adams said, getting up from the edge of the bed where he had been sitting in the aft of the aircraft.

"Yeah, my wife wasn't too happy about that interracial dating stuff. She's old-fashioned. Well, little Shawndra made me a grandfather last year. Wow, that made me feel old. You wanna tour?" General Duke said, motioning toward the bulkhead door. Adams followed him forward.

"This baby's just been refurbished. It's still a 747-200, but it's been zero-timed. Airframe rehabbed. New engines, new comms, new computers. It used to be called Kneecap back in the Cold War, designed so we could run the nuclear war from up here. We could launch the ICBMs directly from this cabin. Still can, of course, but that's not our primary mission. We are a 'mobile crisis response' asset. We still call this cabin the Battle Staff and I'm the director of the Battle Staff, but when we get used, it's usually to fly in a FEMA team to a hurricane area and provide them with an office and communications until they can get things set up."

The Battle Staff cabin was filled with desks with multiple computer consoles, headphones, and microphones. The seats were like mesh cocoons dangling from the ceiling. The lighting was subdued, the cabin quiet, with just the noise of the air-distribution system and the hum of an aircraft at altitude. Only a few seats were occupied. Adams had seen much of the crew bunking out in the aft cabin.

"We're supposed to meet a KC-10 around now to get a drink. If you've never seen two jumbos mating in midair, I'll get you upstairs for the refueling," Duke offered as they continued to move forward in the long fuselage. They went through another door into a smaller room that looked as though it had been designed for briefings or conferencing. "We call this the Sit Room, because that's all you can do here. No, really, it's supposed to have been modeled on the White House Situation Room." The room was devoid of people.

"Very nice, George," Adams said and followed the general's cue, sitting down in one of the big leather chairs that were bolted down around the highly polished wooden table. "But tell me, why is SECDEF using this thing to fly to Turkey?"

"Well, we're going to be flying anyway. If he weren't using it, we'd just be doing lazy eights over Oklahoma for forty hours at a stretch. SECDEF is the guy this plane was built for. Unlikely that the President would use it. Even in a crisis he'd probably stay on *Air Force One* or go to a cave somewhere. SECDEF has all the authority the President has to order forces around, even to launch nuclear weapons. If anything comes up while he is traveling, better to have him on this than on some vanilla 757 with two satellite comm channels.

"Besides, Brad, you should see people's reaction to this thing. In Turkey, all the other NATO ministers of defense will come in Gulfstreams or some other executive jet. Our guy arrives in a big blue-and-white 747 that says 'United States of America' in big letters down the side. It ain't *Air Force One*, but it kinda looks like it."

"Well, I guess that makes sense. It's also probably a lot more comfy up front than some plane we bought to take Congressmen around the world on junkets." Brad laughed.

"Secretary Conrad loves it." Duke beamed back. "He's booked this bird for the next four weeks. We go from Turkey to Egypt. Then we are open-ended. Told to bring aviation maps and airport plans for the Arabian peninsula. How's that for a definite destination?"

"Well, if you get to Bahrain, look me up," Adams said, thinking about locations on the Arabian peninsula. "I'll give you a tour of my emergency command post. It's a little bit longer, not as nice, but it floats better."

Major Chun entered the cabin. "Admiral Adams. The Secretary will see you now."

Chun led Adams forward into yet another conference room, then through another door that had the letters 'NCA' on it. "This is the National Command Authority suite, sir. Around the corner here is the Secretary's office."

"Brad, Brad Adams, isn't it?" Secretary of Defense Henry Conrad said, turning the corner into the narrow corridor. He thrust a hand forward. It was firm, callused. The Secretary was wearing an Air Force leather pilot's jacket, a blue button-down oxford shirt, and tan khaki pants. He looked slightly like he should be at his fiftieth reunion from prep school. "Come on back. Dju eat yet? I was just about to chow down here. Join me, will ya?"

The Secretary's cabin was small, with a table for two, a king-size bed, and a wall of flat screens and telephones. One flat screen showed a map with a little white airplane moving slowly across it. Two others showed dark images of clouds—the view from the nose forward and the view immediately below the aircraft. Two dinners were set out on the table, being kept warm under metal covers.

"Hope you like steak, Admiral. I'm a red-meat man. Don't trust a guy who isn't." The SECDEF removed both covers, revealing two New York strip steaks with mashed potatoes. An Air Force steward appeared with two bottles of cold Heineken. *"Salut,"* Henry Conrad toasted.

He talked as he ate, and carved up the big strip steak. "Sorry to dragoon you like this, but I ran out of time at the office. Got dragged off to the White House for some goddamned NSC principals' meeting on Colombia. Like I give a shit about Colombia. The Middle East is a powder keg, the Chinese are stealing our lunch, and the National Security Advisor has to have a hurry-up meeting on Colombia because some of the State Department's counterdrug guys got taken hostage and they want us to pull their chestnuts out of the fire."

Adams had grabbed a sandwich in the aft cabin earlier, but the steak was so good he was working his way right through it as he listened to this big, gregarious man. He could not remember having had a Heineken on board a U.S. military aircraft or ship before.

"Now here's the thing, Brad. The Chinese are coming on like gangbusters. Their economy has been white-hot now for almost two decades. Their economic espionage in our country has been fantastic. Stole every company's recipes, formulas, designs. They created an automotive industry and are now exporting cars. Amazing. Their cars at home, plus their industry, are sucking down oil and gas like there's no tomorrow. They're importing as much oil as we are.

"That was okay when most of the world's reserves were Saudi and we had long-term deals to get it. Now the Chinese are after an exclusive, first-dibs deal for that oil. We've been paying through the nose for it since the coup there, 'cuz we gotta buy it on the spot market." He spit out a piece of gristle. "But if the Chinese pull it off the market, we will be left with hind titty and paying top dollar."

The steward reappeared with cheesecake covered with raspberry sauce. Conrad passed him the empty steak plate. "So now we hear from this Chinese admiral the Aussies got that Beijing is gonna sneak troops into Saudi to be a kinda Praetorian Guard for these terrorists who have taken over in Riyadh. It will be damn hard for our freedom fighters to throw out the terrorists if they're protected by the People's Liberation Army!"

Adams wondered who our freedom fighters were, but Conrad was on a roll and was not to be stopped for questions.

"Not only that, but the Chinese are sending half their fuckin' fleet into the Indian Ocean and probably to Saudi. That gives the Riyadh regime air cover, too, from the carriers. Maybe they plan to homeport one there to guard their sea lines of communication, their oil lifeline back to China. Who knows? Want some decaf to wash that down?" Without waiting for an answer, Conrad pressed an intercom and ordered the coffees.

"Maybe, just maybe, they are gonna give the Islamies nuclear warheads for the missiles they just sold them. Wouldn't that be great, another nutty regime with terrorist ties and nuclear weapons? Can't let that happen, Brad. No way, not on my watch. My predecessors watched the North Koreans, the Pakistanis, the Iranians go nuclear. The chances of one of those nukes showing up on Wall Street are getting too high."

Finally, Admiral Adams got a word in. "I took the briefing on the Chinese navy and the sensitive intelligence about their plans. That's a pretty good-looking fleet they're sailing into the IO."

Conrad shook his head. "Good-looking, yes, but inexperienced with blue-water combat. If I get the authority for you, can you put them on the bottom?" The Secretary leaned across the little table, almost into Adams's face. The admiral thought he could smell the Heineken.

Adams paused briefly and then answered slowly, "If I can fire first and if I can find their subs, then I would have high confidence, assuming I had my battle group in the Indian Ocean and not bottled up in the Gulf."

Conrad smiled broadly, liking what he was hearing. "CinCPAC has three subs tailing them in the South China Sea. So far, we know where their subs are and they don't seem to know we know. Our subs will follow them into the IO and then they will be your assets," the

SECDEF said, clicking on one of the flat screens that showed a map with icons for ships scattered out along the Straits of Malacca. "Listen, Adams, your battle group and all of our Gulf assets will leave the Gulf and we will tell everyone you're going to Bright Star in the Red Sea, but I want you to spread out a picket line to pick up their two battle groups. One may be heading to the Red Sea, the other to the Gulf. I don't know how long it will take me to get you an execute order. It's still on POTUS's desk. Bunch of worry warts around him. New professor they got for Security Advisor . . .

"You won't have any trouble carrying out this mission when you get the command from me, now, will you, Brad?" As he asked the question, the aircraft hit a pocket of turbulence and began to shake.

"Mr. Secretary, I have my orders from you to move the fleet and set up a picket line, and I can carry them out. For me to fire first, however, I will need an execute order from the National Command Authority. But if they go first, or if they get a few shots off with nuclear-armed cruise missiles, there may not be much of my fleet left. In either case, sir, it would seem that after such an exchange, nuclear or not, we will be in a war with China, which likely would go nuclear."

Henry Conrad was silent for a minute. "You will get all the orders you need, Admiral. From the National Command Authority. As for China going to war with us, you let me deal with that. There is no way they're going to be that stupid. We could eliminate their nuclear missiles in minutes and then fry their economy's infrastructure, send them back to 1945. They know that."

"Aye, aye, sir," Adams replied.

Conrad stood up. "Good, good. Now go get some shut-eye, if you can snooze on this bucking bronco." The Secretary of Defense put his arm around Admiral Adams's shoulders and escorted him to the door of the suite. "You see what it says on the door, Brad? NCA. National Command Authority. That's a power that the President shares with the SECDEF. One of my predecessors tried to get rid of the title, and the CinC's title, too, the regional commanders in chief. I brought them back. CinC. It has a nice ring, like CinCPAC." Conrad winked at him. "CinCPAC Adams. That would have a nice ring, wouldn't it? You'll do a good job out there for me, Brad, won't you?" Conrad slapped him on the back and turned away, walking back into the NCA suite.

Adams started to make his way back to his bed in the aft cabin, holding on to the wall as the plane continued to buck. In the narrow passageway between the two conference rooms, he stood aside to let a civilian come forward. As the aircraft shook again, both men were thrown against opposite walls. "Admiral Adams," Under Secretary Kashigian greeted him.

"Mr. Secretary," Adams replied, surprised that the man would recognize him.

"Did you enjoy your visit to Tampa? Great places to eat there. Although sometimes they're too spicy, too hot. See you in Turkey, Admiral." Kashigian headed off toward the National Command Authority suite.

Fruits of Persia, Limited
Dolab district,
Tehran, Iran

"I will not give you red nuts," Bardia Naqdi insisted. "If you want them red, you must do that yourself."

"That will add greatly to our costs," Simon Manley replied.

"You must teach the South African market to eat them in their natural color. Do you know who it was that started dying them red? Huh? It was the Americans, not the Persians, not us." Naqdi slapped the table.

Brian Douglas, playing the part of Simon Manley, looked at his business partner for a decision. "Well, Bowers, do you think we can educate our market to want natural?"

"I do, Simon. The South African consumer is very health-conscious these days, and if we tell them the red is dye, they won't want it," Bowers replied, looking up from his ledger of notes of the day's discussion. "But it does raise the issue of aflatoxin, which as you know is a carcinogen. The EU has had problems with your pistachios exceeding the fifteen parts per billion limit."

Naqdi threw both arms into the air. "Allah, save me! We Persians have been eating our pistachios for five thousand years of recorded history. Longer before that. Do you see us all falling over of your afla? Pistachios are for lovers. They were the Queen of Sheba's aphrodisiac. When young lovers sit under a pistachio tree at night and they hear the nuts open, it ensures they will live a long life together, long and healthy, Mr. Bowers."

"Very well, but we shall want written into the contract that we are not liable for any foodstuffs rejected by South African authorities on health grounds," Bowers said while making another notation in the ledger.

Douglas looked at his watch. It was almost nine-thirty at night. "Right, then. Shall we go over the list for the first shipment? One thousand kilos of pistachios kernel, hulled, five hundred kilos peeled, five hundred kilos of sweet and bitter almonds, half and half, one thousand kilos of sultana raisins, two hundred kilos of dried figs. Twenty percent payment by wire upon contract signature and eighty percent upon our being notified by an agreed-upon freight forwarder that the shipment is in transit. Bale?"

"Bale, yes, thank Allah it was not more, I would have had to order in breakfast," Naqdi joked, pointing at the remnants of the dinner they had consumed earlier in his conference room.

"Then we shall expect a contract brought round to the hotel in the morning?" Bowers asked, closing his ledger and rising from the table.

"Yes, and we shall expect a wire transfer to our bank by the end of the day," Naqdi replied, walking the two South Africans to the door.

"The very next day at the latest," Simon Manley assured, shaking Naqdi's hand.

Naqdi opened the door out onto the balcony that overlooked the darkened warehouse, filled with piles of sacks and crates. The pungent smell of mixed fruits hung in the still air. The cool of the vast space helped to revive the men, who had been talking and smoking for almost six hours.

"Can you find your way back downtown?" Naqdi asked at the door to the street. "It is a chore. Some street signs are missing. Some lights are out. They do not look after this district, despite the fact that we are the ones out here who are earning foreign currency."

"We have a map," Douglas assured him. "And we made it here, after all. *Salaam.*"

Bowers and Douglas crammed into the small hire car that they had procured through the hotel. As Bowers started the engine, Douglas unfolded a large street map and began examining it under the pinlight of a small flashlight. Naqdi walked back into his empire of nuts and dried fruits.

Bowers checked the car's mirrors. There were no other cars on the street. No one else in this industrial neighborhood working at night. "All right, navigator," he said to Douglas, "you got us here. Let's see you get us back. Which way?"

For ten minutes they took turns down potholed streets, twice ending up at dead ends. If anyone was watching, they would have seemed lost. If anyone was watching, they might have been revealed by the U-turns and driving in circles that Bowers managed. At the end of it, they found a main road, but mistakenly drove northeast instead of northwest toward central Tehran. As they passed a sign indicating that they had entered the Doshan Tappeh district, they stopped again and examined the map. If anyone was listening, the discussion conformed to the erratic driving.

"You're an idiot! You've got us totally turned around, Simon!" Bowers's angry voice rang loudly in the car. "You're less than worthless. After almost screwing up the nut deal, now you can't even get us back to the hotel."

"You couldn't have done that deal alone, Bowers," Simon Manley replied. "And you probably won't be able to find your way back to the hotel alone either. But we're going to find out!" With that, Brian Douglas as Simon Manley grabbed an overcoat and hat from the backseat and got out of the car, slamming the door. He began walking down the street, eastward. Bowers waited for several minutes, then performed a U-turn and slowly headed away. He watched the side streets and his mirror for any sign of surveillance, and saw none.

Douglas walked for twenty minutes, his hands thrust into the Iranian overcoat, the hat pulled low on his head. The snow piles by the side of the road were higher here than in downtown, and whiter. He thought of other nights in the cold, of Mosul, of Baku, where his Iranian network had started to unravel. At 10:10, he stopped at a bus waiting shelter, and at 10:14, he was rewarded by the arrival of a green city bus. Douglas paid the fare and walked past the seven passengers to sit near the rear door. At 10:29, the bus came to the end of the route in the suburban town of Doshan Tappeh.

There were some signs of life around the bus stop. Lights were on in two cafés, and a small market appeared to be open. Douglas entered one of the cafés and ordered a tea and a baklava at the counter. No one followed him inside. Glancing through the window, he could see no sign that anyone was outside. No car had arrived in the little square after the bus. At 10:42, Douglas left the café, putting the appropriate small tip on the counter and wishing the man behind the counter good night.

Leaving the café, he turned left out of the little square and then left again down a side street. Still no tail. At 10:54, Brian Douglas turned a corner into a residential neighborhood and immediately pushed on the gate of the first house around the corner. It was unlocked and opened into an ill-lit white stucco corridor. Halfway down the corridor that led through to the backyard, Douglas turned the knob on a door to the right.

"Punctual as always," Soheil Khodadad said, striding toward the British agent, across the brightly lit living room.

"Glad you have some heat, Soheil. I was beginning to become numb." The men shook hands warmly.

"Please, sit here by the fire. I made tea. My wife is at her mother's or you would have a meal," Khodadad said, taking the overcoat and hat. "Father was not pleased to see you again. He called you an apparition of the spirit that comes to take you when you die." The Iranian looked fit and maybe forty as he sat in a chair surrounded by books and magazines. "But I am very glad to see you. We have a lot to talk about. And I didn't know how to reach you. You should spend the night. Go back into town on the bus in the morning with the commuters. If you walk down the streets here later tonight, it will look odd."

Douglas agreed. He also noticed that the phone line was disconnected from the wall jack. The curtains were down. A radio played a talk program by the window. An old hunting rifle was over the mantel. "We thought it was safer, after Baku, after the arrests of the others, that we just cut off all communications with you for quite a while," Douglas said softly, settling into the chair opposite Khodadad. "As I told your father, the others did not know you, so you were safe. But those of us who used to come in to meet you and the others, those that went to the drops and the meets in Dubai, and Istanbul, and Baku . . . we were possibly known. If I had thought you had been in any danger, we would have gotten you out. Somehow."

"Well, it is good that you did not try. I am under no suspicion. In fact, I have been advanced thanks to my friends from the Madras Haqqani." Soheil chuckled.

"You went there for a while, am I right? The theological school in Qom?" Douglas tried to recall the details from Khodadad's file.

"Yes, I went there. For two years before going back to university. It is where VEVAK, our Ministry of Intelligence and Security, recruits many of its people. My friends from there are now rising to the top of middle management in VEVAK. And so when they needed someone in the Foreign Ministry to be the liaison with VEVAK, they found the deputy director of research in the Foreign Ministry. Me." Soheil spread his arms wide. "You are looking at the director of Department 108 in the Ministry, chief of liaison to VEVAK."

Brian Douglas laughed. "Your promotion into that job would have got me a bonus if I were still running the network. That's amazing. Department 108 is one of those mysterious places we have heard about but never really understood. And now you're running it?"

"VEVAK runs it, Andrew." Soheil used the name by which he knew Brian Douglas/Simon Manley. "I provide them a trusted eye to look at the Ministry for them. But I can also sometimes see the other way, into VEVAK. And what I see now frightens me." Douglas settled into his chair. He had interviewed enough agent sources to know the signs. This one was about to unload something that he had been storing up for some time.

"Andrew, we elect a president and a *majlis*. It does not matter. We have a foreign minister, a Supreme National Security Council. It does not matter. There is a government within this government. Made up of the faqih, the supreme leader, our grand ayatollah. And the Council of Guardians, his minions. They veto the *majlis*. They determine who can run for the *majlis*. When the law enforcement forces kill innocent young students in their dormitory for being dissidents, the faqih lets them do it with impunity. When VEVAK did the serial killing of authors, impunity.

"You know who runs our foreign policy? Not the

Ministry. General Hedvai, the commander of the Qods Force of the Pasdaran."

Brian nodded. "He's a name that does keep popping up. Commander of the Jerusalem Force of the Iranian Revolutionary Guards Command. When I was hunting down al Qaeda in Iraq, I saw his shadow more than a few times."

"Of course!" Soheil shot back. "Qods Force was al Qaeda's greatest source of support. And Hezbollah's, Palestinian Islamic Jihad's, Hamas's. They have unlimited budget, Andrew. They run drugs and black market operations all over the world. In Brazil. In Britain. In New York." Soheil was standing, poking at the fire. Now he sat on the footstool in front of Douglas. "And Andrew, now the Qods has a plan to unite all the Gulf Shi'as. Already with their coup de main in Iraq they have put a Shi'a government in power, loyal to them. The Americans accepted that because it allowed them to say there was stability, so they could send most of their troops home. Then Baghdad told them to get out altogether. But what the Qods and the faqih want to do now, the Americans could not ignore. So they have found a way of checkmating them. And then they will bleed them. And it will begin soon. It is all laid out in the documents on this flash drive I loaded for you, but you will have to read them all and put it together, so let me explain."

Brian Douglas had thought if there was time to contact only one of the people left from the old network, it would be Soheil. He was bright and passionately loved Iran. As a teenager, he had also been the babysitter and then big brother for the baby boy next door. The boy had been among those killed in the 1999 police raid on the Tehran dormitory. That incident had been Soheil's epiphany. All the things that he had rationalized as a junior officer in the Foreign Ministry, all the prices that he had been willing to pay for an Iran that was truly free of foreign interference, then came crashing down on him. The promises of the revolution had been crushed, the people betrayed. A criminal cartel with imperial designs and religious trappings had stolen the government, the real government.

So, on the margins of the Islamic Conference meeting in Istanbul, Soheil Khodadad had walked by the old British Consulate at lunchtime and followed a British diplomat down the street. He had been a great source for the subsequent five years. Now he was a placement of the kind that SIS saw once in a decade. Brian Douglas had tapped a vein of gold. And as he sipped his tea, and Soheil's revelations poured forth, Brian began to think how he could quickly get this story to Vauxhall Cross. He couldn't. Going anywhere near someone from the British Embassy here would be folly. Worse. It would be death.

The fire went out near two o'clock. By then Soheil had finished his story and Brian had walked him back through it several times. How did he know this? Was it possible it was just big talk by people whom he had heard? How could the VEVAK know what the artesh, the army, was doing? Harder still, how could Soheil's friends in VEVAK know what the Qods Force was planning? Why would they tell Soheil? Was it possible he was being fed disinformation? How sure was he that he was not under suspicion? How had he obtained copies of the documents? Wasn't there a risk in scanning them into his computer? Who, besides his father, knew that he had these views?

"Andrew, enough," Soheil said, rubbing his eyes. "Get some rest on the couch. Here is a blanket. You should leave with the early crowd around six. Those of us in the Foreign Ministry are in the late commute, after eight. And Andrew, if you can use this to stop them, *loftan,* you must stop them. Or this whole region will go up in flames, again." He placed the USB flash drive in Brian's palm, embraced him, and walked up the stairs.

Almost four hours later, Brian put the heavy overcoat and hat back on. He was once again glad that his blond beard barely showed after one day. Nonetheless, he felt it and smelled the residue of the night sweat on his shirt. He quietly stepped out into the corridor and felt the morning cold. Then he walked out onto the sidewalk and turned right to walk back toward the bus line. A few others were heading in the same direction. A black Mitsubishi Pajero was headed toward him. Two men were inside. Brian had a sharp stabbing feeling in his stomach and his muscles tightened. He kept walking. The Pajero passed.

Through the corner of his eye, he saw it turn left. Brian was at the corner. The bus line was to the left. He paused. Something. He turned right and right again, walking around the block toward Soheil's. When he reached the corner, he saw the Pajero. It was parked in front of the house where he had met Khodadad. The Pajero was empty.

If VEVAK was arresting Soheil, they would not send just one car and two men, Douglas thought, his mind racing, his heart beating faster. If the two men were security and saw him walk by again, they might stop and question him. He had the flash drive dongle inside his right sock. By all rights, he should just walk away. Now.

He turned back, toward the bus line. *"Crack! Crack!"* They were muffled by the buildings, but they were gunshots. Douglas froze. Then, *"Crack."* One more shot. He needed to clear the area, fast. But he thought about Baku and how his agents had been killed, how some had first been tortured.

Douglas ran down the sidewalk toward the house. His hat flew off. A woman across the street yelled. He was unarmed because there'd been no way to explain why he was carrying a gun if he was stopped. Somewhere in his head a voice yelled, What the hell do you think you're going to do?

He pushed open the gate. The corridor was clear. He moved to the door and stood to its left side. There was no sound from within. Douglas turned the knob and threw open the door. He saw one body immediately, blood still pouring out of what was left of the head. Stepping inside and shutting the door behind him, he inhaled the gunsmoke and then smelled the blood. Soheil sat in his chair, with the books. His head hung down, dripping blood from his mouth and from the back of his skull. A pistol lay in his lap.

The second man was sprawled across the couch where Douglas had tried to sleep. His wound was near his heart and it was large. Douglas saw the hunting rifle on the floor. He checked the man on the couch. No pulse. No gun. The identification folder inside his jacket seemed to say something about security, something about the Foreign Ministry. It was quite evident that Soheil was dead. How had they fingered Soheil? In his mind, he saw Roddy Touraine's face. And then Douglas was aware of a siren, very close.

He moved quickly across the room to the other man. Also dead, but he still had his gun in the holster. He recognized it, a German Heckler & Koch 2000. It was like the Browning Hi-Power, but modernized. He took it.

The siren had stopped. Out front. Was there a back door? Stepping over the body, he rushed through the door at the rear of the room. It opened into a kitchen. There was a pounding on the front door. He saw a stairway, leading down. The house was on a slope. There was a garage and the alley below, in the back. He jumped down the stairs, hardly touching them. He took the HK out of his belt and held it in his hand, inside the overcoat pocket. Quickly, he peered out the window in the rear door. Nothing. He opened the door slowly and moved into the alley.

In seconds, he was down the alley and back on the side street, headed toward the bus line. More sirens. He slowed his walk. There were more people now, moving along the sidewalk in the cold morning air toward the bus line.

A blue light flashed across the building to his right, and instantly a green-and-white police car turned the corner, blaring the up-down siren. He clenched the pistol grip in his coat pocket.

Without slowing, the car shot by. The end of the bus line was no longer a good place to head, Douglas thought. He was suddenly aware that his mouth was bone-dry. He slowed slightly, inhaled. He knew his reflexes were sharp now, the autonomic fight-or-flight juices flowing. He had to be careful, thoughtful, not just instinctive. What was in his head, what was in his sock, had to get out of Tehran today.

Across the street, a man was opening a black wrought-iron gate to his driveway. Douglas strode quickly across the street. "Hello, my friend," Douglas called out to the man in Farsi. He entered the narrow driveway inside the stucco walls. "Can you give me a ride today? I am late. . . ." The man turned at the door of the car as Douglas moved quickly up to him.

"No. Who are you? Go away," the man blurted out. The gun came out. Douglas smashed the shorter man's head, at the temple, with the butt of the pistol. Once. Twice. Douglas caught the body as the man collapsed. He looked around. No one. With a struggle, Douglas got the body into the car and onto the floor of the back-seat. He threw the car into reverse and backed it out onto the street. He realized it was an old Mercedes diesel.

He suddenly wished that he had not taken the gun. If it were still in Soheil's place, the police might think there had only been the three dead men involved in whatever had happened. Not now. Any thought that he had of making the noon Dubai flight from Imam Khomeini Airport was gone. They would be watching the airport once the police realized the three dead men worked for the Foreign Ministry. And that there had been a fourth man. He turned the car away from Tehran.

And then he heard more sirens behind him.

Jaipur Curry House
The Creek
Dubai, United Arab Emirates

"Do you want another Kingfisher, mister?" the Indian waiter asked. He was anxious to have Rusty either order something more or leave. There were few people left in the restaurant.

"Do you have decaffeinated coffee?" Rusty asked. The waiter looked as though MacIntyre had ordered pork. "Well, a Scotch whiskey then, a . . . what was it . . . Balvenie, neat?" The waiter smiled and went away.

Russell MacIntyre stared out at the dhows and tourist boats on the Creek. This was old Dubai. With narrow streets, low-rise buildings, a rabbit warren of walkways through the old Gold Souk. Beyond the Creek he could see the spire of the Burj Dubai, the tallest building in the world, having inched past the last Chinese towering edifice. He felt suddenly alone, powerless. He had been reading *The World at Night*.

Brian Douglas had not shown up. Nor had he sent him any message. It seemed uncharacteristic. He began to wonder whether it had been foolish for Douglas, a senior SIS officer, to go undercover into Tehran. And unrealistic for him to have thought that he could somehow learn one of Iran's biggest secrets by wandering around a place he had not been in several years. Maybe Iran's forces were just exercising, like ours do all the time. Maybe Ahmed bin Rashid's source had not really penetrated an Iranian operation, or the source had just made something up to please Rashid. Maybe . . .

As the Scotch came, he felt the BlackBerry vibrate inside his jacket pocket. Maybe it was a message from Sarah, from Somaliland. He clicked open the file. It was from Susan Connor, back at his office, and it was encrypted.

Rusty, the Boss asked me to send this to you. He still can't make this BlackBerry thing work. He said to tell you that the FBI came by today. Asking about you and your relationship with Senator Robinson. Wanted to know if you had been authorized to brief him on some special compartment. Something about China. Then they asked if you were authorized to meet with terrorists. Was that part of your mission. Rubenstein put them off, but he thinks your friend Secretary Conrad quote has you in his sights unquote. I am not sure what all of that means. I hope you do. It doesn't sound good. Nothing new here, except the anti-Islamyah propaganda machine is in high gear. Congressional hearings. Ads in the papers. Interviews on certain TV networks. The latest is speculation that there are nuclear warheads for the missiles we found. I have gone over every bit of intel that I have access to and there is no repeat no indication that any nuclear warheads have shown up in Islamyah. But Senator Gundersohn says it's reason to "go in there and find them and take them out." Scary stuff if anyone took Gundersohn seriously. Got to go. Be careful out there, Susan.

MacIntyre finished the Scotch in one swig. How could anyone know that he had briefed Senator Robinson about the DIA source in China? It was only a technical violation. Robinson might not have been cleared by DOD to get the information, but he was the Chairman of the Intelligence Committee. Meeting with terrorists? Ahmed. Jesus, he thought, how the hell do they know I met with Ahmed? He signaled to the waiter for a refill.

The BlackBerry vibrated again. This time it was the phone function. He clicked to accept the call.

"Did you hear the news?" It was Kate Delmarco.

"No, I've been sitting here waiting for Brian and he's a no-show. What news?" Rusty stood up and looked north toward Delmarco's office in new Dubai.

"A Navy plane is down. They're saying maybe Islamyah shot it down." Delmarco sounded breathless. "Russell, they say it was Admiral Brad Adams. He was flying back to Bahrain from some NATO meeting in Turkey. They don't think anyone survived. They're searching off Kuwait."

MacIntyre swallowed hard. He felt the world closing in on him.

"Rusty, we'll bomb Islamyah if they did this, you know that. We need to get together."

He thought of what Ahmed bin Rashid had said in that little store in Manama. If the Shura felt pressured, it would reach out for nuclear weapons. And if it did that . . .

"I'm too . . . I need to think clearly," MacIntyre mumbled. "How about I see you for breakfast tomorrow? Where's good?"

She paused. "Okay, my office, Media City, eight-thirty."

"Thanks." He clicked off the phone function. He pulled a wad of dirham notes out of his wallet and threw them on the table. He moved off the porch over the Creek, inside the restaurant, toward the exit.

The Indian waiter chased after him. "Keep the change," Rusty yelled over his shoulder.

"Yes, sir, but the whiskey?"

MacIntyre took a card from a jacket pocket and gave it to the waiter. "If anyone comes looking for me, give them this telephone number." Then he took the glass of Scotch and downed it, thinking about the man who had introduced him to Balvenie in a club in London.

11

FEBRUARY 16

Aboard the USS Jimmy Carter, *SSN-23*
Off Malaysian Coast
South China Sea

"Open the Ocean Interface, aye." The seaman repeated the order and then moved the lever on his control panel. Outside, behind the conning tower, the submarine's hull began to move and the ocean water rushed in. The 12,000-ton ship continued to move ahead at 14 knots, 100 meters below the sea.

"Captain Hiang, Tony, this is where it gets interesting. You might want to sit up here so you can see the display on this screen," Captain Tom Witkovski urged his Singaporean guest.

"So you don't have to come to full stop to launch the ASIPs?" Hiang asked, propping himself up on the observer's chair.

"No, we don't. The advanced submersible intelligence platforms should be called the ABEAUT, because they are beautiful. Beyond my wildest dreams just a few years ago. They swim out of our hull with just their guidance engine running. Then the propulsion kicks in once they are well clear of the *Carter*."

The lieutenant commander standing next to the control panels looked at his skipper. Captain Witkovski nodded at him to begin. "Prepare to launch ASIP-1," he said to the seaman.

Five minutes later, he gave the seaman the last order in the sequence. "Launch ASIP-3."

"Launch ASIP-3, aye," the seaman repeated. "ASIP-3 away."

The two captains watched as three green icons moved away from the blue icon for the *Carter* on the screen. They spread out, three abreast, and accelerated.

"Because they have a very small acoustic and sonar signature, there is no chance that the Chinese will think that there are torpedoes coming their way," Witkovski explained. "They're fully autonomous. Communicate only in an emergency. They know their missions and they just carry them out. When they get to their designated collection points, the ASIPs will switch over to the guidance propulsion to do place-keeping. And they will wait for their targets and then swim up to meet them and swim along their hulls, port, starboard, and right down the keel. Then back to place-keeping until the Chinese move on. Finally, we will swing around from the side and call them to come home. The Chinese will never know they were swept."

The image on the screen jumped out to a 50-kilometer radius. Red icons appeared with alphanumeric designators attached to them. "That would be the first carrier battle group. The *Zhou Man* is the carrier there in the middle. She has two eight-thousand-ton air defense cruisers, one on either side. They carry the HHQ-9 supersonic surface-to-air missile. Highly lethal. Then you can see a lead-and-trail frigate, an underway replenishment ship, two oilers, and what's called a logistics support ship, more like a special cargo ship."

Captain Hiang stared at the icons and the little green dots that represented the ASIPs moving toward them. "Don't they have subs with this battle group, Captain?" he asked.

"There's one with each of the two groups. Their new eight-thousand-ton nuclear attack sub, type 93, Keng-class. A copy of the Russian Victor Threes, but noisy as hell. We can hear it a day away. This one's actually in trail of the carrier. We have a sub, the USS *Greenville*, on her."

The green dots slowed and appeared to stop halfway to the Chinese ships. "Well, now they wait," Witkovski said, hopping off his chair. "And we loop around to the side to get ready to recover them. You look concerned, Tony."

The Singaporean captain had been studying the screen and the briefing materials that he had been given. He looked up from them. "Captain, your boat, the *Carter*, is exactly ten times the displacement of each of my four little Swedish boats at Changi. And almost three times as long. So it's not for me to give you advice, sir."

"Come on, size doesn't matter, Tony. You know these waters better than us. You were a standout in the strategy-and-tactics program at Newport. I checked. And three of those little boats of yours are waiting to pick the Chinese up for a while for us when they start through the Malacca. So what's bothering you?" Witkovski sounded sincere.

"Okay. If I were the Chinese admiral, I would have my sub out front sweeping, or under the *Zhou Man,* looking for you guys. Are you sure, Tom, the sub the *Greenville* is following isn't the lead for the second battle group?" Captain Hiang asked.

"Very sure. Wanna know why?" Witkovski said, sidling up to Hiang's chair. "'Cuz the USS *Tucson* is tailing the Chinese sub that is behind the second battle group. They got two subs and we have one of ours on each one. Makes sense for them to have their subs out back to see if anyone like us is following them. Too bad for them they can't hear us over their own din."

Hiang laughed. "I knew I should have kept quiet."

Forty minutes later, the *Carter* was running at 5 knots 6 miles east of the *Zhou Man.* On the display screen the three green dots were circling their targets, the *Zhou Man,* the destroyer *Fei Hung,* and the logistics support ship *Xiang.*

"Two questions, Captain." Tony Hiang broke the silence in the Special Operations Control Room.

"Shoot," Witkovksi replied.

"One, if the ASIPs aren't communicating, how do we know where they are and what they're doing? And as you say, part deux"—Hiang chuckled at this bit of American humor that he had picked up—"why the logistic ship?"

"Okay, one is easy. We don't know where they are or what they're doing really. This display simulates what we think they should be doing about now, based on their programming and the data we have about where the Chinese ships are," Witkovski admitted.

"Part deux is a little more sensitive. Seaman, close your ears. We won't be surprised if we get radiation readings from the carrier. They may have a few tac nukes on board for the J-11s, their Flankers. We know they have air-to-surface and air-to-ship missiles for the J-11s. The destroyer carries some antiship and possibly some land attack cruise missiles in vertical tubes. I wouldn't be bowled over if a few of them had nukes. And we just might know what kind of radiation signal we're looking for on each of those ships, but I never said that. Now the logy, if we get a signal there, that's what Washington wants to hear about ASAP."

Hiang wondered why they were watching the screen so intently if it was only telling them what they had already programmed into it. He stood and stretched.

"Owweee! Fuck me!" the seaman yelled, pulling off his headset. "Sorry, sir, but acoustics just about blew out my eardrums, sir."

Captain Tom Witkovksi grabbed the headset and held it up near his right ear. "Jesus, what is that?" He dropped the headset and pressed an intercom on the wall. "Exec, what is that on acoustics?"

From the Combat Information Center, the boat's control room one deck up, the executive officer responded, "We're processing it through the database, Captain. Here it is . . . the first sound was 'Similar to a Kilo-class diving.' Then the screeching . . . it just says 'Presumed Collision.'"

"Shit," Witkovski swore, driving his fist against the wall. "I'm going up to CIC. Tony, I need you with me."

The American captain was out the bulkhead and climbing the ladder to the Combat Information Center three rungs at a time. "You got towed array out?" he barked at the executive officer as he entered CIC.

"Aye, sir. The hydrophones back there are what picked it up," the somewhat startled exec replied. The captain flicked a switch and threw the undersea sound on the dashboard speaker. It was an excruciating sound of screeching metal, like steel chalk on a metal blackboard, magnified tenfold.

Witkovski turned down the volume. "What's the depth there?"

"Two hundred fifty meters, Captain," a seaman in front of a control panel answered.

"What's the maximum dive depth of a Kilo-class?" the captain shot back.

"It's nominally three hundred meters," Captain Hiang answered from behind Witkovski. "But the Chinese version, the 877EKM, has a classified rating of 375."

Witkovski spun about. "What else do you know about them? Really, Tony, tell me."

The short Singaporean officer walked closer to the American captain and almost whispered, "They have a range of six thousand miles. They have a new, special sound-dampening and antisonar coating. They have a low-wave bow sonar that's hard to detect. And because they can operate on only battery power for a while, they are very, very quiet. Especially against the acoustic background of an aircraft carrier battle group."

A strange sound came over the speaker. *"Ebup, ebup . . ."* The executive officer turned up the volume on the dashboard speaker and hit the analyzer button. "Don't bother analyzing it. I know what it is," Captain Witkovski said, shaking his head. "Shit!"

"Sir?" the exec asked.

"It's the acoustic distress signal from ASIP-2. There's a Chinese Kilo out there that we missed. It's on top of the ASIP, driving it to the bottom. The ASIP has a crush depth rating of two hundred meters. It will break up in a few minutes." Witkovski sighed. Then he turned to look at Captain Hiang. "It seems the *Zhou Man* did have a sub on point and it's playing dirty."

"Sir, we should butt-fuck that Kilo, sir, come up behind it and ping it," the exec proposed. "They can't know the ASIP is unmanned. They could be killing our guys."

"Not today, Tim. No butt-fucking today. We have two other ASIPs out there to recover and download. That's our mission. Now, let's do it. Give me a course to ASIP-3. Full quiet on the boat."

"Full quiet on the boat, aye." Blue bulbs blinked on throughout the 453-foot length of the USS *Jimmy Carter*.

Almost two hours later, with the *Zhou Man* battle group now turned and heading north into the Straits of Malacca, the word came: "Ocean Interface sealed." The two remaining ASIPs were on board. Captain Witkovski asked Captain Hiang to join him for a meal in his cabin while the technicians downloaded the data from the unmanned mini-subs.

Over Philly cheesesteaks and Diet Pepsis, Witkovski almost apologized. "I should have listened to what you were trying to tell me, Tony."

"I should have been more direct, Tom. Sometimes we ethnic Chinese have a hard time being direct enough for Americans." Captain Hiang smiled. "But we know the Chinese, because we are descended from them. We speak their language. We know their history. The little Indonesian city that the *Zhou Man* is sailing by tonight? Malacca? It was founded by the Chinese navy, six hundred years ago. Besides, what could you have done anyway if you had detected the Kilo sitting under the keel of the *Zhou Man*?"

There was a rap on the door. "Enter," the captain replied. It was the executive officer with a draft message on a clipboard. "It's a summary of the data readout and the automated analysis from the two ASIPs, sir. I have coded it FLASH precedence, sir."

The captain raised his eyebrows and took the clipboard. FLASH was reserved for messages of extreme priority, such as "Someone is firing at my ship." Witkovski slipped on his half-glasses and read:

To: CinCPAC, Honolulu FLASH
    JCS/J-3 FLASH
    DIA, DT-1 FLASH
FM: SSN-23
SUBJECT: Probable Nuclear Weapons on Board *Zhou Man* Battle Group (TS)

Analysis of telemetry from ASIP inspection of PLAN Special Logistics Ship *Xiang* (C-SA-3) indicates neutron and gamma readings consistent with six warheads in bow bulk container area and six in aft bulk container area. Analysis program indicates all warheads have similar size, estimated between 10 and 30 kilotons. Analysis program suggests tentative typing as CSS-27 intermediate-range ballistic missile payload. No readings detected aboard accompanying destroyer. Surveillance of the carrier *Zhou Man* was not performed (details sepchan).

EOT

Captain Witkovski initialed the message board and passed it back to his exec. "Well done, Timmy. That ought to spray feces all over their fans back in Washington. This time we've found them some WMD. Ain't no doubt about it."

New York Journal *Bureau*
Media City
Dubai, United Arab Emirates

MacIntyre drove past the CNN and NBC buildings in the manicured office park that was Media City. His taxi had already passed Internet City and Knowledge City. He wondered if he could persuade them someday to build a Magician City in Dubai. The *New York Journal* did not have its own building but shared one with several European newspapers.

The Pakistani guest worker guard in the lobby was expecting him. As he entered the third-floor door of the *Journal,* he saw Kate on the other side of the suite, standing in front of a bank of screens showing news broadcasts in Arabic and English. She had set up a little breakfast buffet on a table below the television panels.

The audio was on for ABC. ". . . but military sources here at the Pentagon stress that until the wreckage has been examined, there is no way to be sure what happened to the Viking jet that was taking Admiral Adams back to his headquarters in Bahrain from a meeting with Secretary Conrad in Turkey. At the NATO meeting there, the Secretary said that he would take all appropriate steps to respond to any aggression in the oil-rich Gulf region. Martha . . ." Kate Delmarco hit the mute button and turned to face Rusty MacIntyre.

"I was supposed to meet him in Bahrain tomorrow," Rusty said, staring up at the screens. "He left me a handwritten note I picked up when I was at the Navy base. Said he would call my cell tonight when he got in to make arrangements. I can't believe that Islamyah would provoke us by shooting his plane down."

"Maybe they didn't. You heard ABC just now. We don't know yet," Kate said, holding out a glass. "Bloody Mary?"

"No, thanks, I'll take a Virgin Mary. Had enough last night. I'm pretty down. I was also supposed to meet our mutual friend Brian Douglas last night and he no-showed."

"Okay, you want to stay sober. That's fine," she said, sitting down at her desk. "So, where is my mysterious Mr. Douglas? He's got me worried. No, he wouldn't like that. He's got me a little concerned."

"Dunno," Rusty said, looking into the ice cubes. He did know, or at least he knew where he went, maybe not where he was now. But Brian did not tell Kate and I am not about to, he thought. He had meant to ask Brian when he got back just what his relationship with Kate was.

Trying to change the subject quickly, he said, "You heard what Conrad just said. He will respond. Not the President. Not America. Him." Rusty took off his coat and sat down at the desk opposite her. "Look, Kate. I've been thinking. Conrad is the problem. He's the one demonizing Islamyah. Scaring them with some big exercise off Egypt. Scaring Washington into thinking the missiles they got from China have nukes on them. He's gonna get us into a war again out here real soon, and maybe with China, too, by the time he's done. Unless somebody stops him."

"Really? Now what's he doing with China?" Kate said, grabbing her notepad.

MacIntyre placed his hand on top of the pad. "Stop being a reporter for once and work with me here." Delmarco gave him a foul look. "Okay, Kate, you have to be a reporter? Go get some dirt on Conrad, so he's not Mr. Clean on a white charger, saving America. It may be the only way we can stop him."

"You do play dirty, little boy," Delmarco said, crossing her legs.

"So do they. He's got FBI agents snooping around about some charge that I told a Senator something he wasn't cleared for. They may even know about my meeting with Ahmed. Probably charge me with giving classified information to Islamyah."

"What? Rusty, what are you talking about? How do they know about that, and besides what's wrong with you meeting with a source in Islamyah? You are an intelligence officer, after all. It's your job," Delmarco said in her irate reporter voice.

"No it's not. I'm head of an analysis unit. I am out here to learn, not to go skulking about, developing agent sources of my own. I am out of my depth, as well as out of my swimming lane." Rusty sounded tired. "Conrad could intentionally misconstrue it. Sometimes, I think he would do anything to roll over people who disagree with him."

Kate picked up her notepad again and opened it. "Okay, so what's the dirt on him?"

"I'm not sure. Maybe al Saud money and his buyout company. Maybe the exiled royals and the Secretary buying support on the Hill. I have a well-placed friend on the Hill who may know more. He wouldn't tell me everything before, but I think I may know enough now to persuade him to talk to you, persuade him that we need to throw a little sand in the gears." Rusty got up, walked over to the makeshift bar and added a shot of vodka to his tomato juice. "Maybe throw a little mud."

"I said I love it when you play dirty," Delmarco smirked and pointed her pen at him.

"Don't start," MacIntyre said emphatically, returning and grabbing the pen away.

"All business. All right," she replied. "I can leave for Washington late tonight. New York has wanted me back for consultations for a month now. I just hope I don't miss the action out here while I'm gone."

"I can't promise you that." MacIntyre took a pen and held it up to his jacket. "Bada-bing!" he exclaimed, and the pen appeared to penetrate the jacket, half of it coming out the other side.

"You nut. Why put a hole in your coat?" Kate laughed. He handed her the coat. There was no hole in it. She kept laughing.

"I just thought we needed something to cheer us up, and magic tricks almost always do," he said, digging in his coat pocket for the vibrating BlackBerry. "Who the hell is calling me?" MacIntyre put the device to his ear and clicked to answer. "Hello? . . . Well, yes, it's great to hear from you, but have you been listening to the news? . . . How? . . . Here, in Dubai? Lunch at the Four Seasons? . . . I look forward to meeting you, too." He put the BlackBerry down and looked blankly at Kate, shaking his head.

"What's the matter? What was that?" she asked.

MacIntyre didn't answer right away, still stunned by the call. Then he picked up her notepad and handed it to her. "Well, I guess you would say that was an exclusive for the *New York Journal*. How 'bout something like 'Admiral Bradley Adams, Commander of the Fifth Fleet, arrived this morning at Dubai International Airport on a commercial flight from Turkey. It was earlier thought that Adams was on board a Navy aircraft that crashed off Kuwait, but it has now been learned that Adams sent the aircraft on without him when he received a last-minute invitation to visit the Turkish navy. The admiral learned of his reported demise upon landing in Dubai.'"

"Wow!" Kate yelled. "And we're going to meet him for lunch?"

"No. I am. You are going to get ready to go back to the States tonight, remember?" He looked up at the eight channels of news on the screens above. "We have a helluva lot of work to do if we're going to stop Conrad from doing something that could set the whole Arabian peninsula alight."

Doshan Tappeh Airport
East of Tehran

"We get so many people from Monash University at this time of the year, Professor," the ticket agent said. "Here we go. Seat 4B. It's a window, as requested. We try to accommodate all the requests from the Melbourne travel agency, since we do so much business with them now. Any luggage?"

"Well, we have quite the exchange program with Kish University. No, the luggage was shipped ahead, since I will be there the entire semester. Quite a lot to carry. May I say that your English is most excellent. Thank you so much," Professor Sam Wallingford said, taking the ticket for the Kish Air flight from the little airport outside of Tehran to the resort island in the Gulf.

They were boarding when he got to the gate, the only gate. It was an ancient thirty-seat Fokker 50, gaily decked out in the colorful Kish Air livery. Since it was an internal flight to the island of Kish, the security man had barely looked at the Australian passport with Iranian visa and entry stamp before waving him along. If he even had a "wanted" list of passports, he didn't check it. It was nothing like what would have happened at Imam Khomeini International, but in a nod to capitalism, Kish Air had moved its flights to the less crowded, less expensive Tappeh. Tappeh had been an air force base and then closed altogether for a year before reopening for internal flights by smaller airlines.

Sitting in the Fokker waiting to take off, Brian Douglas as Sam Wallingford replayed the tapes of the morning in his head. What had happened to Soheil? Despite his assurance that he was not under suspicion, he must have known that he was. The unplugged phone, the radio, the drapes, the rifle. And he had met with Douglas anyway. Given him the gold. It was Soheil's own ministry security people who suspected something. Maybe they had caught on to the fact that he had downloaded the documents off the ministry intranet. They had sent only two officers to question Soheil. And Soheil had been ready for them, with the hunting rifle. After shooting both, he had taken one of their pistols and killed himself. And now the other officer's pistol was at the bottom of a storm drain, not at Soheil's. He hadn't really needed it; he should have left it at the house. If he had used his hand to hit the Mercedes man, rather than the gun, the man might be unconscious instead of dead in the boot of his own car in a yard down the road from the little airport. He had never killed an innocent man before. He had struck too hard, from the heartpumping rush of fleeing. It was a rookie move. He hated himself for it.

The Fokker began to taxi. It would be over two hours to Kish Island. Two hours in which the police might be notified of the missing man with the Mercedes. Might find the Mercedes, despite where it was parked, despite the mud on the tag number. Might realize that the little airport down the road now had flights to the Kish Island resort in the Gulf. Might call ahead to the Customs or VEVAK at Kish.

He looked down at the slight tear in the lining of the old suit jacket. He had thought it had been a risk to put the Australian identity in the lining, silly to have alternative ways to get out of the country. But Pamela had been right, as always. He hoped she was right about the next bit, too.

As the plane lifted off, he thought of what Bowers would be doing: taking Simon Manley's things out of the hotel room. Paying for Manley as well as himself at the checkout. Flying out on the Joburg run about now. Would their database at Khomeini Airport Customs link Bowers's visa to Manley's? Where is Mr. Manley? Traveling up to Shiraz for a day.

Brian Douglas closed his eyes, but could not sleep on the bumpy flight over the mountains. His heart was still pumping. His mind was still racing. Poor man in the Mercedes. Nothing justified it. But what he had on the flash drive in his sock was at least worth Douglas's risking his own life by running about in the field, solo, overage, undercover. No one else could have gotten it. Soheil and his father would not have trusted anyone else. What if the father had not been at the newsstand? Douglas would have come home empty-handed and looked the fool. But the father had been there, and so far it was working. Very messy, but working. Thank God Pamela had insisted on an emergency egress plan being in place.

The jolt of the landing woke him. So he had gotten some rest. His bones ached. The terminal was bigger than he would have expected and far more modern. He tried to remember the diagram from Pamela's briefings. There was the men's room. His watch said 11:40. They were ten minutes early. Would the Omani be there yet?

He went to the last stall and pushed on the door. "Oh, so sorry, it wasn't locked, you see, I . . ." The Omani, with his pants around his ankles, jabbered back at him in Arabic. The Omani had been there early and had the papers in his hand. The exchange of papers had taken place in three seconds. Brian Douglas went in to the next stall. The papers looked good. A New Zealand passport, with a Kish exit stamp. Ticket on Hormuz Airlines, boarding in a few minutes for Sharjah. Someone had taken some baksheesh along the way, but that was never a problem in Iran.

Nor would you have found another airport in Iran where international arriving passengers could mix with those about to leave the country, but this was Kish. Tehran had allowed it to be a free trade zone, an international tourist destination. The new high-rise hotels on the beach made it look like Dubai. Everything was a little bit more lax here. China had Hong Kong. Iran had Kish, a permeable membrane, a place where needed commerce was permitted, a place where people looked the other way.

He got in line to board. It was some sort of Ilyushin that looked as though it might have been sold off from Aeroflot. He was two people away from going through the gate when he heard the public address system in

Farsi: "Valnford, Professor Valnford. Please see a police or customs officer." His stomach contracted. Had the Omani bungled? But he was not Samuel Wallingford. Not now. He was the New Zealander Avery Dalton. Smile at the ticket taker. Climb the stair up into the old Ilyushin.

The plane had no sooner taken off than it was landing. He feared it had turned around and gone back to Kish at the call of the police or customs officer. But no, this was a smaller airport and this was not an island. Bump. Landing like a ton of bricks. No this was not Iran again, this was Sharjah in the United Arab Emirates. And so the sign said over the customs and immigration booths. Welcome to the United Arab Emirates.

"You will have to come with me, Mr. Avery," the immigration officer was saying. He had run the passport under an optical scanner.

"What? It's Dalton. Mr. Dalton. Avery is the first name, you see," he stuttered.

"We have no record of this entry visa having been issued. It is not in the database. It will just be a moment. This way, please."

The door had one-way glass and a sign that said "Police" in English and Arabic. Inside, however, it was bright and comfortable. "Please have a seat, sir."

"Might I use the phone for a local call? Maybe I can clear this up. Thank you so much." He froze for a moment, trying to recall the number. Then it came to him.

"British Consulate, Dubai," the woman seemed to sing in a rising lilt on the other end.

"Exchanges Office, please," Avery/Wallingford/ Dalton/Manley/Simon managed to get out.

"Exchanges Office. May I help you?" the South London–accented man grunted.

"It's Brian Douglas. I am from Bath," he said using the station's own clear code for Require Assistance. "I am with the customs or the immigration police at the Sharjah Airport. Some problem with my papers."

There was a brief pause on the other end as the officer recalled what being from Bath meant, and then as he realized that the head of station for the entire Gulf was not in Bahrain but twenty minutes down the highway from Dubai, being held. "We will be right there to pick you up, sir, and will call the local service boys in parallel."

It was Avery or someone who had called, but Brian Douglas who hung up the phone. He turned to the young immigration official and said in Arabic, "Might I have a cup of hot tea?"

12

FEBRUARY 16

Security Center of the Republic
Riyadh, Islamyah

"You were the one who told me we could not trust the Chinese to be here," Abdullah bin Rashid said, "and now you want me to trust the Americans?"

"Not all the Americans. Some of them. They are not all imperial warmongers. Many of them are like the Canadians," Ahmed tried. His brother looked at him, unconvinced, but he continued. "My point is just that we do not want them acting against us based on false assumptions about whether we have nuclear weapons or not. And there are some Americans whom I think we can talk to."

Abdullah picked up a folder and handed it to Ahmed. "Read this. A pack of lies. It's a summary of the American media reaction to the crash of their Navy plane off Kuwait. It's full of speculation that we shot it down."

"Did we?" Ahmed asked, scanning the papers.

Abdullah paused, irritated at the question. Finally he replied, "No. No, we did not. Our radar showed nothing near the aircraft and no missile fired at it."

Ahmed passed the folder back to his brother. "So it just blew itself up in midair?"

"So it seems, Ahmed. First they try to blame us for the attack on their Navy base in Bahrain—which you prevented! Now they try to blame us when one of their aircraft blows itself up. They are looking for an excuse, Ahmed, can't you see it?" Abdullah walked back behind his desk.

Ahmed placed his palms down on the other side of the desk. "What I see, brother, is a need to calm things down, to open a channel with the Americans so that we can prevent misunderstandings like these."

Abdullah gathered up files from the desktop. "You want to see what I'm dealing with? How hard it is to convince my fellow members of the Shura that we should be moderate? Come with me, now. The Council is meeting here today. Because they think we need to meet in a highly secure location. The public cannot attend, but you can attend as my aide."

Ahmed bin Rashid followed his brother, the Director of Security of Islamyah, down corridors to a small conference center within the former palace. The room was filled with men in white robes, many with long beards, loudly chattering in small groups before the meeting. In the middle of the room was a large oval-shaped table with a microphone at each place. Abdullah pointed out the Interim President of the Republic, Zubair bin Tayer, a cleric who had spent most of the previous decade in Damascus, Tehran, and London. Bin Tayer was moving to the seat from which he would chair the meeting.

Electronic bells sounded in the room. "In the name of Allah, the most merciful, the most compassionate . . ." bin Tayer started to pray into a microphone. The prayer continued for several minutes and was followed by three readings from the Holy Koran. As soon as bin Tayer stopped and was seated, a man on his right began reading a resolution. Ahmed finally determined that the subject was the appropriate punishment for a group of college students who had been detained by religious police for protesting against the extension of the religious law, the Sharia. The punishment was to be public flogging in a square in Riyadh.

"Does the Shura concur?" the man on bin Tayer's left droned into his microphone.

Abdullah leaned forward and touched a button below his microphone, causing a green light to come on in front of him. "The religious police are supposed to enforce religious practices, not to enforce the civil law." The room went still. Abdullah continued, "I am in charge of law enforcement and security, by decision of this Shura, not the Ministry of Religious Affairs. Publicly dissenting from proposals before the Shura, including those having to do with Sharia law, is not a violation of our religious practices." A chorus of voices disagreed. "These men did nothing to warrant their arrest, let alone their flogging," Abdullah concluded, and he hit his microphone button again to shut it off.

The chorus of disagreement grew louder. A man in

cleric's robes across the table repeatedly pounded on his microphone button. "So what does the director of security propose we should do with these boys who have done *haram*, prohibited acts? Give them sweets?"

Abdullah straightened in his chair and slowly leaned forward to press his microphone. "It is not what I propose, it is what I have done. In the rightful exercise of my legal authority, I have released citizens who were being illegally held, citizens who had violated no law." The room erupted. Ahmed was pleased to see that his brother had supporters who could also scream and point their fingers, wave their arms in the air.

Bin Tayer hit his microphone button and began to speak. "Minister Rashid. Why do you think we fought this revolution, to let the decadence continue that the al Sauds did in private and overseas? To allow anyone to pretend to be a Koranic scholar? To allow Muslims in other lands to practice deviant strains of Islam? To give power to the infidel kafirs and to women? No, it is the mission of government to end such *jahiliyah*, such ignorance. Those who violate the laws must be punished!" More commotion followed.

Finally, Abdullah responded. "First, Zubair, I did not notice that you did fight at all." Cries of outrage followed. *"Munafiqeen!"*

Over it all, Abdullah continued, "Second, those of us who did fight did so to change our country, not to impose something on others elsewhere. Third, it is not the job of *hakimiyah*, of those in governance, to force Salafism or any other school of thought on our own people. The Prophet Muhammad, blessings and peace be upon him, accepted the Jews and the followers of Jesus as children of Abraham. For centuries, Muslims have chosen their own paths. Some choose to be *murtadeen* and live a secular life, but very few choose the ways of Taymiyyah or Wahhab, or the Salafists. We who fought did not do so to change the ninety percent of our Muslim brothers who disagree with you, Zubair."

Abdullah shifted his body, showing his back to Zubair bin Tayer as he appealed to the others on the Shura. "It is the duty of a country to develop its people's full potential, and to allow the smartest to build for the rest of us. So we should, as the government, be promoting education in the sciences, in medicine and mathematics. These are not un-Islamic studies. These are things that Islamic scholars created and promoted centuries ago at the height of our power. This is what we should be doing, not flogging students, not punishing acts which are halal."

After an hour of highly agitated and excited debate, the Shura Council of the Republic of Islamyah adjourned without taking any action. Abdullah left the chamber quickly by a side door near his seat. Ahmed stuck to his side. "I am proud of you, brother," Ahmed said when they slowed down in a corridor leading back to the director's office.

"Now do you see why the sessions are not televised, as you proposed?" Abdullah laughed.

"No, all the more reason why they should be. The people would not stand for it. The people would support you against these Neanderthals," Ahmed urged.

Back in the office, the brothers were joined by six of

Abdullah's supporters from the Shura. "Are you happy now, my friends?" he asked them.

"It was the right issue to pick, Abdullah. It makes it clear to the people that this is not a struggle about religion, but about its place in our government," Ghassan bin Khamis said, patting Abdullah on the shoulder. Ghassan had been with Abdullah in exile in Yemen and was now head of one of his intelligence units.

"It is a struggle about whether we are part of the modern world," Hakim bin Awad objected. "Modern states do not flog people. And people have a right to say what they think about laws. That's why we overthrew the al Sauds, because they locked us up when we expressed ourselves against the things they were doing."

"Ghassan, Hakim, you are both right. We did not fight to become the al Sauds—at least I didn't," Abdullah said, throwing himself down on one of the four couches that formed a semicircle in his office. He adjusted his robes. "I fought so that this country could breathe again, the way it did when our grandfathers were free in the desert. And so that it could be the people's country, its own country, not some privately held company, part of some British or American network. Democracy our way."

Ahmed was stunned. He had never heard his brother so articulate, so passionate, and so much in agreement with what Ahmed himself believed.

"We also need to lead the Arab world back to the leadership it once had in the arts, sciences, medicine, mathematics," Abdullah said, looking across at his brother. "We have lost all that. We have closed the minds of our people." Ahmed smiled, remembering the Arab Development Report he had left with his brother.

"This is all about the Wahhabist clerics trying to do now what even the al Sauds would not do," Hakim added.

"Let me tell you about Wahhabism," Abdullah replied. "They won't even use that phrase, you know, but they say it is the natural way of Islam. Ninety percent of Islam rejects Wahhabism. Muslims who live here should be able to do so as well, if they choose. Our government should not be telling citizens which of the Muslim scholars are right and wrong on interpreting the Holy Koran or the Hadith."

"If you say that out there, they will try to have you killed," Ghassan cautioned. "Bin Tayer fears that you will run against him when we have the elections. That is why he keeps postponing, why his people say only the righteous should be allowed to vote. You are in danger, Abdullah."

"The Corps of Protectors is solidly behind you, Sheik." It was General Khalid, the commander of the united force that was made up of what had been both the Saudi army and the national guard.

"Maybe your men are behind him, but half your weapons don't work anymore. And they are bringing in more Chinese. And how do we know they will keep the Chinese in the desert with the missiles?" Ghassan shot back.

Abdullah turned quickly. "What's this, Ghassan? More Chinese?"

"I haven't had time to tell you yet, Abdullah. My men have confirmed that there are preparations at ports in both the Gulf and the Red Sea, preparations to offload and billet more Chinese. Others will be flying in. This is no troop rotation. These are more."

Abdullah stroked his short beard. "The Shura has not approved this. Why do we need more?"

Ahmed, who had sat back listening to the exchange, now leaned in. "Maybe to protect nuclear weapons?"

"No," Abdullah said emphatically. "We have not agreed to request nuclear warheads for the missiles."

"Maybe bin Tayer has, behind the back of the Shura," Hakim wondered aloud.

"No," Abdullah repeated. Then he turned to General Khalid. "Find out."

The Ritz-Carlton Hotel
Dubai, United Arab Emirates

"Are you Russell MacInytre?" A young man with a British accent was approaching the taxi.

MacIntyre paid the driver and turned. "Who the hell are you?"

"So sorry, sir," the young man said, presenting a business card. "Clive Norman, British Consulate. I am from the Exchanges Office."

"Look, I have an appointment here," MacIntyre said, brushing past.

"With Admiral Adams. Yes, I know, sir. There's been a change in plans and he'd like you to join him at one of our facilities nearby."

MacIntyre examined the business card and looked at what was undoubtedly a young Brit. He doubted that he was looking at a terrorist or kidnapper. "We have a consulate car and driver here, sir, if you'd please . . ." Norman pointed at a Jaguar with diplomatic plates parked down the drive. "The admiral said you could telephone him to verify."

MacIntyre was unsure but said, "All right. Let's go."

The car drove a short distance and pulled up to a gate with two uniformed guards from one of the many Dubai security firms. Inside the compound, the car stopped in front of a large domed villa, one of the shining, oversized homes that lined the beach.

Clive Norman led the way up the stairs and into the high-arched marble foyer. MacIntyre could see through to the glass doors in the back and the Gulf beyond. He was still unsure of what was going on. "They are dining on the patio in back, sir. Please go right ahead through."

MacIntyre walked ahead and pressed open the door to the outside. "Rusty, over here!" It was Brian Douglas. He was bald, there were bags under his eyes, and his nose looked to be a different color from the rest of his face. His polo shirt was too tight . . . but it was Brian Douglas.

"I believe you know of Admiral Adams."

MacIntyre shook hands with the Navy officer and turned to Douglas. "It's good to see you. Both of you, actually. There was a time last night when I thought I would never see either of you, ever."

"Yes, sorry I stood you up. There were . . . complications, but I'm here. And I just got off the secure line with Sir Dennis, who has authorized me to brief both of you on what I found out. On condition that you not report on it, yet. You'll see why."

"Gentlemen, your lunch is served," Clive Norman said from a table nearby. "I will leave you alone, sir, but buzz if you need anything."

Almost an hour later, Norman responded to a buzz by bringing more coffee.

"I know the position it puts both of you in, considering it is your government, or part of it, that seems to be involved," Douglas said, pouring. "But is it really so hard to believe?"

The admiral spoke first. "No, no, it's not. Regrettably, it's all too likely to be true." MacIntyre remembered that Senator Robinson thought the world of this Navy man, who looked too young to be wearing three stars. Adams continued, "I was at Central Command Headquarters in Tampa last week. A guy there, senior guy whom I trust, had some conspiracy theory that the Bright Star Exercise was in fact just a cover for a planned U.S. invasion of Islamyah. Said the exercise is too big otherwise, too many troops, supplies for a month. He thought SEAL Team Six was already looking at landing sites."

"Okay, but shooting down a U.S. AWACS as a provocation and blaming it on Islamyah? Blowing up the Navy base in Bahrain?" MacIntyre asked, skeptically.

"The Iranian documents make clear that the Americans did not know about the planned attack on the Bahrain naval base. The Iranians wanted them to think it really was Islamyah," Brian Douglas clarified. "But, yes, Kashigian did agree to Iran's shooting down an AWACS and making it look like it was Islamyah."

The two Americans looked at each other. "But, Brian, does it make sense that Kashigian, Conrad, whoever is behind all this, would agree to letting Iran land forces in Islamyah?"

"It does, Rusty. Here's why," Douglas replied, "the Pentagon will point to the Iranian landings as another reason why the U.S. has to step in. Iran, of course, will say that the government in Riyadh is being beastly to the Shi'as living in the Eastern Province, and that they have to step in to protect them. Conrad will then claim success, because he has contained the Iranians in a small coastal enclave," Douglas explained, moving cutlery about on the table to indicate the sequence. "But here's the rub. The Iranians also plan to take Bahrain. They expect the U.S. fleet to be gone at the time for some reason."

Admiral Adams pushed back from the table. "It will be. I am to move all surface combatants into the IO, allegedly to join Bright Star in the Red Sea, but actually to block Chinese navy ships from going to the aid of Islamyah. I see now why the Secretary was so intent on getting me orders to do that. He wants the Americans to land before the Chinese do and then to prevent the PLA from arriving by sea."

"Yeah, okay, that part fits," MacIntyre said, pounding the table absently with his fist. "Conrad does believe the Chinese are coming. He thinks they even have nukes for the missiles they sold Islamyah. But if you try to block their fleet, that's an act of war."

Adams shot MacIntyre a glance. "Tell me about it.

Their fleet is well equipped. And they actually are bringing nukes for the missiles. I got that from my office this morning when I called in on the consulate's secure phone. We confirmed it by scanning them off Malaysia."

"So Conrad was right about that," MacIntyre muttered.

"But he's wrong about what Iran is up to," Brian Douglas said, trying to get the conversation back to his point. "He believes Iran is only landing near Dhahran. They actually plan to take the whole Gulf coast of Islamyah—and Bahrain. He thinks they will then withdraw after they cut a deal to protect the Shi'a, but in fact, Tehran plans to use their enclave to supply a terrorist guerrilla war to evict the Americans and the al Sauds, again, from the rest of the country. They want to bleed America dry in a long desert war."

"Great. So Conrad has done a secret deal with the Iranians to give him cover to reinstall the Sauds, and Tehran is actually double-crossing him, taking half the Gulf, and suckering us into another occupation war in an Arab country. Fucking great!" Adams shook his head in disgust. His pale face was reddening with anger. "We gotta stop this motherfucker."

"Yes," Rusty added quietly, "yes, we do."

The three men sat silently for several minutes. Russell MacIntyre, the American intelligence analyst, looked out at the Persian Gulf and then, after a while, seemed to know what to do. "I had a debate the other day with a friend over whether I was arrogant. She said I wasn't, but maybe I am, because at the end of the day I think I work for the American people, not Conrad and company. And nobody has asked the American people if they want more of their children killed out here in another war."

MacIntyre had chosen sides. "If we act, we act alone. We will never be able to get anyone in Washington or London to go along with what we will have to do. But I have an idea of how we might be able to change things." He turned to Bradley Adams. "Admiral, you have orders to take Fifth Fleet out of the Gulf, and I know you are going to have to follow those orders, but maybe Brian and I can manage events back here so you will be free to do the right thing—at the right time.

"Brian, you and I will be freelancing. If it goes wrong for us, we lose everything, our jobs, our pensions, maybe a lot more, but I swore an oath to protect my country, not a bunch of liars who happen to be in power." Rusty swallowed. "You in?"

"I am. And I have some friendly assets around the Gulf that we can use. I bet you do, too, Admiral." The British spy smiled. "Besides, if it goes wrong, I doubt London will be anywhere near as mad at me as some folks in Washington will be with you." He reached across the table to shake MacIntyre's hand.

Admiral Adams stood and placed a hand on the shoulders of the two civilians. "You guys may think I'm just a big cornpone, but when I was a kid there was a TV show about Davy Crockett, King of the Wild Frontier. The theme song had a line that I just remembered, sitting here. They sang 'Be sure you're right, and then go ahead. It's up to you to do what Davy Crockett said.' Gentlemen, I'm sure we're right. If there's any way to stop another deceitful war out here that's just gonna kill thousands more Arabs and Americans, the right thing is to stop it. You two create the right circumstances and I can put a pretty potent force on your side."

"It's a long shot, and everything will have to work, and in the right order," Rusty admitted, looking up at the naval officer, "but it is the only shot we've got. Brian, can you get the two of us into Islamyah?"

13

FEBRUARY 17

Aboard the USAF E-5B AWACS
Call Sign Quarterback Golf
38,000 Feet above the Persian Gulf

"You know, Major, it's like them Iranians tired them-selves out," Master Sergeant Troy White said over the intercom. "Last few weeks they been flying like crazy with all their old MiGs and shit. Today the sky over there is almost clear. Just a couple of scheduled passenger flights. This shift's gonna be a piece of cake."

The revolving radar dome on top of the modified 767 gave Sergeant White a view almost 200 miles into Iran as the big twin-engine Boeing slowly moved up the middle of the Persian Gulf off Abu Dhabi, headed toward Kuwait.

"Copy, Troy. What about the other side?" Major Kyle Johnson asked from his position in the forward compartment. "Old Islamyah has had a hard time getting their birds up, now that we cut off their spares. You see anything goin' on over there this morning?"

"No, sir. Not much there either. The northern Global Hawk over Kuwait sees a coupla big guys circlin' up north. Looks like maybe Air Islamyah practicing. Maybe checkout flights. Otherwise routine."

The Global Hawk was a Bistatic UAV Adjunct, one of two unmanned aerial vehicles constantly doing high-altitude loops at either end of the Gulf, one over Kuwait and the other over the Musandam Peninsula of Oman, at the mouth of the Gulf. Each flew at over 60,000 feet and had look-down radars whose signals were bounced up to a satellite and down to the AWACS. In addition to its own active radars and those on the Global Hawks, the unarmed AWACS aircraft was equipped with passive sensors to detect and categorize emissions from radars and radios in the air, and those transmitting from below on the land and at sea in the Gulf. All of the data the aircraft collected was integrated, analyzed, and beamed directly up to a satellite for relay down to the U.S. Central Command's forward headquarters in Qatar, the U.S. Fifth Fleet headquarters in Bahrain, the U.S. Army air defense missile batteries in Kuwait, and back to stateside military and intelligence facilities.

"Intel, what you seeing?" Major Johnson asked into his chin mike.

Two compartments back from Johnson, a young Air Force officer, two noncommissioned officers in their late thirties, and a forty-year-old National Security Agency civilian listened on headsets and watched on flat screens. The young officer, Lieutenant Judy Moore, answered for the section. "Concur with Sergeant White, sir. Quiet as a mouse on the Iranian side. On the west, the Islamyans have got some of their Patriot radars blinking on every once in a while. First time I've seen them up in a long time. But they don't stay on for long. Must be having problems. And Troy's right about the two birds circling up by Ar Ar on the Iraqi border. They've been ID'ing themselves as Air Islamyah checkout flights. I think they're both four-engine jobs." She swiveled in her chair and looked at another flat screen that was showing data relayed from the Global Hawk circling at 65,000 feet over the Straits of Hormuz. "Down south it's mainly us making noise. Navy is beginning to head out to Bright Star and is really lighting the Straits area up as they go through."

"Okay, gang. It's the usual racetrack loop today," the major confirmed to the crew over the intercom. "We'll go into Kuwait, do some links down to the U.S. and Kuwait Patriot missile units, make a tight turn, and head back down to Qatar and then . . . do it again."

Beyond the range of the AWACS radar, five SU-27 SMK Flanker aircraft took off from the Iranian air force base at Dezful. Each of the twin-engine interceptors carried a combination of eight heat-seeking and radar-guided air-to-air missiles. Two boys on their way to a high school on the edge of Dezful thrilled to see the powerful Russian-built fighters launching, even though they had often seen Flankers in the air around Dezful. Today, they agreed, was different. There were five together, instead of the usual two, and they did not do the near-vertical climb on takeoff. Instead, these Flankers clung low to the ground, their radar reflections lost in ground clutter, their ten engines laying down a thick black trail as they headed west. If the boys had looked through binoculars, they would have noticed something else different on this day. The paint scheme was new.

Flying west-southwest, the Flankers left Iranian airspace in a few minutes on a heading taking them into Iraq between Al Kut to the north and Al Amarah to the south. They spread out five abreast at one-mile intervals as they swept 2,000 feet over the Tigris River, still heading southwesterly. Their course took them between the Shi'a holy cities of Najaf to the north and Nasiriyah to the south, right over the Euphrates River. Near the riverbank, a man working atop a cell phone tower saw the unusual five-ship formation to his north and called a friend to see if he could see it, too.

The fertile land around the two rivers had been a battleground for as long as there had been governments on the planet. The land ahead of the aircraft now, however, was empty, vast sweeps of vacant desert. Into it, each aircraft dropped a depleted external center-line fuel tank, lightening its load. They were flying slower than normal now in these unpopulated stretches, trying to compensate for the heavy fuel consumption of low-level flight.

As they approached the border with Islamyah, the aircraft pulled into a close formation and descended lower toward the desert sands. The lead pilot was indicating to his wingmen with hand signals. Their radios, like their radars, were turned on but not emitting. Only the IRST, the infrared search and tracking system, scanned out ahead. At this low altitude it was limited to about a 40-kilometer forward view, but unlike radar, no one could detect it. The IRST showed a clear field of sky ahead.

They crossed the border north of Rafha and south of Ar Ar, with only dunes beneath them. The lead pilot waved his arm to his wingmen, indicating an approaching left bank. The aircraft rose slightly before executing the maneuver, then rolled gently around to a south-southeast heading. There were no surface features below to confirm to them that they were where they were supposed to be, but the Galileo global positioning satellite signal in their cockpits told them they were right on course. The desert town of Baqa was coming up off to their right, off to the south. That also meant that their lowest-level flying was coming up. After they passed Baqa on the right, the twin military complexes of Hafr al Batin and what had been known as KKMC, King Khalid Military City, would be miles off to the left of the aircraft. Both locations had been relatively moribund since the coup that had toppled the house of Saud.

Iranian Qods Force observers dressed as camel herders were near the two military bases. They confirmed for Tehran that nothing had taken off from either airstrip all morning. From their positions outside the fences, they could see the flight lines. No one was even preparing an aircraft. Each observer clicked his small satellite radio, firing off burst transmissions on frequencies being monitored by Qods Force. The signals indicated all clear. There was no need for Tehran to use the emergency satellite link to the Flankers.

From their lowest-level flight, the Flankers planned to climb quickly after they were south of KKMC and banking left, toward the Persian Gulf south of Kuwait. The lead pilot checked his fuel gauge. He had consumed a little more than he had planned for at this point in the mission, but only a little. His eyes went to the Russian Phazotron Zhuk coherent-pulse Doppler radar screen. It was warmed up, but not yet switched to emit. When he did flick that switch, it would give him a track-while-scan capability and a look-down/shoot-down system linked to his missiles. It wouldn't be long now before that would happen. As he looked at the radar screen, he caught the electronics intelligence screen to its left blinking an icon on. Then quickly it was gone. The lead pilot thought he had seen that happen a few minutes earlier as well. He had ignored it then. Now he tapped the button below the screen to call up a readout. The data showed that four times in the last sixteen minutes a signal had hit the Flanker, but too briefly to cause the automatic alarm to come on. He tapped the control again for a diagnostic of the signal.

"APY-2," the screen read. That made no sense to him. The APY-2 was the signal he would home in on in a few minutes, the powerful, sweeping radar atop the U.S. AWACS aircraft. He looked at his watch: 0835. If the U.S. AWACS was on its usual, highly predictable schedule, it was coming up the Islamyah coast right now about fifteen minutes south of Khafji, about twenty minutes from Kuwaiti airspace. That would place the Americans to his east. Yet the ELINT screen placed the origin of the signal to the northwest. AWACS signals were also usually sustained, not quick little bursts. These readings made no sense. The Russian ELINT system was so unreliable.

Now his navigation system beeped. The flight of Flankers had come to the GPS coordinates where they were supposed to begin their climb. He signaled to his wingmen and then throttled back with pleasure, making the Flanker almost stand on its tail as it soared up from below 1,000 feet on a climb out to 40,000.

As the g-force pressed him back into his seat, the Iranian struggled to hit a digital tape machine jerry-rigged to his radio. The radio began to transmit the tape of several fighter pilots speaking in Arabic, coordinating their formation, headed toward a target. It would make the Iranian jets seem to be Islamyah fighter pilots, if anyone was listening.

Sergeant White was reading a *Sports Illustrated* spread across his lap, glancing up occasionally at the radar screen in front of him. "Whoa, looks like KKMC damn come alive," he yelled into his chin mike as he dropped the magazine on the floor. "I gots me three, four, five fighters on a fast climb out headed east toward Khafji. I thought those motherfuckers been dead for a while. Guess they done come back from the crypt."

"Keep it clean," Major Johnson responded, looking up at his own screens. "Intel, what you make of that?"

"They are twin-engines. I'd say they'd be some of the F-15s that Islamyah can still get working. But I am not getting a radar emission from them, so maybe not everything's working," Lieutenant Moore answered. She paused while the NSA civilian, headphones still on, passed her a note. She read it and continued her report:

"Confirm Islamyah Air Force chatter from several fighters on climb-out. Keep you posted."

The Iranian Air Force has sent fighter interceptors into the general vicinity of the AWACS a few times, just to let us know they are there, Johnson thought, but Islamyah had not done so before. Maybe they are going to do it now, too. He thought he'd better remind the aircraft commander to review the procedures for dealing with visitors. Although she was junior in rank to Major Johnson, the pilot, Captain Phyllis Jordan, was the aircraft commander. He was just the mission commander. Another example, Johnson thought, of the tyranny of the pilots in the Air Force. He touched his mike. "Captain Jordan, we may have bogeys visit us in a little while before we enter Kuwait airspace. It could be a first for these guys; it's Islamyah this time."

"Roger that," the aircraft commander replied. "We'll keep an eye out. Right now, no joy." The unarmed AWACS continued to lumber north.

Listening to that exchange and now watching his screen intently, Sergeant White saw another surprise. "Major, they keep a-comin'," Troy White barked. "I swear I got six more coming like bats out of hell from the north, climbing out of angles twelve for twenty. Don't know where these bad boys came from."

Kyle Johnson spun his head around to the screen. He saw the new icons moving fast from the west. They broke into two groups of three, one flight on either side and in trail of the group of fighters they had spotted a few minutes ago. At the rate they were moving, they would not be trailing for long. So there were now almost a dozen fighters racing toward the coast, racing toward his AWACs. "Major, intel here," Judy Moore called.

"Whatcha got, Jude?" Major Johnson answered.

"Sir, I have two airborne radar signals coming from near Rafha. Sir, it's two AWACS. The Islamyah Air Force AWACS," she said with incredulity in her voice.

"Well, we did sell the Saudis five AWACS, but I thought intel said only one of them was operational. And you got two up and, what, flying in formation?" Johnson asked.

"I know it sounds crazy, but that's what we're seeing. Don't know where they came from. They just all of a sudden appeared. They are at forty thousand," the intelligence section chief reported out. "And this second group of fighters are definitely F-15S birds. Their radars are working and pinging out strong."

Johnson was suspicious. He hit the keyboard on his console, merging intelligence and radar data onto one screen, focusing the cursor near the city of Ar Ar, and running the tape backwards like a TiVo. He would now see what had happened a few minutes earlier, what they might have missed. There on the screen were the two icons they had designated as "Probable Air Islamyah A-340 or 747." Neither aircraft seemed to be emitting a radar signal. Then, briefly, a narrow radar beam shot out westward, then another to the southwest. The automatic diagnostic software labeled the radar beam "ASY-2 AWACS." He moved the tape ahead. Suddenly three radar icons bloomed from the 747, or AWACS, or whatever it was. The icons moved away quickly. The diagnostics software quickly labeled them "F-15S," the version of the U.S. Air Force Eagle that had been sold to the Saudis.

Then, as Johnson watched, the other big aircraft also seemed to eject three icons, and they were quickly labeled "F-15S." What he had assumed were two airliners on checkout rides had actually been two Islamyah AWACS flying in tight formation with three F-15s each hiding right beneath them. Now, Johnson thought, the six fighters were headed his way. As were the five others.

He hit the mike. "Phil, you might want to think about diving to the deck and speeding up toward Kuwaiti airspace." He wondered if there were U.S. fighter aircraft on alert in Kuwait. He checked for the call sign of the detachment there and switched to their frequency. "Kilo Light, Kilo Light, this is Quarterback Golf, request CAP ASAP, repeat, request CAP ASAP. We have multiple bogeys, possible hostiles . . ." He needed U.S. Combat Air Patrol protection to scare these fighters away.

Before he could finish his transmission, a loud horn blared in his cabin. A tape-recorded female voice spoke the alarm: "Alert. Missile radar lock-on. Alert . . ." The fighters had not launched their missiles—not yet, anyway. As the Flankers were closing on the U.S. AWACS, their radar-guided missiles still sitting on their launch rails, had started to track the AWACS at a distance.

Major Johnson felt the 767 airframe lurch forward as the aircraft commander put the big plane into a dive. In the cockpit, that commander, Captain Phyllis Jordan, was also flicking three countermeasure switches in quick succession, spraying aluminum chaff in the air, shooting infrared flares out the side of the aircraft, and sending electronic warfare signals back toward the fighters on the same frequencies that their missiles and radar used. Johnson now heard the U.S. detachment in Kuwait responding to him: "Quarterback Golf, this is Kilo Light. Say again your request."

The lead pilot in the Iranian Flanker was still climbing when his radar warning receiver started beeping. The flat screen flashed on, with an orange background and the letters "ASY-2 AWACS." Then, as he watched, three different headings appeared. He was being painted by three AWACS radars, only one of which was the American target. He checked his own targeting radar. It had locked on the American AWACS out over the Gulf, still well beyond his firing range. Then the radar warning receiver beeped again, faster and in a higher tone. The screen switched to a red background and the words "APG-70 lock-on."

That meant an American F-15 was out there. Multiple F-15s. Or, he thought, maybe the Saudis? What was happening back there? he wondered as he sped eastward. He switched on his radio and turned it quickly to low power, enough power to reach his wingmen. Then he called in Farsi to two of the four Flankers with him, "Break off. Clear our tail. See what's back there." He flew on. The radar lock-on he had on the AWACS was blinking on and off. He laughed. The American aircraft was trying to jam him, but the 767 was too big a target for his powerful radar to miss. He turned up the gain on the target acquisition mode.

Two of the Iranian Flankers broke from their formation, one right, one left, rising and looping, rolling over in modified Immelmanns. As soon as they had righted themselves, the Flankers each had a visual through their long-range cameras of six Islamyah F-15 Eagles speeding toward them. One of the Iranian Flanker pilots radioed his commander, asking for two more of their squadron to turn around and join what was about to become a major dogfight. Coward, the squadron leader thought, but I can do this on my own. He ordered his remaining wingmen to break off and go after the Islamyah F-15s on his tail.

As the U.S. 767 dove lower, the detection range of its sensors dropped, too, but the northern Global Hawk had moved from scanning into Iran and was now augmenting the AWACS. Major Kyle Johnson saw the "Missiles Away" alarm pop up on his screen. He quickly keyed a text message in and hit Transmit: "CRITIC: Air-to-Air Missiles Launched." A message slugged CRITIC would literally ring bells in command posts all the way to the White House Situation Room. Then Johnson realized the missiles had not been fired at his AWACS. The fighters were firing on one another!

"Major, I have an ELINT readout that says at least one of those fighters is a Flanker, Russian export version. Islamyah doesn't *have* Flankers." It was Lieutenant Moore back in intel. "Could be Syria or Iran, maybe even Iraq."

Johnson switched the display on his screen to see how close they were to Kuwaiti airspace. They had leveled off at 3,000 feet over the Gulf immediately south of Khafji, a few minutes from feet dry over Kuwait. As he watched, an icon blipped on the map at Khafji: "SAM: PATRIOT (X)." Now a Patriot missile's air defense radar was emitting, one of the export versions the U.S. had sold the Saudis. The neighborhood had gone from quiet to chaotic pretty fast. What the hell was going *on* out there? He called to Troy White at the master radar console.

"Major, its fuckin' amazing. They—whoever *they* are, the second group of fighters—splashed one of the first group at range with a Slammer, AIM-120. Shot 'em down! And now they're all mixing it up. There are a bunch of ALQ-135s jammers fuckin' up some of the lock-on radars. But Major," the sergeant said, catching his breath, "one of these guys is still coming at us."

Two of the Islamyah F-15S Eagles soared to 40,000 feet and hit after-burners, sending them into supersonic flight toward the fleeing Iranian Flanker. Below them, four Eagles and three Flankers had begun firing close-in heat-seeking missiles at one another and using their guns as they banked and rolled, weaving in and out in a confused interlaced dogfight. Then the lead Islamyah Eagle got radar lock-on of the lone Iranian Flanker still heading toward the Gulf. The F-15's flat screen flashed "Probability of Kill: 60%." The Islamyah pilot was trained to wait until he was closer, had at least 80 percent, but his fuel light was blinking red. The afterburners had drained what was left of his tank. He flicked back the safety cover over the firing button on his joystick and hit Launch. The

Slammer missile shot off the wing, leaving a trail of smoke as it sped toward the Flanker.

Below, on the beach near the Kuwait border, another Islamyah officer was watching the chase and the aerial ballet on a flat screen in a tan camouflaged trailer. He was the commander of a Patriot missile battery that had just set up there the day before. He had a cursor over the icon for the Iranian Flanker as it moved closer to the U.S. AWACS. "Fire two," he said and almost instantly heard the *whoooshh* of missiles leaving launchers behind sand berms to his right and left.

In the Iranian Flanker, "Air-to-Air Missile Away" and "Surface Missiles Away" messages were flashing. A horn and a beeper were blaring in the pilot's ears. His radar lock-on with the AWACS was intermittent. There was intense jamming, and he suddenly had four distinct radar images for the 767. He had no idea which one was real or where the missiles would go if he fired. He punched anyway. A missile left each wing, one heading left and the other banking straight up. He thought he could see the AWACS below and in the distance, through the glare. If he went to afterburners, he could get a gun kill with the Flanker's cannon. . . .

Standing in the door of the Patriot launch control trailer, Lieutenant Colonel Yousef Izzeldin saw the airburst as the Iranian Flanker exploded into an orange ball and chunks of aircraft were thrown higher and to the side.

The colonel was convinced it was his Patriot missiles that had hit the Iranian.

On the American AWACS, Major Johnson sat slack-jawed in front of his screen. He had seen the Islamyah battery fire Patriot missiles and thought he was about to die. Then he'd realized the Patriots were aimed at the lead fighter, which had exploded a second later. The frequencies were being so heavily jammed, it was hard to tell what else was going on. Then he heard Sergeant White in his earphone. "Well, it looks like it's over. Six aircraft down. Seven, if you count the one the Patriot got. Can you fuckin' believe it? Does *anyone* have any fuckin' idea what that was all about? What the hell *was* that? Who were all those guys?"

White's voice was overridden by a high-priority secure voice message from Headquarters, United States Air Force, Air Combat Command, Langley Air Force Base, Virginia: "Quarterback Golf, this is Blue Squire. Can you confirm your CRITIC message: Missile Launch? Over.

Admiral's Suite
Aboard the USS Ronald Reagan
Straits of Hormuz

"Turn it up, Andy. I want to hear this," Admiral Adams asked the *Reagan*'s captain, Andrew Rucker. The captain grabbed the remote and turned up the volume on the MSNBC broadcast appearing on the screen. A reporter was standing in front of the large blue-and-white 747 used by the Secretary of Defense:

> . . . an apparently unsuccessful revolt within the Is-
> lamyah Air Force, according to a senior Pentagon offi-
> cial on Secretary of Defense Conrad's aircraft as we flew
> here to Cairo with him today. The source said several
> pilots, apparently unhappy with the new regime in
> Riyadh, seized fighter aircraft and took off, but were
> chased and shot down by forces loyal to the regime.
> The senior Pentagon source makes it clear that there
> is widespread discontent in what used to be called
> Saudi Arabia and we should expect to see more such re-
> volts in the weeks and months ahead. Barbara Nichols,
> Cairo.

The news anchor added, "Earlier today an Islamyah government announcement said that several foreign aircraft were shot down after violating the country's airspace. When we come back, the new diet craze . . ."

"Bullshit!" Adams spat out. "That's utter and complete nonsense."

"Sir?" Captain Rucker asked.

"Look, you read the tactical reports coming off the AWACS, just like I did. It was an ambush and it saved our ass, saved the AWACS. The Islamyah Air Force somehow knew these guys were coming and they were waiting for them. If they hadn't been there, those bandits woulda shot down the AWACS. Our own limp-dick Air Force couldn't save its own plane, you saw that." Adams waved a stack of message traffic printouts at the ship's captain.

"Yes, sir, but if they weren't rebel Islamyah pilots, who were those guys?" Rucker asked sheepishly.

"Well, let's see, they were the new export version of the Flanker, which Iraq does not have. That kinda leaves Iran, doesn't it?" Adams walked up to the large map of the Gulf on the wall.

"Yeah, but the AWACS or the Global Hawk would have seen them flying across the Gulf, no?" Rucker said, pointing to that section of the relief map.

The admiral moved around Captain Rucker to a point farther down on the map. "Not if they started up here somewhere in Iran and cut across Iraq on the deck below radar coverage. Then bang, they pop up in Islamyah."

"But why would someone on SECDEF's plane say . . . ?" Rucker asked with a smile.

Adams just gave him a frown. "Let's go up to the tower, Andy," the admiral said, spinning about and heading toward the door.

Several minutes later, the two emerged onto the observation deck ten stories above the flight deck of the *Reagan*, twenty-five stories above the surface of the water below. "Admiral on deck!" a seaman barked as they entered, and then, "Skipper on deck." The fleet's chief intelligence officer, Captain John Hardy, had already found this pleasant perch and was staring out through heavy binoculars when the additional brass appeared.

"Johnny, I knew you were on board," Adams said, patting him on the shoulder, "but I thought you'd be in CIC." The Combat Information Center, the brains of the ship and the entire battle group, was a darkened computer-filled war room several decks below. It was also windowless and, after a time, mind-numbing.

"Needed the air, Admiral. Besides, the intel picture is pretty quiet down this end of the Gulf. The Iranians look like they're on holiday. You think they'd, like, check us out. Here we are moving almost the whole Fifth Fleet from the Gulf, through these little narrow straits, out into the Arabian Sea and the Indian Ocean. What an intelligence opportunity. Shit, if it were them doing this, I'd be flying overhead, sailing along by, putting guys on these little islands with cameras and electronic gear. Not these guys, nothing." Captain Hardy shook his head.

"Not quite the entire Fifth Fleet leaving, Johnny. I'm leaving two new ships behind. There's the new littoral combatant, the *Rodriguez*, and the newest cutter, the *Loy*. Plus two minesweepers and two patrol craft," Adams said, taking the binoculars from Hardy.

"Like I said, Admiral . . ." Hardy joked. "We haven't had so few ships in the Gulf since 1979. I checked."

"Well, as Arnold said, 'I'll be back.' But not until we deal with the Chinese. What's the latest on their deployment?" The admiral guided his intelligence officer to a corner of the tower. Hardy spoke in a lower voice, briefing the fleet commander.

"Both of their battle groups are now well into the Indian Ocean, but after they came through the Straits of Malacca, one stayed to the north, the other to the south. Our P-3s flying out of Diego Garcia are also following a bunch of Chinese Ro-Ros that are spread out ahead of the battle groups. Basically, sir, it all fits so far with what you got briefed on at the Pentagon. We're sailing into a wide-open dragon's jaw, filled with very sharp teeth."

Adams inhaled, filling his barrel-chested torso. He looked down on the big flight deck, at the F-35 Enforcers, the most advanced strike fighter aircraft in the world. "When will we be able to resume flight ops, Andy?" he yelled over to the ship's captain.

"As soon as we get out of this narrow, Admiral, probably while we are sailing by Qeshm Island if the wind stays in this direction. But I have four F-14s and two F-35s up now. They can recover in Oman, at Seeb or Masirah Island, if they need to. We also have Air Force F-22s on strip alert on Masirah and down the Omani coast at Thumrait. F-22 Raptors, F-35 Enforcers . . . If we have to do it, the Chinese will be outclassed," Captain Rucker said, nodding his head.

"Never underestimate the enemy, Andy. Never underestimate them," Adams said. He bit his lip, turned, and walked out.

"Admiral off the deck!"

Security Center of the Republic
Riyadh, Islamyah

"I know I've been here before, Rusty," Brian Douglas whispered to MacIntyre as the elevator descended into the basement of the Security Center. When it stopped, the door opened to reveal Ahmed bin Rashid standing in a darkened corridor, waiting for them.

"I hope your flight from Dhahran was good," the

doctor said, shaking hands with the Brit and the American. He then turned to the two Islamyah Army escorts. "It's all right. I'll take them from here."

They walked past large windows through which they could see room after room of what was clearly a large command post. "This was Schwarzkopf's command post in Desert Storm," Ahmed observed. "You guys should really have left after that, like you said you would. We could have avoided so much." They came to a door with two guards, who nodded at Ahmed and let him and his two guests pass inside.

"Sheik Rashid, *salaam alaikum,*" Brian Douglas said, offering his hand to Abdullah, who had been alone in the small room. After brief introductions by Ahmed, they sat on the two couches, the two Arabs on one side, the American and Brit facing them. A man in Army uniform appeared and served hot tea in glasses. Another placed a dish of dried fruits and sweets on the table. When the waiters were gone, Abdullah began the conversation in English.

"Ahmed explained to me what you have told him." He paused, in thought. "So you tell me the Americans are about to invade my country, and you, MacIntyre, are an American, an intelligence officer. So am I supposed to believe that you are, what, a traitor? Why should I believe you?"

Rusty looked at Brian, who signaled for him to answer first. "Earlier this morning, your aircraft stopped an Iranian attempt to shoot down an American Air Force jet and blame it on you. You stopped it, acting on information that we, that Brian, gave to your brother. Yes?"

Abdullah nodded, looking at his brother for confirmation.

Rusty continued, "I understand that your government has factions. So does mine. I am in the faction that favors exhausting peaceful approaches before we go to war, the faction that believes that your country and ours do not have to be enemies. But if a decision were made to introduce nuclear weapons here, or if this country were to become a base for training and exporting terrorists, I might have a different view. For now, there may still be a window of time in which we can avoid a catastrophe."

Abdullah spoke in a low voice, but with precision: "Mr. MacIntyre, Mr. Douglas, if foreign troops land on our shores without our permission, be they the Americans again or the Iranians, all people of this land will fight them, forever. In whatever way they can. You may call that terrorism. To me it is duty. It is why I fought you Americans when you were here before, why I helped the Iraqis when you invaded their country. Why do you think you can go around the world, putting your army in other people's countries? Germany, Japan, Korea—you have been in these places for decades."

"Sheik Rashid, I did not come here to argue." Rusty could not let the record go uncorrected. "But you must know that the reason we sent forces to Japan and Germany is that those countries attacked us. After we defeated them, we gave them money and democracy. We went to Korea at their request when they were invaded. We also sent American boys to fight and die trying to help Muslims in Bosnia, in Somalia, in Kuwait. We tried to rebuild Iraq and give it democracy. We are not the satanic force that you seem to have convinced yourself we are."

Abdullah cut the air with his hand. "You gave them democracy? Don't you understand that you cannot give democracy with your armies, except to give it a bad name? That you have done. Democracy must spring from the ground like native flowers, different colors and textures in every land. You have made it harder for us even to discuss democracy with our people, because they think it is Washington's idea."

Ahmed and Brian looked at each other, sharing a fear that this meeting would degenerate into a debate between the American and the Arab who had fought against Americans in the recent past. "Whatever, this is history," Ahmed interceded. "We must deal with what is right now. American, Iranian, and Chinese forces are now all very close to invading this country, not to rebuild it or to give it democracy. We are in the process of creating our own form of native democracy. *They* all are coming here to invade to get the oil, but what they will get is a long war in which many from America and Islamyah will die."

Rusty took the cue. "It is our goal, Sheik Rashid, to prevent that. It would be a tragedy for both our countries. And we have both had tragedy enough. That is why we told you what Brian learned in Tehran."

Abdullah nodded in agreement that there had been enough misfortune. "But you do not tell us how to stop this next tragedy, how to stop this triple invasion," Abdullah pointed out.

"No, but we, and some others, will help you if there are ways in which we can," Rusty explained. "I am going back to Washington because I believe that I might be able to stop things there, by informing the right people about what Secretary Conrad is planning."

Abdullah shot a glance at his brother, and asked, "You gave the American woman reporter the accounting paper that Muhammad did for me from the files he found? It shows that this Conrad was just a paid puppet for the al Sauds."

"She has it," Ahmed assured him, "but I will get a copy to Russell as well."

Although MacIntyre did not fully understand the last exchange between the brothers, their audience with Sheik Rashid seemed to be over. Abdullah bin Rashid stood, forcing the other three to rise as well, and then said, "I have already taken some decisions, before I had your information. And I have asked Ahmed to develop for me a plan, a gate, to keep out what he calls the scorpions, the Chinese, the Iranians, and . . . the Americans. You have done this, Ahmed?" The younger Arab waved a folder that he had been carrying in his hand. Abdullah continued. "There will be fighting. We are about to become what you would call 'proactive.' But maybe we avoid the big fight."

"*Inshallah,*" Brian Douglas prayed. "*Inshallah.*"

14

FEBRUARY 21

Aboard the USS George Herbert Walker Bush
The Red Sea, Just South of the Suez Canal

"Thank you so much, for the briefings and the tour of the ship—for everything, Mr. Secretary," the Egyptian minister of defense said as he walked down the red carpet on the deck, toward the awaiting V-22 Osprey. "We are doing the right thing. And I know, when the time comes, my President will do the right thing, too. And you and I will be ready to carry out his instructions." The Egyptian stopped and placed his hand on Secretary Conrad's arm. "We cannot let these people in Islamyah think they can change regimes and replace rulers with religious fanatics and terrorists. We should never have let this happen. We should have acted sooner, but now, with your help, we can correct this mistake and restabilize the region. *Inshallah.*" He stood back, saluted the Secretary, and climbed into the big vertical-liftoff aircraft.

Conrad, wearing a Navy flight jacket, returned the salute and then walked back inside the ship before the big rotors started to turn, creating a strong prop wash across the entire carrier deck. The Secretary was escorted to the CIC and to a small conference room just off the floor of the war room. "Well, I thought that went well, Ron," Conrad said as he shut the door.

Under Secretary of Defense Ronald Kashigian had been alone, waiting for his boss. "We'll see. When he tells President Fouad that we're going in to stop the chaos and to stop the Iranians, then we will know if we have Egyptian troops with us. Not before."

"Ron, it's critical that we have another Arab state going in with us. A big one, not some little pissant sandhill," Conrad said as he sat down at the little table. "How's the press play on the dogfight fuckup?"

Kashigian handed him a pile of printouts. "Actually, quite good. Not what we wanted. The Iranians all got shot down, amazingly. But I think it adds to the impression of instability in Islamyah. The Pilots' Revolt, that's how the *Chicago Courier* headlined it. What bothers me is how it got screwed up. I can't believe that Islamyah's air defense system was that good. All the intelligence briefings I got said—"

"Christ! How many times do I have to tell you that you can't believe intelligence!" Conrad said, throwing the papers back at his subordinate. "But it worked, well enough. Now, what else can go wrong?"

"Well, let's see. The Saud princes leave Los Angeles and Houston tonight and fly forward to Geneva. The rioting in the Shi'a neighborhoods in the Eastern Province in Islamyah should begin tonight, and then Tehran will hold a big rally tomorrow afternoon to protest the persecution of the Shi'a in Islamyah. They have stood down their air and naval forces to get them ready for the assault. Our fleet has just about left the Gulf, so you need to sign out the order to Adams formally modifying his mission from Bright Star to setting up a picket line to block the Chinese. . . ." Kashigian went down a timeline and checklist in a black leather folder. "Has the President signed the order yet to intercept the Chinese ships with the troops and the nukes?"

Conrad looked up with a disgusted grimace. "No, the President hasn't signed the order yet," he said, mimicking Kashigian. "Goddamn lawyers in the White House are debating whether it's an act of war. Of course it's an act of war! So what? I'll order it myself if it comes to that. National Command Authority, right?"

"Yeah, but I thought we wanted to save that card in case you have to, shall we say, spontaneously decide to go in to Saudi to stop the Iranians, after their landings," Kashigian said.

"Stop the Iranians from spreading across from the enclave they will have on the Gulf side, but also to stop the chaos in Jeddah and Riyadh, which will be threatening Westerners," Conrad added.

"Right, although I don't know how much evidence we will actually have of any chaos there to show anybody," Kashigian admitted.

"Evidence? This is not a court of law!" Conrad pounded the table. "The press will report it, if we say it."

The two men sat for a moment, looking at the map of the region on the wall in the small room. "What else . . ." Conrad thought out loud.

"There's that guy MacIntyre from IAC, who has been snooping around," the Under Secretary replied.

"Nah," Conrad scoffed. "He's a pipsqueak."

"Our Special Forces will seize the oil infrastructure right away to prevent any destruction. We want to get the production up and going to us directly again as fast as possible. But that oughta work. Let's see, what else? I'm not confident about this guy Adams in Fifth Fleet," Kashigian suggested. "I've had Counterintelligence checking on him, too."

"Oh, I know you aren't happy with him, but I met with him on the plane. He's fine. Good Navy officer. Wants to be a CinC someday. He'll handle the Chinese," the Secretary assured Kashigian.

"What if they don't want to be handled?" the Under Secretary asked.

"They are in way over their head and they know it. The admiral, Tian-something, the Australian source, says that if it comes to a possible shooting war, they will back down because they don't want to lose to us. Face, and all that. And right now they would lose. Maybe not in ten years, but, shit, they only just started with carriers a few years ago. They can't take on the United States Navy. And besides," Conrad said, stroking his chin, "remember, I have a surprise for them."

"Let's hope Tian-something is right, Mr. Secretary." Kashigian smiled back. "I just don't like to ever believe intelligence."

"Fuck you," said the Secretary of Defense.

The Second Scenic Overlook
George Washington Parkway
Fairfax County, Virginia

"I have confirmation on almost all of it now, Ray, and it all checks out, from what Ahmed gave me," Kate said into the cell phone. "I'm about to meet a guy from Dominion Commonwealth Partners who is going to give me more." She sat in the rented Ford in the parking lot off the parkway, looking down at the Potomac.

"Who's the guy?" Ray Keller, managing editor of the *New York Journal,* asked. He was in his office on the 42nd floor, looking out on Manhattan.

"When I went out to Tysons Corner to this hedge fund's office, they sent out this flack to deal with me. I didn't get past reception, but I gave the flack my card. Then, two hours later, he calls and says he couldn't talk there, but he has the answers to the questions I faxed them. Said he would meet me after work at the Second Overlook and give me the files," she said, scanning her notes on her PowerBook.

"Well, at least he's got a sense of the dramatic, or humor." Keller laughed. "You do know that the Second Scenic Overlook was where some of the Watergate figures met Tony Ulasciewicz?"

Kate laughed, too. "No, I didn't know that. But I know it's just down the parkway from Turkey Run. Isn't that where the conspiracy theorists say that Bill Clinton killed Vince Foster? Nut jobs."

"Yeah, which reminds me, be careful. This is big stuff and I don't like that your hotel room was broken into down in Houston, or that you thought those thugs were following you up here," Keller said, using his deeper tone, which meant he was serious.

"Now who's being dramatic?" she replied. "Listen, I want four columns above the fold when this runs. Here's the first four 'graphs." Kate read from the laptop, which was plugged into the car's outlet,

Secretary of Defense Henry Conrad has been championing the return of the Saud family to their royal thrones in Islamyah. Now, in information obtained exclusively by the *New York Journal*, it is clear that Henry Conrad's highly successful leveraged buyout (LBO) firm was funded almost exclusively with al Saud money. Much of the campaign contributions Conrad raised for the President also appear to have originated with the Saud family.

Over $2 billion was laundered from the Sauds to Conrad Conversion Partners. Conrad left the firm he founded to become Defense Secretary. The Saud money was hidden through layers of offshore firms and banks, as well as investment houses in the United States (see chart). The *New York Journal* has confirmed that the funds originated in al Saud accounts, although it is unclear whether the money belonged to the government or the royal family.

Late last year Senator Paul Robinson asked the Treasury Department to investigate which Saud funds in the U.S. were personal and which belonged to that nation. Many funds remain frozen, awaiting the results of the report. Robinson's request, however, did not include the funds in Conrad Conversion because it was not known that they were Saudi monies. The Conrad Conversion funds are not frozen by the Treasury order.

Over $200 million donated to a series of political committees supporting the President were given by employees or investors in firms that were owned by Conrad Conversion. If those donors were acting as pass throughs for the former royal family, they may have been engaging in a criminal conspiracy to violate U.S. campaign financing laws. U.S. laws prohibit foreign contributions to U.S. campaigns. Violation of those rules is a felony.

Ray Keller responded with his usual line to reporters. "That's close, Kate, but it's going to need some polishing. When will you be back?"

"By the time I'm done with this source tonight, it may be too late to get the last shuttle up to New York. I haven't even checked out of the Marriott yet, so I'll come up first thing in the morning. Be in the office around eleven. See you then," Kate said, stretching and realizing how tired she was from jet lag and all the running around she had done since she returned from the Gulf. A Park Police car drove slowly through the parking lot. She looked to her right, where, in the distance through the bare trees, she could see the Washington Monument, brightly lit, standing guard over America's capital city.

But, Kate thought, it is really an active, investigating, questioning media that guards the capital against people like Conrad. Against people who put the welfare of their rich friends over the national good, people who would so easily send the children of the poor and middle class off to fight their wars instead of trying to solve the problems that cause the wars. Like the failure to find alternative energy. God, she thought, if I wrote that, they'd fire me. Her reflections on power were broken by flashing headlights in her mirror.

Kate Delmarco turned around to get a good look at the car. That was the car he had said he would be in, the gold Lexus.

She was about to get the proof that Dominion Commonwealth Partners was a hedge fund with twenty investors, all of whom ultimately were funded, through layers of fronts, by a Saudi government account. And every employee at DCP had made big donations to the same set of political action committees within a week of a special dividend distribution. If that isn't foreign financing of a U.S. election campaign, she thought as she got out of the Ford, I don't know what is.

Her blood raced in anticipation as the man got out of the Lexus.

The Hussein Mosque Naval Base
Iranian Revolutionary Guards Command
(Pasdaran)
Bandar Abbas, Iran

"I will leave you here," the Pasdaran general said. "You do not participate in the prayers enough, General," the cleric said, changing into a robe for the service he would lead.

"There is much still to be done," he replied, tightening the lacing on his boot. "But you saw in the tour, they are ready to go into this battle, they are well trained and equipped."

"I cannot judge such things." The cleric's voice was soft and his tone mild, unlike what it would be when he gave the sermon later in the hour. "That is why I place my trust in you. Just as I trusted our airplanes would perform their secret mission: kill the Americans, cast blame on Islamyah, and return home."

The general straightened up, standing tall above the cleric. "It was a minor piece of the puzzle. It did not work perfectly, but the Americans are telling the world that it was a revolt in the Islamyah Air Force, a further sign of the chaos in that country. When the explosions take place in the Shi'a cultural centers in Islamyah tonight, it will add to the chaos, to the persecution of our religious brethren, whom we must then rescue."

The cleric looked up from the Koran that was open on the table. "The American Navy base in Bahrain did not blow up. The American spy plane was not shot down. Both because Islamyah stopped them from happening. Have you thought that perhaps Islamyah has a spy in our midst, General?"

The general had not told him about the discovery made by the Foreign Ministry security staff. About the man who had downloaded sensitive documents, killed two security staff, and then committed suicide. The fingerprints they had found were those of a British spy, who was still at large. Not of a spy from Islamyah.

"I can assure you that we have looked very hard and that there is no evidence of any such Islamyah spy," the general said in a crisp military way.

The cleric moved toward the door of the anteroom. He adjusted his robes and placed the Koran in his right hand. He turned back toward the general. "I must pray for our forces. I must pray with our forces. For Allah to give us another victory!" With that, the cleric left the room, empty except for the general.

"We shall have another victory," the general said. "I will give us that."

15

FEBRUARY 22

Near the CSS-27
Missile Base, Al Juaifer
Islamyah

So many Chinese. What were they *doing* here in his desert? the guard wondered. What were they preparing for? And why in the name of Allah did he have to live among their filthy foreign ways? He sighed, his mind drifting. No one told him anything.

It was soon after dawn, and as the guard at the front gate sat musing, his reverie was interrupted by the sight of three columns of black smoke rising from behind the dune to the north. And then he heard the noise. It was like something screaming in agony, something made of heavy metal. His hand was on the telephone in the guard booth when the three M-1A2 tanks flew through the air above the dune and then crashed to the surface, creating a sandstorm below.

Stunned by the apparition, the guard stumbled out of the booth to join his colleague by the Humvee. The metal screeching noise was becoming unbearable as the giant tanks emerged from the sand and drove at the high chain-link fence around the missile base. With more screeching and black smoke, the tanks flattened that section of fence, then a machine gun on the front of the closest tank turned and sprayed the guards and the Humvee with .50-caliber ammunition.

Men in green uniforms and khaki uniforms poured from the buildings in the camp as a klaxon sounded and voices from the speaker systems shouted in Arabic and Chinese. A large green truck moved between two rows of warehouse buildings, carrying two stages of a CSS-27 mobile missile. But one of the M-1 tanks was right on its tail and seemed to crawl up onto the truck's flatbed. With a roar, the missile burst into a fireball, engulfing the truck, the tank, and a nearby building.

At the port of Jizan on the Red Sea, the guards saw the big helicopters coming in time to sound the alarm. The chief of the port police ordered his men to fire, yelling that the helicopters were American, painted to look like Islamyah's army. He grabbed a machine gun mounted on a pickup truck and started to fire, and his men joined in a hail of bullets, shooting up at the approaching Chinook CH-47s. The lead chopper seemed to stop, then it burst in two in an orange flash.

The remaining Chinooks broke left, away from the port, and then a wave of smaller Apache AH-64 attack helicopters appeared. The port police could see the smoke as missiles left the rails of the Apache and rockets shot out of pods hung below their fuselages. Almost instantly, explosions erupted in the piles of shipping containers stacked high in the yard. The police chief looked behind him to see a Chinook whipping up debris as it hovered over a dock, troops rappelling down ropes out of its rear cargo door. Above the noise, the port police chief started yelling, "Surrender, surrender!"

In the basement of the Security Center, Abdullah bin Rashid's deputies manned the telephones and radio consoles, fielding reports on the progress of the Protectors, as their combined army and national guard was now called. The reports were mostly good. The oil refineries and shipment facilities were secured. The religious police at the Two Holy Mosques had been quietly replaced. At the ports and airports where the additional Chinese were scheduled to arrive, patrol boats blocked the harbors, and tanks sat on the runways. The CSS-27 missile bases were now in the hands of the Protectors, and the Chinese guests well cared for.

There was, however, fighting in the Hadramaut region near the Yemeni border, where the local army unit remained loyal to a governor tied to Zubair bin Tayer and his faction on the Shura. Also, when the Dhahran base commander had read out the communiqué about the change in the Shura membership, two F-15s had taken off and then strafed the field. A Navy patrol craft captain loyal to bin Tayer had ordered his sailors to lob rounds into an army facility near Jeddah.

The worst fighting, however, was in and around Riyadh. Bin Tayer had placed loyalists in several military and police units, and his brother, a colonel, was in charge of a regiment of infantry twenty miles north of the capital. The regiment had converged on an office, warehouse, and housing compound once built for an American defense contractor. It was walled and easily defended.

"It's confirmed, bin Tayer is in the Vanilla compound," an officer announced in Abdullah's underground command post. "He's got most of his Shura supporters with him, and he's calling it a meeting of the Council. Their guys are well positioned to keep us out. We got two tanks burning from antitank missiles. We got a lot of casualties."

Abdullah stroked his beard.

"Bomb it, Abdullah," General Khalid urged. "There is no need for us to take casualties. Just blow them up. I will order up a squadron of Tornadoes and it will be over."

"No!" Abdullah yelled. "You are right, Khalid. Our boys should not take casualties. But neither should theirs. We are all brothers." Then, walking toward his friend, Abdullah stood in front of the general and directed him, "Pull our boys back a bit. Then launch your Tornadoes, but have them drop their bombs outside the compound walls. What the stupid Americans called shock and awe. Then talk bin Tayer into surrendering."

"I will do the bombing, Sheik, but who can talk bin Tayer and his Shura fools into surrendering?" Khalid asked.

"I will. I'm going over there," Abdullah said as he went for the door. "Khalid, you are in charge. Ahmed, you are his deputy. And, Ahmed, see that the scorpion gate videotape is ready for when I have arrested bin Tayer, and then call the Chinese Embassy." Before anyone could object, Abdullah bin Rashid had left the command room.

As he pulled his Range Rover up to the forward command post outside the rebellious compound, Abdullah could see Tornadoes circling in the distance. "What are they waiting for?" he asked General Hammad, who was leading the assault.

"For you," Hammad said, smiling and signaling to an officer standing beside a radio-laden Humvee. Two minutes later, three Tornadoes swept in low, dropping bombs in front of and on either side of the compound. As the center Tornado pulled up, it was hit by a shoulder-fired rocket. Smoke trailed behind the Tornado, which disappeared from view. Then there was the noise of an explosion, and a black column billowed upward in the distance.

"They just killed a pilot. So, do it again, Hammad," Abdullah ordered. "Throw the bombs out forward of the planes. Don't fly over the compound. And put the bombs inside the walls this time."

Four minutes later, two F-15s could be seen approaching over the city at low altitude. As they approached the forward command post, both Eagles seemed to stand on their tails, arch over, and begin to fly back in the direction they had come. Halfway up their short climb, a large bomb separated from each Eagle and arched in the opposite direction, toward the compound. Abdullah pulled General Hammad down behind the Range Rover. A second later the detonation shook the vehicle, and the roar continued on for several minutes.

When they looked up, the front gate and most of the front wall of the compound were gone. Fires burned in several places inside. "You have been talking to bin Tayer's brother, the colonel, inside?" Abdullah asked General Hammad. "Call him back and tell him in four minutes the entire compound will be obliterated unless they surrender. Call him. Now!"

Fifteen minutes later, General Hammad walked up from the communications Humvee. "The compound is secure. They all surrendered, and they have bin Tayer and the others in custody."

"They must be treated with respect," Abdullah told the general. "Let's go see them." The two men climbed into Abdullah's Range Rover and drove into the compound, around chunks of wall and burning vehicles. "We will put them under house arrest. In the Saud's desert villas in the south. Until the elections. Then they can run, make their case peacefully to the people. Maybe they will win."

An officer directed them to a large white villa in the center of the compound. Its windows had been blown out and curtains hung askew. Abdullah and his general met bin Tayer and three other Shura members being held by the guards near a fountain inside. Abdullah spoke first. "Zubair bin Tayer, I place you under arrest for conspiring with foreign agents, for planning to bring additional foreign troops into the country without the consent of the Shura, and for planning to put in jeopardy the welfare of the nation by introducing weapons of mass destruction into the land of the Two Holy Mosques."

Bin Tayer spat at him. "It is you who will be arrested. For killing our citizens. For exceeding your authority as security chief."

"Zubair, we differ. Maybe in an election, the majority of the men and women of our country would agree with you, but I doubt—"

Bin Tayer cut Abdullah short. "There will be no elections with *women*." He brought something out from under his robes and pulled at it.

Time seemed to freeze—and then there was a roar, followed by more roars, and flashes inside the gleaming white villa. Guards ran in to find bodies strewn on the floor. Many, including General Hammad, were wounded, sitting up or leaning against the fountain. Nine others were dead: the four rebellious Shura members, blown to bits from the blast of their four hand grenades. Four guards.

And Abdullah bin Rashid.

Blood poured down General Hammad's face; his eyes bulged out. He struggled to respond to an officer who had just run in to take charge of the scene. "Call the Center. Get me Dr. Ahmed bin Rashid. . . ."

Hideaway Office of Senator Paul Robinson
Chairman, Senate Select Intelligence Committee
Hart Senate Office Building, Capitol Hill
Washington, D.C.

"Call the President," Russell MacIntyre urged the Senator. "Tell him what his Secretary of Defense is about to do."

Sol Rubenstein answered his deputy on the Senator's behalf. "He can't just call up and get the President and have a one-on-one chat. Besides, the President is at the Asia Pacific meeting in Chile."

"They moved Chile to Asia?" Robinson joked. "Look,

Rusty, all of this has taught me something, and I intend to build a coalition and act on it. We can't go into this century with our energy policy being to fight wars over who gets the remaining oil. The Chinese growth has just exacerbated it, but we already had a problem. We have a market failure here. The private sector cannot pay for the massive costs and risks of developing alternative energy. So we have to. With new tough conservation regulations, with tax credits, and with an unprecedented R & D program. As to what's happening today and tomorrow . . ."

"Look, Rusty, it's not that we don't believe you. We do," Rubenstein added. "It's just that we don't know how to stop it. The intel brief this morning shows the Chinese fleet is more than halfway there. Conrad is right to try to stop them from landing troops and sending in nukes."

Rusty bristled. "We haven't done enough diplomatically with the Chinese to stop them. Remember the Cuban Missile Crisis. How did we stop the Soviet ships from bringing in nukes? Not with just the Navy. Besides, he's not just stopping the Chinese from landing, he is having Americans land and take over the fucking country," MacIntyre said in exasperation. "Except for the part he bargained away with Iran."

The two older men looked at each other. Rubenstein spoke. "Rusty, you can't prove Conrad did that. At best those documents you have prove that some Iranian wrote that he had met with Kashigian and he agreed. Of course, Kashigian will say it's a setup . . . he was there to threaten them. At best we get Conrad for not coordinating with the State Department."

MacIntyre stared at his boss. "Look, Sol, I know I'm too close to this thing, but the way I look at it, we are only a day or two away from a war with China and an occupation by a division of U.S. Marines of the most holy land in the Muslim world." MacIntyre looked from Rubenstein to Robinson. "Am I missing something here, Senator?"

Neither man answered.

"All right, well, what about the fact that Kate Delmarco is about to blow the lid off the whole Saudi funding deal with Conrad? Isn't that enough to get him recalled from Egypt?" Rusty asked.

The Senator walked over to a stack of newspapers. "Did you say the Kate Delmarco story?"

"Yeah, did she run it already? I just got off the airplane two hours ago. Been in the air and airports for twenty-two hours," MacIntyre said, rubbing his forehead.

Senator Robinson picked up the paper and put on his reading glasses. "Here it is. Made the late edition. Pulitzer Prize–winning reporter for the *New York Journal* Katherine Delmarco was found dead tonight, an apparent victim of a heart attack. . . ."

"What!" Rusty screamed. He felt a sickening lurch in the pit of his stomach.

The Senator continued, "Ms. Delmarco, forty-five, was found by Park Police in an area off George Washington Parkway, where she had apparently stopped while experiencing chest pains driving to an appointment in McLean. . . ."

Rusty sat down and looked at the rug. "They killed her!"

"Who killed her?" Senator Robinson asked.

"Who? The Saudis, Kashigian, I dunno. The same

guys who blew up Admiral Adams's plane, the guys who compromised Brian Douglas's source and damn near got him killed in Tehran. The ones who sicced the FBI on me for meeting with terrorists . . . *them*." Rusty sat back in the chair and closed his eyes. What was the point? Maybe like the characters in Furst's book, he was just a little person who had to stand by and watch the war come, get swept up in its vortex, have everything he loved destroyed.

"Here, what's this?" Sol Rubenstein asked, pointing at the television. "Paul, take that thing off mute. Turn up the volume, will ya?"

Senator Robinson found the remote and turned up the audio on CNN. ". . . fighting. A statement issued in the name of the Shura Council Vice Chairman Abdullah bin Rashid said that there had been an attempted coup by Iranian-sponsored elements and that Shura Chairman Zubair bin Tayer had died in the fighting. The statement said that full stability had been restored. It gave no further proof of the alleged Iranian involvement, but said that Rashid would address the nation tomorrow. In other news from . . ."

Rusty looked up and smiled. "That's it. They've started. Abdullah and Ahmed!"

"Sounds to me like what you feared would happen is happening," Sol Rubenstein answered. "Both Iran and Conrad can claim there is chaos there. And Iran can say that this bin Rashid guy is blaming Tehran so he can beat up on the Shi'a."

"No, no," Rusty countered. "Don't you see? Ahmed and Abdullah are taking over. They are going to try to stop this engine that's coming down the track. How ironic. We three sit here and can't think of how to affect our own government, and it's the guys in Islamyah who are doing something."

"I dunno who Abdullah and Ahmed are, Rusty, but from where I sit, it's going to take a helluva lot to stop the U.S., China, and Iran from invading Islamyah," the Senator observed.

16

Combat Information Center
USS Ronald Reagan
Northern Arabian Sea

"How far are you from the lead element of their battle group, Captain?" Admiral Brad Adams asked the skipper of the cruiser USS *Ticonderoga* on a secure voice hookup.

"Admiral, I am on the bridge and I can see one of their ships on the horizon through the glasses. Looks just like a U.S. Burke-class, and he's closing on me," the voice said over the speaker.

"Too close," Adams said to Captain John Hardy, who was standing next to him in CIC. Then the admiral pressed the mike to talk to the cruiser *Ticonderoga*. "Captain, pull back. Maintain twenty-five-mile separation, but let him know you're there. Turn everything up so he knows." Hanging up the phone, he turned to his intelligence officer. "If we have to fight them, we're going to get bloody. I don't want to start that fight by mistake or miscalculation." He exhaled. "Johnny, do the Chinese still think that the *Ticonderoga* is us? The *Reagan*? Do they think we're down there in the Indian Ocean?"

"From what I can tell from the intercepts, that's exactly what they think"—Hardy laughed—"and from the daily plots the Pentagon issues, I'd say Washington thinks we're down there, too!"

"And the Iranians, Johnny?" Adams asked.

"Them too," the captain answered. "Their plane followed us out past Hormuz into the northern Arabian sea, but then it went back. I don't think anybody knows we've been circling since we went EMCON and then electronically lit up the freighters from Diego Garcia to look like warships. I think the trick is working, just like it used to do with the Soviets."

The *Reagan*'s commander, Captain Andrew Rucker, had been listening, and he walked over. "I gotta hand it to you, Admiral. I didn't think you could hide a U.S. carrier battle group, let alone from the Pentagon."

"Well, it's a Cold War trick. You put out radar corner reflectors and radio and radar transmitters and suddenly a destroyer looks like a carrier, a freighter looks like a cruiser to the satellites and the radio intercept towers. It worked on the Chinese. The only reason that the Pentagon thinks we're down there is because that's what we are reporting to them. And because Bobby Doyle and a few other friends are playing along . . ." Adams replied in a low voice.

"But at some point, sir, we're going to have to hightail it down there if we're going to block the Chinese fleet," Rucker said, looking at the location of the ships on a wall projection.

"If we have to, we will. We'll crank the reactors and scoot, but we'll do it under emissions control, quiet, so they don't see us coming." The Admiral continued: "If we get caught out by the Pentagon, I'll take the fall. You're just following my orders." At the door, he turned back to the two captains. "I'm going topside to get some air. Let me know if anything changes. Rucker, you want to join me?"

On the flight deck, Brad Adams and Captain Andrew Rucker walked among the aircraft in the predawn dark, hands thrust in their pockets. They had seldom seen an aircraft carrier so still. No flight activity under way. The normally spinning radars turned off. Most of the lights out. Adams stared out at the water, wondering if he was doing the right thing. He wanted to be in two places at once, in the Gulf to stop the Iranians from invading Bahrain and Islamyah, and in the Indian Ocean to intercept the Chinese troop ships and maybe shoot it out with the Chinese fleet. Right now, he was in neither place, but bobbing up and down in the Arabian Sea.

"Andy, what we're doing here is on the razor's edge of insubordination. Look, I believe in civilian control of the military. It's what has kept us from having coups and the kind of chaos other nations have had. But when the civilians' decisions aren't subject to checks and balances, when they distort information, when they cow the media into going along with their shit, I dunno," Brad mused.

"Sir, they taught us at Newport how when Colin

Powell's generation of young officers came back from Vietnam, they all swore that they would never let the civilians take the Army to war again if there was no good need, no endgame, no informed popular support. Maybe we gotta get back to that attitude in the military," Rucker suggested.

"Admiral," John Hardy called out across the flight deck. The captain ran across the steel plate. "The Iranians have set to sea. Everything they've got. Amphibious assault ships, car ferries, freighters. Moving toward Islamyah and Bahrain. NSA reports that they've launched almost one hundred sorties from their air bases."

"How long do you think that they can fend them off?" Adams asked, taking the reports.

Hardy shook his head. "Not long. Islamyah is holding forces in the West, in case we invade them, too."

"Well, it's decision time, Johnny." Adams looked back out to sea. "I cannot go back into the Gulf. Not while we still have the Chinese coming our way."

A sailor approached them, carrying a large manila envelope. Hardy opened it. "Shit. It's a CRITIC from ASU Bahrain: 'Iranian aircraft dropped bombs on Fifth Fleet headquarters at 0530 local.'"

"Good thing we emptied it out, Johnny." Adams looked at the CRITIC message. "But we still have a lot of Americans nearby. Let's go back inside."

As they reentered CIC, the battle group commander, Rear Admiral Frank Haggerty, was directing a flurry of activity. He was speaking into the secure telephone. "Commander, this is very important. Can you confirm that the *Zhou Man* has done a one-hundred-eighty-degree turn?"

A voice responded over the speaker box on the wall. "Yes, sir, Admiral. I'm looking at her stern through the periscope. She did a big wide turn."

Adams went over to Haggerty. "Who is that?"

"It's the CO on the *Tucson*. She's been submerged, following the *Zhou Man*. But I also have the P-3 that's been tracking the Chinese Ro-Ros. It's reporting that they are sailing in toward Karachi. *Ticonderoga* says the destroyer that was out front turned around, too. I think they're bugging out, Brad." Haggerty was clearly excited. "What the hell happened?"

"Admirals, if I may, a couple of things happened," Captain Hardy said, poring over his papers. "Almost all of the Indian Navy has put to sea in battle formation and they were sailing up behind the Chinese." Hardy almost chuckled. "And the *Zhou Man* and *Zheng He* both got a high-precedence, special encryption message from Beijing. But we don't know what it said."

"I do," Adams asserted. His colleagues looked surprised. "It was sent over five hundred years ago from the Chinese Emperor to Admiral Zheng He in the Indian Ocean. It said, 'Return at once.' When he got back, the Emperor burned the fleet and almost every record of its great expeditions. Later, the Emperor relented and let him go to Mecca on the hajj . . . but without the fleet."

Adams walked to the small podium sometimes used by briefers in the CIC. "Gentlemen, and ladies, here is the situation as I see it. We are unable to complete our mission to intercept the Chinese ships because they are either headed into port in Pakistan or have turned tail and are heading back to China.

"On the other hand, we have a CRITIC saying our headquarters in Bahrain has just been bombed, and we have intelligence that Iran has begun an amphibious assault on both Bahrain and Islamyah. I don't need orders when I am told Americans are under attack.

"Captain Rucker, bring the *Reagan* about into the wind. Launch both Enforcer squadrons with full weapons loads across Oman toward Bahrain and Islamyah. Execute Plan Ten Zero Nine, as modified. Forty-third Squadron is to take out the Iranian Navy. Forty-fourth is to take out the Iranian coastal air and Navy bases. The U.S. Air Force Raptors in Oman will escort.

"Admiral Haggerty, get in touch with the Gulf allies. Tell them what we're doing and ask them to execute, as planned in last week's modification to Plan Ten Zero Nine. We will recover the Enforcers in Qatar, refuel, and rearm. That wing of new Super F-16s the Emirates have, they will be flying over Hormuz as we go through. If anything moves on the Iranian islands, they'll pickle it.

"Captain Hardy, terminate the deception operations. Let's light up the battle group's electronics and let the Iranians know we're coming.

"All right, everybody. Any questions?" Adams almost yelled. A loud "No, sir" rang in CIC. "Then let's go to war. Captain Rucker, strike the battle ensign."

The lights on the tower of the *Reagan* lit up, its radars began to spin, a horn rang out, and a small blue flag covered in five-pointed white stars was run up the flag mast. The huge ship lurched forward, accelerated, and began to execute a U-turn, spreading a giant curving wake behind it. Giant elevators rose from below, carrying aircraft to the flight deck. Men and women in brightly colored jump-suits ran to the planes, in red, in green, yellow, purple . . .

Back in CIC, Captain Hardy waited until Adams had walked around the command center, checking on the execution of his orders, patting the seamen on their shoulders. Then Hardy quietly asked the Fifth Fleet commander, "What modification to the plan?"

"The one the Gulf allies got from me last week," Adams mumbled while reading a message board. "The one approved at CENTCOM headquarters by General Bobby Doyle."

"Not by the CinC, General Moore?" Hardy asked.

"Bobby's the J-F. He can approve plans, Johnny." Adams smiled.

"And did you also arrange to have the entire god-damn Indian Navy, including its two little aircraft carriers, sortie out to trap the Chinese in between our two fleets, Admiral?" Captain Hardy whispered back.

"You overestimate me, Johnny. I think maybe Secretary Conrad had that little maneuver planned. God only knows what he gave them to do it." The admiral laughed as he handed Hardy the message board. "But that's not why the Chinese turned back. Look at the message traffic. The government of the Islamic Republic of Islamyah formally requested that the Chinese terminate their military assistance program and withdraw all Chinese military personnel. Abdullah bin Rashid's office announced it publicly late last night!"

"No fuckin' way—ah, excuse my French, sir," Hardy said, flustered.

Admiral Haggerty joined the discussion. "Looks like I

missed something. Anyway... Admiral Adams, shall I send a message to Tampa and Washington telling them what we're doing?"

"Of course, Frank, that's standard operating procedure. And we *always* follow standard operating procedure. Bring it to me to sign out," he said, looking at his watch, "in about a half hour or so. I'm going out to watch the air wing launch. Maybe after that."

Haggerty and Rucker both laughed. Haggerty saluted. "Aye, aye, sir."

Boardroom, Banc Bahrain
Thirty-fifth floor, Bank Bahrain Building
Manama, Bahrain

"The Iranians may bomb the Ministry of Defense, but I doubt they will attack this bank," the Bahraini Defense Minister, General Ibrahim, said to Brian Douglas. "And from here we have good lines of sight and communication." Behind him, soldiers were connecting radios and telephones, setting up long-range telescopes and television monitors. Below, in the city, Brian could see fires and smoke rising from several locations throughout the area, where the predawn Iranian air raid had penetrated the Bahraini air defenses.

"We are protecting the mouth of the port with patrol craft, divers, our frigate, and a U.S. cutter. And we and the Americans laid a minefield last night. The American SEALs are assisting. They did not sail away with everything," the Bahraini general said, pointing to the east.

"How much damage did the Iranians do at the air base?" Douglas asked. Sheik Issa Air Base was behind them to the south, a view blocked from where they stood.

"Pretty bad, but we had rolled some of our F-16s off the base and moved others to the corners of the International Airport, so we still have eight or nine F-16s operational," the Bahraini general admitted. "We expect the Iranian landing to be at the northern beach area, and that's where I have most of the army. We have some American-built multiple launcher rocket systems, and I have them aimed there."

The sky was turning from black to gray in the north, the direction from which the attack would come. In the east, fingers of light pink were appearing on the scattered clouds as the sun began to rise. "I have a visual. I can see their fleet," an officer yelled in Arabic. Brian looked through his telescope. He could see through the midst the hulk of a destroyer and then a smaller warship to the west. Then, between the two, he saw water sprays, and below the sprays fast-moving hydrofoils laden with armored vehicles and trucks.

"They will be within range in two minutes," Ibrahim said.

The sun broke the horizon and shone brightly, blinding those who looked east. Brian slipped on his polarized sunglasses just as the flying wedge of American F-35 Enforcers appeared from out of the sun. He swung the telescope around and focused in on the aircraft. They were smooth, with no external missiles, bombs, or fuel tanks. As he focused the lenses, missiles shot forward from inside the aircraft. To the north, Iranian MiG-29s appeared over the ships. To the west, the first wave of Bahraini rockets soared up from the MLRSes near the beach. Brian looked north again. Almost simultaneously, the Enforcers' missiles hit several ships, the rockets from the beach smashed into other ships, and Iranian aircraft exploded in midair. Above and behind the Enforcers, a line of Air Force Raptors were firing on the MiGs. As he tried to make out Raptors, Brian saw an Enforcer explode, hit by a missile from one of the MiGs. Then the windows shook as something blew up at the mouth of the harbor. A ship had hit one of the mines.

"I guess the Iranians lacked the element of surprise," Ibrahim said to Douglas, "thanks to you."

"General, I'd say it's beginning to look like maybe two of the three scorpions have been stopped at the gate," Douglas replied.

From behind Ibrahim, another rocket volley shot up from the beach. "By the way, Brian, the Shi'a imam from their big mosque is on the beach urging on our troops, along with our Crown Prince," the general said, giving himself a thumbs-up.

Sweeping west from behind the bank tower, Douglas saw the contrails of another group of Enforcers and Raptors speeding west. Iranian MiGs flew after them, firing missiles. Douglas turned to General Ibrahim. "What Churchill would have given for a view like this over London during the Battle of Britain!"

"May we fare as well as he did," the general replied. *"Inshallah."*

The windows shook again, and below them, a wing of the Bahraini palace exploded.

Meanwhile, off the coast, the bulk of the Iranian force

was heading toward Islamyah's beaches. Hovercraft carrying light armored vehicles and trucks flew just above the water and then just above the sand as they came ashore. Above Islamyah's beaches, Iran's MiGs and Sukhois were dogfighting again with the American- and British-origin fighters that Islamyah could still get to fly. What had been the Royal Saudi Air Force was significantly smaller in number now because of cannibalizing for parts, and the Iranians were winning the air combat by putting more fighters up than Islamyah could, even over its own territory.

Behind the hovercraft came rehabilitated amphibious landing craft, disgorging troops into the surf. Islamyah's forces rained artillery and tank fire down on the landing zone with deadly results, but some Iranian troops were getting ashore and off the beaches. Islamyah had more shoreline to defend than Bahrain and so the defense forces were more spread out. Iranian special forces employing mini-subs and semisubmersibles were placing commandos ashore in port areas, their goal to seize control of facilities for Iranian ferries and Ro-Ros to dock.

It was not going well for Islamyah. The general in charge of the Protectors in the Eastern Province, in a bunker in Dhahran, was beginning to think he would have no choice but to order his units to fall back to regroup against the Iranians, when he received reports that several Iranian troop-carrying ships had just exploded offshore. Seconds later, Islamyah's AWACS reported that another wave of Iranian fighters coming across the Gulf had also erupted.

What was going on? Islamyah's forces were not responsible for this, the general knew. There were no solid radar images of any new Air Force units arriving. Who was killing the Iranians?

Then the Iranian flagship *Zaros* was reported hit. In his Dhahran bunker, the general turned to the chief of his battle staff, who grinned and said, "I just picked up their comms, sir. It's Enforcers. Raptors."

What was it the Americans said in those movies? The cavalry was coming?

The general nodded to himself. Yes. The cavalry had come. Al-Hamdu Lillah.

17

FEBRUARY 22

Security Center of the Republic
Riyadh, Islamyah

"Play the tape," General Khalid ordered.

All television channels in the country switched to an image of a plain green flag flying against a blue sky. A martial song played in the background. Above the music, a voice said, "And now to speak to the nation, Abdullah bin Rashid, Chairman of the national Shura."

Abdullah, dressed in formal robes, stood against a green background. The camera zoomed in on his face. "Although you have not selected me, it is my task now to lead this nation until you choose one who will lead us. We who are members of the Shura have been chosen only by those who fought to unseat the usurpers who stole the wealth of our nation for their one family.

"But the day will come this year when you will choose those who will lead us. Let no one stop you, brothers and sisters, from making that choice.

"When you choose, think about the future. Think about how we Arabs can restore our greatness, how we can contribute to the world's progress. We must contribute more than just the energy from fossils millions of years old. Once again, we must turn the power of our minds to math and science, to medicine and engineering, to learn to unlock the secrets of what Allah has given to us. It will take tapping the skills of all our people, men and women.

"If this republic can survive, we can look forward to a day when the peace of Allah may prosper in this world. When weapons of mass destruction will themselves be destroyed. When we unlock Allah's other gifts, to replace the ancient fossil fuels that Allah provided to the world. Allah placed them in our land, providing humanity with the fuel for the phase of emergence, which is now passing.

"To hasten those days, we will take leadership. Today we destroy the long-range missiles in our nation, missiles that one day might have carried weapons of mass destruction. We have brought the diplomatic representatives of many nations to our deserts to see this destruction. We invite international inspection, anywhere, anytime. And we call upon Iran, Israel, and other nations to follow our example.

"Today we invest two billion euros, the first of a much greater amount, to create the Future Energies Institute here in Riyadh, an international center to develop and deploy new methods of electrical and other power beyond the fossil era. Here, too, we invite the international community to join us in funding and participating in open discovery. Until we help the world emerge from the fossil era, we shall share our oil on the world's market, open to all to buy, at the rate of one percent of our known reserves every year. No more, no less. Ten percent of our revenues will go to the Future Energies Institute. If anyone uses force to seek more of our assets, all of our oil facilities will self-destruct. Thus, there is no point in invading our lands.

"And we must recognize that just as Allah has placed this special reserve in our land, we hold a special responsibility to Allah to preserve and protect the Two Holy Mosques he has also placed within our borders. These places are sacred to almost two billion Muslims. Muslims of all communities, Sunni and Shi'a, for there is no one right community of Islam. And our government must protect them all and support no single view.

"You, in turn, must protect our government and our nation. Especially now, in this time of transition. There are those who may be tempted to invade our territory, to drain our sands of the fuels below. You can scare these scorpions away. You can demonstrate your support of the revolution. March to the Red Sea, line it with thousands of patriots and believers. Show that you are ready to sacrifice to preserve our nation. Members of the Shura are organizing transportation in every city. After this broadcast, join me. March for Islamyah." The camera zoomed out and now showed dozens of men and women on either side of Abdullah.

"You will not march alone. Let me introduce you to the new Shura Council. Here is my brother, Ahmed, a man of medicine, who now is my right hand seeking to heal this nation and who has developed this plan. Here is General

Khalid, who leads the Protectors. Here Fatima Khaldan, a scientist, who has returned to her native land from . . ."

When the introductions ended, the screen dissolved to an image of General Khalid and Ahmed sitting side by side. Khalid spoke. "After he taped that speech for broadcast today, Abdullah was killed by enemies of the revolution. Now potential enemies lurk off our coasts. Our forces are scaring off Persians in the east. As Abdullah asked, you must be our forces in the west, on the Red Sea. Join with Dr. Rashid as he carries the body of his martyred brother to the sea."

Aboard the USS George H.W. Bush
Red Sea

"Sir, we have to make a decision. Do we make the landing on the east coast or west coast in the morning, in Egypt or Islamyah?" General Moore, the commander of U.S. Central Command, asked the Secretary.

"Have the Iranians achieved a beachhead?" Secretary Conrad asked General Moore.

"A limited one near Jubail, but the aircraft from the *Reagan,* the Emirates, Qatar, and Kuwait are pounding it pretty hard. And it looks like their invasion of Bahrain has been repulsed altogether," the general said.

"They weren't invading Bahrain, General," Secretary Conrad insisted. "That was just a feint, probably."

"Fucking Adams! I knew it," Kashigian said to the Secretary. "But we can still claim the need to go in to protect the oil from a second-wave Iranian attack . . . and from the chaos in Islamyah. There is definitely chaos there. They're changing leaders by the day."

Conrad exhaled, loudly. "Maybe. What about the Chinese troops and the nukes?"

"Well, the two Chink carriers are definitely heading home. The Ro-Ros have docked in Karachi, where they seem to be delivering military vehicles to Pakistan, along with a bunch of military advisers and technicians," General Moore read from his message traffic.

"So no Chinese threat," Conrad muttered at Kashigian.

"Mr. Secretary, ever since that speech this morning by the Shura fella, we have been getting reports of movement toward the beaches, the landing areas we planned. Lemme show you the feed we're getting from Global Hawk of what we call Nebraska Beach, or landing area Alpha Two."

The image that appeared on the large screen showed a coastal area, then zoomed in to show a beach, then in farther to show people massing in groups.

"I don't see any tanks, artillery. What are they armed with? Zoom in more," Conrad blustered at the general.

"Mr. Secretary, that's just it. They're not armed. They're civilians. And they're, like, holding hands and praying. Every so many yards there's some imam with them."

The secretary had walked up to the screen, trying to peer down onto the beach. He turned back to Kashigian. "Ron, what do you make of . . . Ron, stop reading the goddamn news clips. I have to make a decision."

Kashigian walked over to the Secretary, carrying the newly arrived news summary. "This just came in. Front page on the *New York Journal*. A story written by that Delmarco reporter. It says although her laptop was missing from her car when she was found, it had automatically backed up her draft onto their server." He handed the Secretary the paper.

Conrad's eyes widened as he read. He seemed to pale. "This is scandalous, it's libelous, it's untrue lies."

"Sir?" the general asked, confused by the exchange between the civilians.

The Secretary of Defense looked down at his subordinate. "You fucked this all up. Nothing is working."

"Don't blame me. You gave me orders to set things up so you and your Saudi friends could get back in. Well, this was the best thing that anyone could come up with. It doesn't matter what the facts are, Henry, we need to invade!" Kashigian yelled at his boss. "We just use the Big Lie. It's worked before."

Henry Conrad walked closer to the screen showing the image of the beaches lined with civilians, praying. "Don't you see? There are no nuclear weapons there. There are no Iranian invaders there. There are no Chinese. And the chaos you promised me has turned into a fucking prayer rally! Do you think we can tell our constituency back home that we bombed a *prayer rally*?"

"Sir?" General Moore asked again.

"Fine, fine," Ron Kashigian said. He turned to General Moore. "The Secretary has decided to go ahead with the planned exercise with Egypt. But he will be returning to Washington to take care of something that has just come up. So we need a COD flight to Cairo, where the 747 is parked."

"Yes, sir," the CinC replied.

"And I'll need onward flight reservations from Cairo to Geneva for me," Kashigian added.

Command Post,
Revolutionary Guards Navy Base
Bandar Abbas, Iran

"We can mount another wave, expand the beach-head," the Iranian general said, looking up from the map.

"My brethren in Tehran say that our air force chief is refusing. He thinks his losses are already too high, unacceptable," the cleric said, as though he were commenting on the weather.

"We can't just leave them there," the general insisted.

"Oh, yes we can. We left many more Pasdaran and Basiji in Iraqi jails for over a decade. Many more," the cleric said, gathering up his papers. "That war failed. So did this one. Accept it."

"But we didn't have nuclear weapons then," the general said, moving to block the cleric's exit.

"I told you the nuclears are only for defense. Not for you, Qods Force, Hezbollah, or anyone else," the cleric explained. "If a nuclear weapon goes off in the United States, they will not hesitate to incinerate our entire country, and Korea, too, just for good measure.

"General, you must look at a longer time horizon. In 1986, we ended the war with Iraq without victory. By 2006, we had won, thanks to you and others. And we won without arms. We let the Americans do the dying for us. This operation today was too direct, too overt. Not subtle. But don't worry, General, we will prevail. I have another plan. We will discuss it in Tehran. Join me

there in a few days, after all of this . . . has been cleaned up.

"The long view, General." The cleric glanced at the map, then back up at him. "Our day will come."

FEBRUARY 28
The Ethical Culture Society
Central Park West
New York City

"My word, she knew a lot of people," Brian Douglas observed to Rusty as the two emerged from the memorial for Kate Delmarco.

"Well, a lot of those in attendance were reporters. That was one hell of a job of reporting. It took smarts and guts," Rusty MacIntyre said, walking down the stairs. "And it may have taken her life." He thought of their night together, her smile, her scent—and guilt rolled over him. Had he been responsible?

"Oh, come on, don't start that again. You saw the autopsy report, even though you probably had no right to. She had a heart attack, Rusty," Sol Rubenstein added as he caught up with them.

"Ray Keller, her editor, doesn't think so. He has three reporters on it," MacIntyre told his boss. "He's trying to get the FBI to look into it." And I'll make sure they do, he said to himself.

"Good luck to them and the Mets," Rubenstein retorted. "You just should be glad that your own FBI

thing is going away, now that it looks like Dr. Rashid is no terrorist—more like the next president of Islamyah."

"He's invited me back," Rusty reported. "Ahmed is going to run in the national election."

"And you're going when?" Rubenstein asked.

"No time soon, boss." he said. "Brian here is en route to a sailing vacation out of Virgin Gorda and he needs a crewmate. So, with your permission . . ."

Rubenstein laughed. "Oh, I suppose for averting a major war you two probably deserve a week off. Although I am not sure how Sir Dennis will view the two of you bonding, turning into some kind of Anglo-American version of *I Spy*."

"I expect he'll have to get used to it," Brian said, grinning. "It's his fault anyway. He introduced us."

As they walked down the street toward Columbus Circle, Rubenstein asked in a fatherly way, "So, how's Sarah? She going along to Virgin's Girdle, too?"

Rusty looked across the street at the park and then back at Rubenstein. "No. No, she's not. Sarah is saving Somaliland for ninety days."

Rubenstein looked disappointed, not surprised. He started to say something, but the expression on Rusty's face . . . No, better to leave it alone.

At the end of the park, they turned into the Time Warner Center, where they were due to have their delayed celebratory lunch. A television was showing CNN in the lobby.

"Hey, look at this. The President is holding a press conference," Rubenstein said, walking over to the screen. As they approached, they could hear the audio:

". . . will decide which of these unproven allegations should be looked into, but while the Attorney General is doing that, I just want to say that we are blessed to have Henry Conrad in public service. His Reconfig Program is changing the armed forces and saving the taxpayers billions of dollars. He has rebuilt bridges to our critical allies around the world, something that was very clear to me recently at the Asia Pacific summit. It was in Chile, Santiago . . .

"Look, the bottom line is that Henry Conrad is the best Secretary of Defense we have ever had. Now, what was the second part of your question . . . ?"

"Unbelievable," said MacIntyre.

"Best we ever had, huh?" said Rubenstein.

"I wonder if they serve Balvenie here?" said Douglas, and walked past the television into the restaurant.

The President was still talking.

Rusty looked out at Central Park, at the leafless trees, and thought of Kate, of Abdullah, of all those who had died so needlessly. And he promised them that he would fight back.

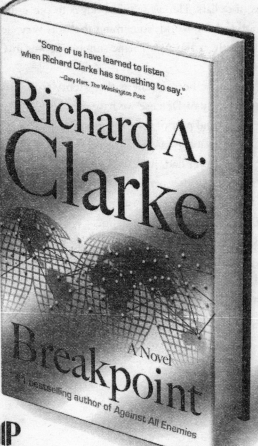